A
LIGHT TO
GUIDE US
HOME

BOOKS BY DIANNE HALEY

DIANNE HALEY

A
LIGHT TO
GUIDE US
HOME

bookouture

Published by Bookouture in 2023

An imprint of Storyfire Ltd.
Carmelite House
50 Victoria Embankment
London EC4Y 0DZ

www.bookouture.com

ISBN: 978-1-83790-096-1
eBook ISBN: 978-1-83790-095-4

For my family

NOVEMBER, 1943

Neutral Switzerland is still surrounded by war.

In occupied France, the terror continues, with more round-ups of Jews who are sent to Nazi concentration camps across Germany and Poland. In Italy, Mussolini has been replaced and the country has switched its allegiance from Hitler to the Allies. The north of the country sees violent battles between Fascist sympathisers and partisans fighting to overthrow their German occupiers who are becoming ever more brutal with the Italian population.

PROLOGUE

Paris
November, 1943

David ached all over, the least movement making the pain worse. He lay on the hard wooden surface among rows of men in the bare hut and pulled his coat more tightly around him, as the cold of the Drancy refugee camp seeped into his bones. The groans and whimpers of his fellow inmates created a background noise of misery and despair, subdued in the darkness. Everyone knew that from here they would be taken to a concentration camp and that they had left their old lives and loved ones behind forever.

The blows from the German interrogators throbbed painfully but he didn't think they'd broken any bones. They kept asking him about the document but, because they hadn't found it on him, they had finally left him alone. He knew the questions wouldn't stop and he was as good as dead. David shivered when he remembered their harsh accusations. They knew who he was, but, more than that, they seemed to know what he'd taken: the document with evidence of high-level military and industrial spies in the British establishment who were sympathetic to the Nazi cause. They would go to any lengths to find it.

His physical suffering was nothing compared to the horror in his mind, the thoughts of the dangers facing his family. He screwed up his eyes and thought about his wife, Ruth, and daughter, Clara, trying to flee Paris without him. Ruth would have to follow the plan they'd agreed; he hoped that his shy, nervous wife would have the strength to carry it out alone. At least they wouldn't still be in the apartment shown on his papers so might not be found for a few days. He groaned and tried to turn over but his whole body protested so he lay still. Then his thoughts drifted to his sister, Hannelore, drawn into the danger too.

He was only a scientist, he kept telling himself, but he felt a huge weight of responsibility that he'd left the people he loved most in the world so exposed to the Germans. He knew he should have got rid of the document before now, but hadn't trusted anyone enough to hand it over. Before the German borders had been closed to them, he'd only managed to give his friend Jacob the composition of the nerve gas he'd been working on, but the other document he'd taken was what they really wanted. Getting the names and plans of Nazi sympathisers deeply embedded in the Allied war machine to the Allies could change the course of the war. And now it was his daughter, Clara, who had to get into Switzerland and give the document to the British. She was only thirteen years old but she was brave and knew what she had to do. He'd tried to protect her by dividing the document between her and Hannelore. If either of them were caught... he shuddered to imagine the fate that would befall them.

The door to the hut opened. In the early morning light coming through the opening, he saw the guards waiting outside. A burst of cold air blew into the room but it couldn't take away the smell of so many men sleeping packed together in the fetid room. Although he buried his nose in the collar of his coat, nothing could dull the stench of broken humanity and fear. He closed his eyes to shut out the reality of the life around him.

The shouts of the guards forced the men to stagger upright, the slower and older ones beaten when they did not move quickly enough. David trudged behind the others to the court-yard outside, the grey dawn hardly lighting their way as they were led towards the wooden goods vans that made up the train. Those who couldn't keep up were shot and thrown into the gutter, the noise of pistol shots punctuating the still air.

The cold November rain started to fall and the guards hustled them into the carriages, trying not to get wet. He couldn't think about the horrors ahead of him, and concentrated on taking a step at a time. As the door slammed shut behind him and the other men jostled against one another to keep their balance, he grasped the wood on the side of the carriage to stay upright, wondering if he would ever see his family again, and whether any of them would survive the hell of this war.

ONE

HANNELORE

Paris
November, 1943

Hannelore heard a harsh shout at the window. *Juden.* Heart pounding, she crouched down behind the sofa and leaned her head against the soft leather. The darkness of the ground-floor apartment on the Rue Pavée seemed like very flimsy protection, but she was grateful that she'd switched the lights off in the front rooms to hide her presence. She heard banging at the front door and more distant shouting in other streets in the Marais district. French vigilantes or German soldiers, it hardly made any difference these days in Paris.

She looked out into the hall of the apartment, expecting the door to crash open, and feeling very alone, but it held firm and the banging stopped. She hung her head in relief, her light brown hair escaping from the pins and falling onto her face, then stifled a scream when the window shattered and a rock crashed onto the carpet. They were still outside, watching for someone they wanted to hate, someone they could terrify. Anger filled her mind and she almost ran to the window to scare them away, determined not to become their victim, but she sank back onto the floor, knowing that she was powerless.

She sat behind the sofa for hours, terrified a bigger group of vigilantes would come back. Finally, she heard a key in the lock and Ruth and Clara rushed inside, their voices sharp with fear.

'Hannelore? Where are you? Are you okay?'

She staggered out of the living room and threw herself into her sister-in-law's arms, unable to speak with relief. Then she pulled back and looked towards the door. 'Where's David? Why is he not with you?'

Ruth led her into the kitchen at the back of the apartment and they sat down at the table. 'The police took him away.' Her voice broke and she covered her face with her hands, before she visibly took control of herself. Hannelore's quiet, sweet-natured sister-in-law was showing a strength she had never revealed before.

'Clara, go and pack your suitcase. We're leaving to go somewhere safer.' After Clara had left the room, her face white with shock, Ruth closed the door behind her and came back to the table.

'I thought they'd come here and got you too,' she said finally. 'When we heard there was trouble here, we came to find you.' Ruth leaned forward. 'It was so dangerous out there tonight. Did they try to get in?'

'Yes,' Hannelore answered, her voice trembling, shocked that the Germans had taken David and what that meant. 'They were shouting outside and banging on the door, and then they broke the window.' She felt the tears come, hot streaks running down her cheeks.

'They wanted us as well as David,' Ruth said. 'We hid with the Beckers until they'd gone, but they'll be back. We must get out of Paris and quickly, it's far too dangerous now. David hasn't got what they were searching for, so they'll be back here to look for it. We'd better not be around when they come.'

A shout from outside made both women look at the window and then Ruth carried on. 'It's not just vigilantes who are after us, the Germans are carrying out raids across the whole community.'

It was just like what had happened in Germany at the start of the war. First, Jews were banned from professions and universities by the Nazi party and then the round-ups had started. After years of studying, Hannelore had been forced to leave her medical classes at Frankfurt University, her hopes of becoming a doctor dashed in a matter of days. And now in Paris things were even worse, the short walk to her job at the hospital laundry full of threat and danger.

Ruth sighed, the stress on her face making her worry lines even more pronounced. She seemed to have aged years in one short night. 'I never thought I'd say this, but I'm glad your mother and father aren't alive to see their son taken away by the Nazis,' she said, shaking her head, her dark hair now flecked with grey. 'It isn't safe for any of us to stay here any longer.'

The year before, David had taken them to live in Paris, as it felt safer than Germany despite the occupation of France by the Nazis. After working in a leading chemical company in Frankfurt, he had easily got a job in one of the smaller companies near Paris. 'But what about David's work? Won't they try to get him back?' asked Hannelore.

Ruth shook her head. 'We didn't tell you, but David said the company was being threatened and were going to get rid of everyone who came here from Germany. He thought the authorities would be taking over the factory very soon and they want all Jews out of Paris. He was warned that he was vulnerable even though they encouraged him to come.'

'Did they know about the information he took from Germany?

'I don't think so, but somebody did. We have to get it away from the Germans if there is any chance of giving it to the

Allies. You know what that means. At least David prepared us for that.'

Hannelore thought about her beloved older brother and knew what she had to do. She'd always been close to David, who'd set her riddles and puzzles from a young age, helping her to work out the answers and making her burst into peals of laughter with his clumsy attempts at giving her clues. Their close relationship hadn't changed with his marriage to Ruth, who had become like a sister to her. And the arrival of her niece, Clara, gave her such joy, she became the little girl's playmate and confidante in Frankfurt and then Paris.

Ruth looked up, her warm eyes full of sorrow. 'We have to split up and travel separately. You head for the Allies in neutral Switzerland, go wherever you can to stay safe. Clara will do the same by a different route. She will take half of the document and David has given you the other half. That means that if one of you is caught, at least some of the information is safe. It is the most important thing we have to do.'

Hannelore looked at Ruth speechlessly. She would need to live alone, leaving the only family she had left in the world. She knew the plan David had outlined for their safety, but her heart sank when she realised what it meant.

'I'm sorry Hannelore, but it's the only way to protect the information, survive this and to have any chance to be together again once the war is over.'

She heard the hopelessness and finality in Ruth's voice and realised that they had no good options left. There was simply nothing else they could do.

'So, I need to leave the hospital?'

'You can't go back. Just don't tell me how you're going to get to Switzerland, it will be safer for everyone. We have to hope that we will all get there.'

They heard the distant sound of breaking glass and Hannelore clutched Ruth's arm, the fear rising up again.

'You go and pack,' said Ruth. 'You should leave early tomorrow morning. We'll go later. Just take the minimum that you'll need.'

Hannelore nodded and left to go through to her small bedroom, simply furnished with an old-fashioned iron bedstead, wardrobe and dressing table. Inside the room, she sat on the bed and couldn't stop the tears from flowing down her cheeks. After all the upheavals trying to keep the family together and moving constantly to hide from the authorities, they now had to split up. The thought of being on her own was terrifying.

Hearing the sound of shouts fading into the distance, she stood up from the bed and pulled out her small suitcase from the bottom of her wardrobe, starting to put clothes inside and anything else she felt it was important to take. With a sigh, she picked up the photograph of her parents from the dressing table and a picture that Clara had drawn for her when she was very small of the little dog in the next apartment in Frankfurt.

As she finished packing her suitcase, there was a hesitant knock on the door and Clara came inside, her face blotchy from crying and her straight dark hair tucked behind her ears. The usual sweet smile was absent and her dark eyes were like pools of sorrow. Although she was only thirteen years old, Clara was tall for her age and wasn't much shorter than Hannelore. She ran up and hugged her aunt tightly and Hannelore pulled her close, not sure how she was ever going to let her go.

Clara pulled away from Hannelore's arms and collapsed onto the bed, dangling her legs over the side. 'Maman says you must leave tomorrow and then we have to go, so you're not coming with us. Why can't you come with us? I don't want to go without you.'

Hannelore sat down next to her and put an arm around her shoulders. 'Liebchen, you're a smart girl. You know how difficult it is in Paris just now. Your mother thinks that we should all leave and I think she's right. I wish I didn't have to go separately but your father and I decided a long time ago that it would be best if we weren't together.'

'But you'll be all on your own,' wailed Clara.

'It won't be for long, my darling. This war won't go on forever. When it's over, we'll be in a safe place all together.'

She could tell that, whatever words she used, Clara wouldn't be happy. Hannelore leaned over to her dressing table and picked up a picture of herself, David and Ruth in Geneva. She handed it to Clara. 'We'll meet there again, I promise.'

Clara clutched the picture to her chest. 'But when will you be there?' she asked.

'I don't know Liebchen, but I'll try to get there when I can.'

It was the best she could come up with, unsure of what was going to happen to all of them and not wanting to scare the girl. As if she was trying to imprint Hannelore's features in her mind, Clara stood up and looked searchingly at her. 'Will I see you tomorrow morning?' she asked.

Hannelore nodded. 'Of course, you will. I won't leave without saying goodbye.' Clara walked across the room, pausing at the door to take one last look at Hannelore before closing it quietly behind her.

Hannelore came down the next morning into the kitchen. Ruth and Clara, their faces white and drawn, looked up when she came in. They'd all decided, by some unspoken agreement, that they weren't going to cry this morning because it would make everything worse. There had been too much crying already. Ruth bustled at the kitchen table with a bag, putting bread and cheese into it carefully, then handing the package to Hannelore. 'Here you are. You must have something to eat on the train. Take it before you go, please.'

There were dark circles under Clara's eyes and the face that stared at her aunt was pinched and sad though she'd clearly decided to keep herself under control. Hannelore couldn't bear to see her pain and ran towards her, holding her arms out. Clara threw herself into them, and Hannelore pressed close, her eyes closed, trying to imprint the feeling of the thin body in her mind so that she would never forget her. Clara pulled back. 'You promise you'll find me,' she said in an urgent voice. 'Wherever I am, will you come back to me?'

'Yes, my darling, I promise,' said Hannelore.

They stood gazing at one another for a few moments, Clara's dark eyes wide and pleading, before Ruth came up towards them. 'You need to go now, Hannelore, if you're going to get away this morning.'

She nodded, but before she could pull away from Clara, the girl sobbed and ran out of the room. Hannelore went to follow her but Ruth stopped her. 'Leave her now,' she said quietly. 'There's nothing more you can say.'

Ruth came with her to the door. 'You go now and get the train south. You should get to Switzerland without being stopped and will have to take your chances at the border.'

'What about you? What will you do?' asked Hannelore.

'We'll be safe for a few days if we aren't here when they come and search. Then we'll go to the station. David has contacted someone who has said they will come and get Clara and take her to safety.'

'What about you? If you go to the station, won't they pick you up?'

'I know that's possible but my husband has gone now and my most important duty is to save my daughter's life. I don't care what happens to me now, all that matters is Clara.'

'But the Germans won't let you go, they'll take you away.'

Ruth caressed Hannelore's cheek and spoke in a calm tone. 'Whatever God decides is my fate is what will happen to me. Whether they take me this week, next week or next month, it will make no difference. So long as you and Clara are safe, then I'll be satisfied.'

Hannelore wanted to protest, wanted to say that Ruth must escape too but her sister-in-law shook her head. 'There is no escape for me now. It's what David and I knew. You and Clara have the document between you and you're the ones who must be protected.'

Ruth opened the door and looked outside. 'It's clear out there now so you must go.'

Hannelore clutched Ruth one last time and then went into the street, hearing the door clicking shut, her heart feeling leaden in her chest when she thought about the look on Ruth's face and the calm acceptance of her fate. Hannelore knew her own destiny was just as fraught, the risk of being stopped in France and deported to a concentration camp always alive, not to mention the challenges of getting across the border into Switzerland. She would just have to work it out when she got there. Raising her head and straightening her back, she walked through the Marais district towards the Seine, on her way towards the Gare de Lyon to catch a train to the south.

It was a cold, sunny day, the winter sun glancing off the ornate, stone apartment buildings and shining on the metal balconies set below the tall windows. The streets were deserted apart from a few bicyclists riding along the wide boulevards. Hannelore walked through the Place de la Bastille, dominated by the July Column stretching into the sky, and paused under one of the trees to stare up at the statue at the top of the column. Then she decided to take one last look at the River Seine, not knowing if she would ever see Paris again. Despite all the mistrust and hate she felt in the streets, she had grown to love the city.

On her way to the river, she passed a group of German soldiers, who looked at her curiously but didn't approach. Pulses racing, aware of the document hidden in her suitcase, she

felt herself stiffen under their gaze and looked down as she kept
walking along the Quai de la Rapée under the Pont d'Austerlitz.
She stopped briefly to watch the dark grey water swirling
through the stone arches of the bridge. With a heavy heart, she
looked at the wide flowing river that cut through the heart of the
city, patches of sunlight dappling the surface. The beauty of the
city all around was one constant among all the upheavals she'd
witnessed there.

She heard a shout behind her and saw the group of German
soldiers push a man to the ground and start to kick him. Sick-
ened by the sudden violence, she turned away from the scene,
her powerless to help compounded by the need to avoid trouble.
She hurried on her way, knowing that she couldn't linger any
longer and had to get to the station before she was caught up in
the fight.

But then she took a closer look at the man being
attacked. He wasn't very old and his brown hair looked familiar.
She heard him shout again and realised with a cold certainty
that it was Marc, her friend Chantal's husband. Plunged into
indecision and fear, she looked ahead at the clock tower that
dominated the station and then back at Marc being dragged
away. What would happen to him? And more importantly, how
could Chantal survive without him? Nausea rose in her throat
as she tried to decide what was best to do. Then she watched
him being bundled into a van and the noise of the vehicle taking
him away echoed down the street. She knew she couldn't leave
Chantal on her own. She had to go back, despite the importance
of getting the information safely to the Allies. It could make the
difference between a Nazi future where countless more innocent Jewish people were brutalised and murdered, and one
where they could finally be safe. But Chantal was sick and
needed to be cared for. If Marc wasn't there, then she wouldn't
survive. Hannelore couldn't forget her friend, she had to
help her.

Once she'd made her decision, Hannelore turned away from the station and went back towards the Marais, her heart beating as she walked away from her chance of safety. It was still very quiet in the city and there were only a few people on their bikes as she walked towards Chantal and Marc's apartment a few streets away from where she'd left that morning. She looked straight ahead as she walked, terrified of bumping into Clara and her mother, not knowing when they'd leave the apartment in the Rue Pavée. It was bad enough saying their goodbyes once; she didn't want to have to do it again and risk their safety.

Hannelore breathed a sigh of relief when she reached the Rue de Rosier and the apartment in the rundown tall building. Her feet kicked through some rubbish on the street, leaflets from the Nazi party and an old shoe that must have belonged to a poor soul dragged from their home. She went into the damp musty hall and towards the apartment. The door was unlocked and she went inside, calling her friend's name. There was no reply and she continued into the main room of the apartment where she found Chantal sitting on a chair looking vacantly into space, seemingly unaware of Hannelore's presence. She dropped her suitcase and ran across the room, crouching down in front of Chantal. 'What's happened? Are you all right?'

Chantal coughed painfully and Hannelore stood up to get her a glass of water. She handed the glass to her and felt Chantal's freezing cold hands. Hannelore looked at the small stove in the corner of the room but it must have gone out hours before, leaving no trace of warmth in the poorly furnished room.

Chantal took a couple of deep breaths and, when she could finally speak, said, 'I was waiting for Marc but he hasn't come home. We were going out to get some food.' She glanced at Hannelore and then at the small suitcase at her feet. 'You were leaving Paris?' Then she started coughing again and Hannelore waited until she had finished and could speak again. The doctor had said that Chantal was unlikely to recover from her tuberculosis, particularly since they couldn't afford the medicine that might ease her condition.

'Has something happened to Marc?' asked Chantal. 'Is that why you're here?'

'I'm afraid so. I saw him. He was picked up by the Germans.'

Hannelore started to take off her coat automatically and then changed her mind and kept it on. 'I'll stay until he gets back. Let's get this fire going.' She went to get a blanket and put it over Chantal's shoulders before going to the stove to light it and try to warm up the room. Neither of them said what they were both thinking. What if Marc didn't come back and Hannelore was picked up by the Germans? What would Chantal do then?

It was only later in the evening when Hannelore went into the spare room that she felt the tension drain from her body and she went over everything that had happened in the last few hours. Feeling icily cold, she wrapped her arms around her waist. She felt so alone and wondered where Clara was, realising how much she missed her and wanted to see her again. Hannelore closed her eyes, remembering the feel of her body in her arms, the joy of her laughter. She'd always felt more like a daughter than a niece and Hannelore's pain at their parting burned. She pushed away the thought of the days, maybe months, that had been robbed from them, taking Clara away from her. She didn't know if she would ever see her again and felt her eyes fill with tears.

TWO

VALÉRIE

Geneva
November, 1943

Valérie knew someone was following her; the prickling feeling at the back of her neck was unmistakeable, and she glanced around nervously as she pushed her bike away from the Café de Paris and across the Place du Bourg-de-Four. She paused in front of Bernard's grocery shop to stare at the reflection in the window but only her auburn curls and green jacket looked back at her and no one in the gathering dusk of the cool autumn evening was watching her. Outside the café, her friend Geraldine's red dress and blonde hair weaved between the busy tables on the pavement, a bright patch of colour against the grey military uniforms and business suits.

Further down the square, a group of women sat on a bench under the trees, chatting while they kept an eye on their children playing in the dry brown leaves, kicking them into the air in swirling clouds. Two men in light raincoats emerged from the Rue de la Fontaine at the base of the hill and began to climb up the cobbled street, the warmth of the climb prompting the older

man to take off his hat and wipe his brow. While he paused to
take breath, his younger companion took photographs of the old
square, its tall stone buildings and wooden shutters stretching
along both sides around the fountain in the centre.

Unable to shake off the unsettling feeling of being watched,
Valérie pulled her bike away from the window. The scene
around her seemed too commonplace for her growing sense of
danger, but she continued to glance all around her as she left
the square and walked home along the cobbled streets of Geneva's old town.

She'd learned to trust her instincts and her instincts were
telling her to be alert. If her secretive follower wanted to make
themselves known, then she would be ready.

The rattling noise of closing shutters followed her down the
street towards the open square in front of the imposing pillars of
the Cathédrale Saint-Pierre. She stopped to wait for the proces-
sion of white-robed clergy to pass before pushing her bike over
the uneven cobblestones, past the Hôtel Les Armures, heading
for the quieter streets towards home.

Suddenly, she heard a step behind her and whipped round.
Her bike tyre scraped the dry cobbles and sent up a cloud of
dust. She grasped the handlebar with shaking hands to steady
herself. A small, well-dressed woman stood in front of her,
looking scared but determined, her face pale and her jaw
tightly clenched. She was older than Valérie, her well-cut, dark
hair shot through with glints of grey, but her expensive navy
dress and jacket fitted her slim figure to perfection and the
patterned blue and white scarf round her shoulders adding a
stylish touch. She came up close to Valérie and spoke in a low,
soft voice.

'Are you Valérie Hallez?'

'Yes....'

They heard men's voices close by and the woman glanced
behind her, waiting until they had gone. When she looked back,

her brown eyes wide and desperation written across her face, she grasped Valérie's arm in a painful grip.

'They're following me. I can't stay for long.'

The woman's fear throbbed in her low voice and Valérie felt her heart pounding in response.

'Who's following you, madame? How can I help?'

'You help the Resistance, like I do, you get people out of France?'

Valérie hesitated.

'Please, you should look for a girl called Clara Lieberman. The Resistance will get her across the border, but will you make sure she's safe? She's only thirteen and her father was taken to the death camps by the Nazis. We think her mother will be taken too. The Resistance will get Clara out of Paris and take her to a children's home near Lyon, but she has important information and the Gestapo will be looking for her. It will only be a matter of time before they find her if she doesn't leave France very soon. She'll be looking for her aunt, Hannelore, when she gets to Geneva but we don't know where Hannelore is. Clara has my name but I might not be here to help her. Can we rely on you?'

'Yes, of course. I'll find out where she is and be here when she comes across.'

'Thank you,' said the woman, her voice slightly calmer and her grip weakening on Valérie's arm. 'Just before he was taken away, Clara's father left a message with the Resistance to say that Jacob Steinberg would help Clara when she reached Switzerland, but I couldn't find him. I was told you would be the best person to help, and that your mother knew Jacob.'

'Jacob Steinberg who owned the bookshop here?' It had been years since she'd heard that name. Her late mother had worked with Jacob before the war, and he had left Geneva after her mother's accident.

'Yes. Hannelore, Clara's aunt, was the woman Jacob loved.

She might be the only family that Clara has left in the world, but she is missing. Our job is to save the child.'

'Our job?'

'The job of the Resistance.'

They heard more voices approaching from the Cathédrale Saint-Pierre.

'Come back home with me, please. You'll be safe there,' urged Valérie.

The woman shook her head.

'No, I have to get away. I wouldn't want to lead them to your door.'

'Lead who?'

'German spies. They are everywhere in Geneva.'

Valérie tried to follow the woman's words.

'Jacob trusted your mother. It's up to you to protect what he left behind.'

'What do you know about my mother?' The sharper tone of her voice caught the woman's attention.

'Only that he relied on her.' The woman pulled away her hand. 'I have somewhere I'll be safe. Don't follow me.'

'Wait, what's your name?' asked Valérie.

'It's Isabelle,' she replied.

Before Valérie could stop her, the woman left as quickly as she had appeared, slipping down one of the narrow alleys leading to the lake that threaded through the old town. A group of youths burst on to the street behind her and, sending up a prayer that Isabelle would be safe, Valérie turned her bike and walked steadily away through the cobbled streets.

Despite the warmth of the evening, she felt a cold weight on the back of her neck and a shiver run down her spine. She knew all too well what it was like to be in possession of vital information needed by the Allies and coveted by the Nazis. The constant terror of being caught, the strain at the thought of failing the war effort, that feeling of always being on guard.

How could a thirteen-year-old girl, all alone in the world, possibly hold up under such pressure? And could Valérie help the Resistance to smuggle her across to safety, before it was too late? What had become of Hannelore, who might be the child's only remaining living relative? Hannelore, who had once been in love with her own mother's friend, Jacob. Perhaps Hannelore and her mother had even known each other? Either way, Valérie knew her mother would have done anything to help Clara and bring her to safety. For Jacob's sake, she would surely have tried to find Hannelore, too, and reunite her with Clara. But how could Valérie help Hannelore, with no clue as to her whereabouts?

Valérie knew from her mother that Jacob Steinberg had left Nazi Germany in 1935. As a Jew, he had lost his job and faced increasing danger and discrimination. So he'd come to Geneva, opened his bookshop and her mother went to work for him, although neither of them had looked on it as work. She could still see his tall figure, surrounded by books, creating a community of culture-lovers who had escaped the Nazis as he had, seeking solidarity and companionship as well as a shared appreciation of literature.

She paused, her hand on the doorknob of their tall townhouse, and glanced back along the familiar cobbled street, wondering whether she should have gone after the woman. Her fear and tension still lingered in the air along with the feeling that someone was out there lurking in the shadows. But the street was deserted. With a sigh, Valérie turned back to her home, knowing how lucky she was that a warm meal and the love of her father waited for her inside. *Hold on, Clara,* she whispered to herself. *I'm going to find you soon.*

THREE

VALÉRIE

Geneva

Valérie took a step back in surprise when the door crashed open in front of her as she stretched out her hand to open it. A figure came rushing out, almost colliding with her on the steps.

'Excuse me, mademoiselle,' said the small, balding man from the German consulate, his accent still as strong as it had been the first time she'd met him.

She stood to the side to let him pass.

'*Guten Abend*, Herr Hoffman.'

He bowed to her without stopping, sketched a wave and scuttled up the street, disappearing round the corner as she went inside.

'Valérie, is that you?'

Her father Albert looked up when she entered the dining room, his calm gaze sweeping over her face with a broad smile. She kissed him and then sat down at the long wooden dining table in front of all his watchmaking tools.

'What was Herr Hoffman doing here?'

'Oh, he was just giving me those export licenses he promised me.'

Her father waved at the papers at the end of the polished table.

'He was only here for a minute or so. Wouldn't wait. Unlike his predecessor at the German consulate, he really does only seem interested in supporting German trade with Switzerland. It's good to deal with someone like that.'

'Good,' was all Valérie replied.

Her father carefully put away his watchmaking tools into a leather pouch. He was wearing one of his fine woollen waist-coats, finished off by a smart collar and tie. While he seemed as calm and controlled as ever, in the pool of light from the oil lamp shining down on the table she couldn't help but notice the fine lines on his face and the grey hairs taking over his head. The stresses of the last few years had sapped his energy, aging him rapidly.

'You're working late tonight, Papa,' she said.

He gestured towards the delicate watch mechanisms on the table in front of him, next to his eyeglass and favourite tools. 'I prefer to do some of the more valuable pieces here rather than in the workshop. It's safer for everyone.'

She nodded. He trusted his workers, but he made sure that they concentrated on making the products for their German clients. It was only Valérie who knew that some of her father's watch mechanisms and jewel bearings were destined for use in Allied weapons.

'I expected you earlier,' he said as placed the valuable parts carefully in small boxes and locked them in a large metal strongbox at the side of the table.

'A woman came and spoke to me on my way home,' said Valérie, resting her chin in her hands. 'She wants me to help the Resistance get a young girl across the border to Switzerland.' She looked up at her father. 'The girl's father told her to look for

Jacob Steinberg, that he would help Clara. She couldn't find him so she came to me instead.'

'You know that Jacob's been gone since before the war,' said her father abruptly.

'I thought you might have some idea where he might be; he might have said something to you or to Maman.'

He didn't reply and looked back down at the table until Valérie spoke again.

'I just get the sense that there's something else going on, something Jacob was involved in. Something Maman knew about too.' Valérie didn't want to tell him she had evidence from the Allies that Jacob was passing German secrets to them before the war but didn't know how involved her mother might have been. 'I understand why you hate talking about that time, about Maman's accident, but please, Papa. You must know something.'

Her father sighed and she leaned across the table to grasp his hand. After a few long minutes, he looked up at her.

'I don't know much more about Jacob than you do. He set up the bookshop and asked your mother to run it for him. They both loved literature and surrounded themselves with artists and writers. Your mother sourced the books and managed the business side. He provided all the funds and created a community of artists and writers, people from across Europe who had fled from the Nazis before the war, trying to escape from a desperate situation.'

He paused, staring not at her but into the past. 'I never quite trusted Jacob, but your mother wouldn't hear a word against him. And you seemed to like him.'

In a flash of insight, Valérie could see it all, everything he wasn't prepared to say. He'd been jealous of Jacob and quietly resented her mother's desire to spend so much time in the other man's company. She could see him in her mind's eye, as clear as if he were right in front of her. He was a tall, well-dressed man with a perfectly trimmed beard, his deep voice booming out as he welcomed people into the bookshop. Her father's crisp Swiss formality was very different from the gregarious German exile.

Her father continued to speak. 'I know he previously worked for Deutsche Bank in Frankfurt. He was quite senior and used to travel to Switzerland for his job, which is why he came to Geneva when he was forced to leave the bank. He hated to talk about the past. Given what was happening in Germany even then, we could understand that.'

'And he didn't say where he was going when he left?'

'He just came here one day and told me he had to leave, that there was something he needed to do.'

'Isabelle – the woman tonight – talked about a woman Jacob was in love with. Her name is Hannelore, and she is the little girl's aunt. She is missing too. Do you know anything about her?'

Her father hesitated. 'Yes, I remember Hannelore, she became a great friend of your mother's.' He got up, went to the dresser and searched through some papers, then came back to the table with a photograph that Valérie had never seen before. In it were two women walking along the path at the lakeside arm in arm, wrapped up against the cold on what was clearly a winter's day. One of the women was her mother, laughing towards the camera, her dark, curly hair framing her face. The other was shorter, her wavy brown hair caught beneath her cloche hat. She was very pretty, strikingly so, even in the black-and-white image.

'That's the last photograph I have of your mother,' said her father. 'She looks so happy. She always was, when she was with Hannelore.'

'I feel like I've seen her before, but I don't know where.'

'Well, she sometimes went to the bookshop, so you might have seen her there. She came down to Geneva quite regularly to visit Jacob, but after your mother died, I never saw her again. And then Jacob left too. I never really asked or thought about what happened to them, not after your mother died. It took all my energy just to keep going, and then the war began.'

He rubbed his forehead as she blinked back her tears.

'I'm sorry to make you think about it all again, Papa...'

He tried to smile, but his eyes were full of pain. 'I can't believe it's five years since we lost her. Sometimes it feels like she's going to walk in again through that door, as if nothing had happened...' He sighed. 'I blamed Jacob for her death. Honestly, I was glad when he left and closed up the bookshop.'

'But Maman died in an accident, Papa. You said the driver had a stroke and it wasn't anyone's fault.'

'It might have been an accident, but she wouldn't have been out if it hadn't been for him. She was out that night seeing someone connected to him.'

'Do you know what she was doing there?'

'No. She asked me to pick her up at the Place de Cornavin, but when I was late she started walking to meet me. Then the car slid off the road in the square. They said the driver was dead before he hit your mother.'

He couldn't carry on and bent his head. Valérie leaned forward and rested her head on his shoulder.

'I'm sorry, Papa.'

They were quiet for a while, until Valérie found a way to change the subject.

'I'll speak to Marianne about the girl tomorrow when I'm out seeing Philippe. She has the best contacts in the Resistance.' She still couldn't believe that her fiancé, Philippe, was in Geneva and hadn't been called back to the fort above Saint-Maurice to play his part in defending the Swiss Redoubt in the Alps. He had saved her life by taking a bullet that had been meant for her and had spent months recovering over the summer.

Her father tried once again to summon up a smile. 'How is Philippe? The doctors think he's fully recovered now?'

'Yes, they're very pleased with him. He was so lucky the bullet missed his spine.' She shivered. 'A few millimetres to the left and he wouldn't have been able to walk again. It was that close.'

Albert grasped her hand. 'Don't think about what might have happened. It's all turned out well. And once this war is over, we'll have a wedding to look forward to.'

He glanced down at her fingers. 'You're not wearing your engagement ring.'

Valérie unclasped the silver chain round her neck and slipped the ring on to her finger, the diamonds sparkling in the looped platinum setting as they caught the light.

'Just keeping it safe.'

They exchanged a smile.

'You'll miss Philippe when he goes away,' said her father. 'It's been like the old times since he came out of hospital.' He stood up and kissed her forehead. 'Go to bed, mignonne. It's late and you're tired. Once you've found the girl, your part is done. You can forget about Jacob Steinberg and leave the past behind.'

But as Valérie climbed the stairs slowly and went into her bedroom, she knew it wouldn't be that simple. The past had barged into her life and she could not stop thinking about Jacob, Hannelore and her mother, and how much she wanted to reunite Clara with Hannelore. She leaned out of the window and looked down at the cobbled street, breathing in the cool night air before closing the wooden shutters and lighting the brass oil lamp next to her bed.

She propped up the photograph of her mother and Hannelore on her dressing table and stared at it, wondering what else she didn't know about her mother or her past.

Shaking her head to banish her unease, she brushed her fingertips across her favourite photograph of her and Philippe laughing together. The first few weeks after he was shot had been so painful, when they didn't know if he would ever fully recover. She'd spent hours with him, watching him try to stand and then to take a few hesitant steps, trying to encourage him not to push himself too hard and to be patient with his healing body. But once he'd started to move around more easily, his progress was swift. And now, she knew that he would soon leave her again to go back to Saint-Maurice. He loved her but he missed his unit. Switzerland was under constant threat of a German invasion, and Philippe wouldn't be content until he was able to resume his role in defending his country.

Her eyes rested on her bookshelves, which were full of the books Jacob had given her mother. What secrets had he been hiding in Geneva? She twisted round to open the top drawer of her dressing table and pulled out the background file note her old Special Operations Executive contact, Henry Grant, had found and given her before he'd left Geneva. She held it up to the dim light.

Jacob Steinberg, no known family. Reliable intelligence source, ample funds available, source unknown. Book-shop used as cover for spying activities. Likely target for German counter-intelligence.

The words *no known family* made her think again about Hannelore and Clara. They must be feeling so alone, hunted by Nazis with little hope for survival – let alone of seeing one another again.

She picked out of the drawer a notebook she'd found in the bookshop and flicked through the pages. The notes in her moth-er's neat handwriting, so like her own writing, were all related to book orders and deliveries, meetings with the bookshop accountant and lawyer. Jacob's scribbled notes in black marker pen were difficult to read, but she could make out some random words that seemed unconnected. She threw the notebook down onto the table in frustration. They wouldn't have left anything important in the disorder of the bookshop; she would have to find answers somewhere else. But as the notebook fell open at one of the pages with her mother's handwriting, she picked it up again, holding it to her heart. Just like her father, she too often felt as though her mother might walk through the door one day, like nothing had ever happened. She imagined conversations with her where she advised Valérie on everything from her work with the Resistance to her future with Philippe. But her mother was gone, and all Valérie had left were fragments of memories, photographs and books, little reminders of the empty space she'd left behind.

She looked around her bedroom, at the familiar furniture and well-worn shutters and felt a pang of pity for Clara, torn from everything she knew and split up from Hannelore. She knew exactly what her mother would advise her to do: reunite the broken family if it was still possible rather than delve into old secrets from the past.

Valérie went over to the bookshelves and pulled out a couple of novels at random, slotting the notebook at the back of the shelf before replacing them. She was surprised by her own desire to hide the notebook but she had so many questions now about the bookshop and what her mother might have been doing there that Valérie wasn't going to leave it lying around until she knew more. She tried to shrug off her feeling of foreboding. She would see Philippe tomorrow and that would surely cheer her up.

FOUR
CLARA

France

After three days in hiding, jumping at any noise outside and scared of a knock on the door, Clara went with her mother to the Gare de Lyon. They'd discussed it many times, the plan her father had prepared now being enacted. She blinked as the cold wind blew dust into her eyes. The only difference was that they'd never planned on doing it without him. Clara glanced at her mother walking next to her; neither of them spoke. She saw other families going along the familiar city streets in the same direction, trying to flee south to Vichy France, in case their lives would be better there.

As they neared the station and its familiar clock tower, people were converging from all directions and it was loud and chaotic. German guards were shouting at the passengers, herding them towards one of the goods trains in the sidings beyond the platforms. Clara and her family had only come to Paris the year before, when they thought that France would be safer than life in Germany, but they knew now that nowhere in

France was safe for them; the Nazis were in control everywhere.

It had happened as quickly as her father had warned her it would. *When someone approaches you, just go with them, don't try to stay with us. I've found a way out for you, people who can help get you to safety and you can trust them. But they can't take us as well. I've given you the names you will need if you reach Geneva.*

The thought of separating from her parents had terrified her. *How can you leave me?* she'd wanted to cry. *I'll be all alone.* But the pain in his face and her mother's tears stilled her protests. Her father gave her an envelope and made her promise never to show it to anyone, not unless she was in a safe place and she was sure they were working for the Allies. Only then could she hand it over.

And now he had been taken and his words echoed in her ears with added weight. *We can't be together and you need to protect the document I've given you.* Always the document, she thought bitterly, but she knew how important it was.

She shivered as they walked. It was starting to get cold, the late autumn weather casting a covering of grey cloud over the town. Her mother had given her the best warm coat she had to wear, saying that it didn't fit her any longer.

Despite all the preparation, she was still taken by surprise when a young woman pushed through the crowd and walked beside them as they came closer to the station.

'Is this Clara?' she asked in a low voice. When her mother nodded, the stranger took Clara's arm and whispered, 'Come with me now.' Clara felt the pressure on her arm as the young woman steered her away. She tried to share a last message or look with her mother, craning her head around as the solitary figure walked swiftly towards the goods yard. Her last glimpse seared itself onto her memory as another woman she didn't know put her arm round her mother's shaking shoulders and supported her, before they disappeared into the crowd. And behind her, she heard shouts and cries from the people being herded into the wagons, younger children separated from their parents. Her companion walked even more quickly when they heard the noise of gunfire coming from the siding, pulling her along and resisting Clara's attempts to go back and find her mother.

Eyes full of tears, Clara looked up at the young woman, realising that she was still only a teenager, barely five or six years older than she was. Her father had told her that she would be helped by an organisation that was trying to rescue children from France and take them to Switzerland. 'You could come too,' she'd said desperately, but he'd shaken his head. 'They can only help children; it's the best we can do.'

The woman led her to a quiet street behind the Gare de Lyon, away from the bustle of the station, towards a church. She rang the bell at the gate, which was opened immediately and Clara followed her inside. Two old black cars, covered in dust and grime, were parked in front of the church and the young woman took her to the first one and opened the back door so she could climb inside. 'We'll need to wait for the others. Then you'll be taken south, away from Paris. It'll be a long drive.' She squeezed her arm, closed the door and stood at the side of the car.

In the other car, Clara saw younger children in tears, being comforted by a nun dressed in a white robe. An older boy, about her age, was sitting in the front of the car she was in, hunched down so that she could only see a few sandy-coloured curls on the headrest. He was staring forward, his stance repelling all contact.

Before long, two other teenage girls scrambled into the back seat next to her. They must have been sisters, maybe twins, and they held one another tightly. Clara squeezed into a smaller space in the corner and the girl next to her mumbled an apology. The young woman got behind the wheel of the car and turned to the back.

'We'll be driving for most of the day. If anyone stops us, we're moving you from one children's home in Paris to another out in the country. Just keep quiet, whatever I say.'

She took a baguette out of a paper bag and gave them each a piece before they drove away. 'Eat first and then you'd better sleep. We won't get to our destination until it's dark.'

Clara nibbled at the bread, feeling sick to her stomach as she looked out of the window at the outskirts of Paris, wondering where they were going and trying not to think about what could be happening to her mother and where her father was now. She felt as if everything she'd seen that day had happened to someone else, it couldn't be real, but she knew that nothing would ever be the same again. She might never see her mother and father again or know what had happened to them. Biting her lip until she tasted blood, she pushed down the panic and the tears, knowing that if she started to cry, she would never stop. Her father had told her to be strong, to keep the envelope safe and to try to find Hannelore in Geneva. She wouldn't let him down.

FIVE
VALÉRIE

Geneva

Valérie tossed and turned that night, her dreams about Clara and Hannelore fleeing from Nazi soldiers mixed up with Isabelle's fear of the spies following her. Unable to sleep, she rose early the next morning and left home when it was still dark, pushing her bike along the cobbled street leading to the Cathédrale Saint-Pierre and past the opening to the cul-de-sac where Isabelle had stopped her the previous night.

As it was so early, and she had fewer watch deliveries to make for her father that day, she leaned her bike against a tree and walked down the short flight of steps, past the statue opposite the Hôtel Les Armures, going a few metres towards the lake along the route the woman had taken the night before. Unsure what she was looking for, she scanned the cobbles and scuffed them with her shoe. On her right, an old woman was vigorously brushing the bottom step leading into her apartment, her back turned to Valérie.

'Hello Madame Moulin, I wonder if you could help me.'

The woman turned round and leaned on her brush,

breathing heavily from her exertion. The apron strapped around her stout midriff was faded and her nose was smudged with dirt where she had rubbed it. She stared at Valérie, unsmiling, and waited for her to speak. Valérie took a step closer.

'There was a woman who came this way last night as it was getting dark and I was worried someone might have been following her. Did you see or hear anything?'

The woman shook her head.

'I'm too busy looking after my husband to pay much attention to what's going on outside.'

She waved towards the window and Valérie saw the silhouette of a man sitting in a wheelchair staring at them through the thin curtains.

'In any case, it's safer if you mind your own business these days. I don't want to know what devilment might be going on outside my own front door. I've got enough to deal with trying to keep us both alive to worry about anyone else.'

'I'm sorry... I just wanted to ask...'

The woman's expression thawed a fraction and, encouraged, Valérie persevered.

'I don't suppose your husband heard anything, did he? Or maybe saw something out of the window?'

'He's a bit deaf, but his eyesight isn't bad. You could come in and ask him, if you like.'

'Yes please.'

Valérie followed the old woman inside the building and turned into the living room, where the old man was sitting in front of the window, the small room dominated by his wheelchair and the solid table in front of him.

'Monsieur Moulin, how are you?'

As always when Valérie spoke to him, she was careful to stand directly in front of him and speak slowly and clearly. Whatever his wife said, Valérie knew the old man could understand her. However small the chance he'd seen what had happened to Isabelle the night before, she wanted to know.

'Same as always,' he replied. 'How's your father getting on, these days?'

'He's well, thank you. I wondered if you saw a woman going past the window at around supper time, yesterday evening.'

Almost before she'd finished speaking, he was shaking his head.

'My son comes every night and then he helps put me to bed later on. I didn't see anyone outside when he was here.'

Valérie tried to hide her disappointment.

'Thank you, monsieur.'

'I saw some men earlier in the evening acting a bit oddly. They seemed to be looking for something. Two of them, wearing light raincoats. The young one had a camera and was taking photographs. The older one was shorter and heavier, looked like a bull.'

She stared at him and caught her breath when she remembered the men she'd seen walk into the Place du Bourg-de-Four the previous evening.

'They seemed to be arguing, but I couldn't hear what they were saying.' He shrugged. 'Can't tell you anything else, I'm afraid.'

'That's all right. If you see them again, I'd like to know. If it's all right, I might drop by again next week.'

He nodded and Valérie left the apartment, picked up her bike and rode towards the cathedral square through narrow streets, shivering in the cool morning breeze. She was relieved to feel the warmth of the sun on her back when she emerged into the square and pushed her bike past the tall pillars at the front of the cathedral.

On her way out of the city to see Philippe, she would call into the Café de Paris and find out if her friend Geraldine had seen Isabelle the night before. She might even be able to tell her who she was. If there was any news about what could have happened to her, Geraldine would be sure to have heard it. And she wanted to say thank you for all the food she'd sent to Philippe and his grandfather over the summer. Geraldine might want to forget about the war, but the practical support she provided to her friends and neighbours was generous and constant.

Valérie crossed the Place du Bourg-de-Four amid the bustle of the shopkeepers opening their shops and unloading deliveries. Once at the café, she leaned her bike on the side of the old stone building. Geraldine had just finished setting up the outside tables and was unfurling the dark green canopy above the café windows. She took Valérie's arm. 'Hello, you. Come inside. I have a meal for you to take to Philippe and his grandfather. I assume you're going there. It's too early for most of our customers so we'll have the place to ourselves.'

Valérie followed Geraldine into the wood-panelled bar, comforted by the familiar atmosphere and smell of coffee. She leaned on the glazed partition that protected the entrance from the worst draughts in the winter as Geraldine pulled out one of the bar stools for her and placed a package and bottle of wine on the counter.

'A piece of gruyere and a bottle of Fendant. We got a wine delivery yesterday.'

Valérie opened the package, and the strong smell of cheese filled her nostrils.

'It smells wonderful. Even Agathe hasn't been able to find any gruyere for months now and she gets all our supplies.' She sat on the stool. 'How can we thank you for all the food you've sent? You've been so generous.'

Geraldine smiled, her blonde curls bouncing.

'It's the least I can do. My father never notices if I give away a little bit now and then.' She thought for a few seconds. 'Or maybe he does notice and thinks I'm doing the right thing.'

Valérie watched her skilfully prepare two coffees and place one on the bar in front of her.

'How is Philippe now?' asked Geraldine, taking a sip of her rich espresso. 'You must have been so worried about him.'

'He's fine now, thank goodness.'

'When's the wedding going to be? Are you still waiting until the war is over? I don't see why you can't get married now, it would cheer us all up.'

Valérie shook her head.

'You know why. We want to wait until everything gets back to normal, the whole madness of war is over and we can properly be together.'

Geraldine pulled out a cloth from under the bar and rubbed the wooden surface energetically.

Valérie took another sip of coffee, resisting the impulse to go into the reasons she couldn't contemplate having such a happy occasion when they were surrounded by so much misery. The faces of the Jewish children and families she'd helped escape from occupied France haunted her thoughts and she knew their plight needed to be over before she could truly be happy. And now there was another girl she had to keep safe. Clara was in as much danger as any of the other children she'd helped.

Geraldine stopped polishing and her lips curved into a satisfied smile. 'At least I've got some good news for a change. I've met someone new.'

'That's nice. Who is he?'

'He's called Klaus Werner. Works in banking, very tall and handsome. He's interested in the history of the old town; he's always taking lots of pictures and asking questions about Geneva.'

The mention of a camera brought back the memory of the men she'd seen the night before that Monsieur Moulin had talked about. 'You'll need to introduce me to him.' Valérie smiled, as she glanced at the clock and jumped off her stool. 'I need to go, or I'll never get out of town and back again in time. Thank you so much for the coffee, Geraldine, and for the cheese and wine. I had a question for you. Was anyone looking for a woman last night? Did you hear anyone asking in the bar for someone called Isabelle?'

Geraldine stopped polishing the shiny wood. 'They're always talking about women in here. What is she like?'

'She's older than us, with brown eyes and dark hair going grey. She was wearing a blue suit with a blue and white scarf.'

'No one who came in last night said anything about a woman like that. Is she a spy?'

Valérie shook her head.

'Just someone helping the French Resistance, but she said she was being followed, so I'm worried about her.'

Geraldine's face fell and she shivered. 'That sounds frightening. I'll ask around today, see if I hear anything.'

'Thanks Geraldine.'

She leaned forward over the counter, still clutching her duster.

'If you're seeing Marianne, ask her to come and see me. It's been ages since she's come over for a drink. She's always working these days and never seems to have time for her friends any longer.' Geraldine's red lips drooped. 'She's either working at the telephone exchange or on the farm. I never see her at all.'

'You know it's only her and her mother left now, and with having to get the harvest in, I'm not surprised she hasn't been in town so much.'

'But I thought they had help. Haven't they got a couple of internees on the farm, some English airmen shot down last year?'

'Yes, but they still need to take advantage of the good weather.'

She felt a pang of sympathy for her friend. An uneasy mistrust of Geraldine's various admirers had taken firm hold in

Marianne's mind and she had avoided going to the café, even on the days when she worked at the telephone exchange.

'Apart from you, Bernard's the only one who still comes to see me. And most of the time, he looks at me in that disapproving way he has.'

Valérie wasn't going to get dragged into her friend's relationship with her neighbour. Ever since they'd been children, Geraldine and Bernard had squabbled and then made up their differences.

'You know he's very fond of you, deep down.'

'So deep down it's invisible,' retorted Geraldine.

Valérie burst out laughing and Geraldine responded with a reluctant smile.

SIX

VALÉRIE

Geneva

Valérie cycled out of the city towards Philippe's grandfather's house in Vessy, townhouses and apartment blocks thinning out and giving way to warehouses and factories, the green patches of grass and trees expanding into fields of crops. She cycled past the men working on the land, internees drafted in to help the local farmers with their crops. No one looked up at her as she passed, their backs bent over the heavy work of clearing the fields and planting the seed for next year. The chill of the early morning air had given way to a clear day, but it was still cold. Valérie looked across at the hills to the south of Geneva. They weren't high enough for snow, but this late in the year, the Alps would have got the first snowfalls of winter.

She turned off the main road leading to the border with France and stopped for a few moments to look at the frontier post only a few hundred metres away. For most of the year, the Swiss border police had been boosted by German soldiers watching the crossing for escaped refugees. Her eyes scanned the border in each direction and she saw more soldiers dotted along the fields, alerted to some desperate soul trying to cross over. She saw them all run to one spot and heard shouts across the fields. The beauty of the day dimmed in that moment, tainted by the ugly scene unfolding only a few metres away and she bent her head, pedalling more quickly along the narrow country road, trying not to think about the hunted human being so close to safety. She could not save them all, but she would do everything she could to save Clara.

As she approached the house, cycling past the outbuildings on the farm, she saw Philippe digging the large garden, his back towards her. He stood up and leaned on the spade, his movements smooth and sure. She breathed a sigh of contentment. There seemed to be no weakness left from his injury and he looked fit and muscular from a summer and autumn spent outside. Sensing her presence, he looked up and smiled, then dropped the spade and strode towards her to open the gate.

'I hoped you'd come over today.'

He clasped her close to him and kissed her. She drank in the warmth of his hazel eyes. She had been next to him every step of the way in his recovery, sitting with him in hospital and then spending hours at the house in Vessy. She felt closer to him than ever before and didn't think that anything or anyone could come between them again.

He took her bike from the gate.

'Come and sit down.'

She followed him to the table and chairs on the grass sheltered by the side of the house and he poured them some water from a heavy glass jug.

'Where's your grandfather?' asked Valérie.

'Sleeping. He wasn't feeling well this morning so I told him to stay in bed.'

'Is he all right?'

'I think so, but I caught him tidying up the old barn this morning. I don't know what he was doing in there but he wouldn't come inside until he'd finished. You know he's not good at resting.'

Philippe handed her a glass and she drank thirstily. 'I can't stay for long, I need to speak to Marianne. Someone asked for my help last night, to get a girl out of France and to safety in Switzerland. She's in a children's home, so I thought Marianne's friend Genevieve might know where she is. I think she works in one of the children's homes.'

He nodded, but she could tell that his mind was elsewhere. 'I got a letter from Christophe.'

'Oh, how is he? What news did he have from the fort?'

'He doesn't know when I'll be called back but he said that they need all the experienced marksmen they can get. There are more rumours of an invasion. With the Allies coming through Italy from the south and the Germans taking over the north of the country, we're right next to the fighting. We've got to hold the mountains against the Germans if they decide to attack.'

The determination and resolve resonated in his voice.

She ran her fingers down his cheek. 'I know that you can't stay here for much longer.' Like everyone else in Switzerland she had listened to the news of Mussolini's downfall and the impact on ordinary Italian citizens. The Germans had occupied the north of the country to stop the Allied advance from the south. The Italian population was buffeted uneasily between them, mistrusted by both sides.

'But that isn't all he said...' Philippe held her hand, as if he didn't know how to go on. He stared down at their hands, and she felt a flash of fear, an emotion that she hadn't felt for months, but one that took her right back to the day she'd almost lost him.

'Philippe, tell me. What else did he say?'

He looked at her finally and sighed heavily.

'He said Stefano has left the army and gone to Italy. His

cousins and some of their friends joined the partisans and are fighting the Germans in the mountains down from Ticino. Stefano was virtually brought up with them, his aunt was like a mother to him, and they haven't heard anything from them for days. Stefano went across to Italy to find out what happened and he's gone missing now too.'

'That's awful. I'm so sorry. But what can you do?'

'Well, I don't have to go back to the fort just yet, I have some time.' He leaned forward, gripping her hands tightly, his voice deepening. 'I have to go and find him, get him back.'

Her heart plummeted. 'But Philippe, the whole area is occupied by the Germans. It's all over the news. The place is lawless, fascists and partisans tearing it apart.'

'I know, Valérie. But Stefano saved my life, and he's one of my men. I have to do whatever I can to bring him home safe. And I won't be alone, Christophe says Yves will go with me. He speaks fluent Italian.'

'No, Philippe. Please, don't go. It's too dangerous, you'll be risking everything and so soon after we nearly lost you. Not just your life, but mine too. I don't want to live without you.'

He looked at her steadily. 'That's very like what I once said to you.'

She released his hand and sat back in her chair. 'I know and I went into France anyway. I was just waiting for you to throw that back at me.' She felt the tears prick her eyes and dashed them away angrily.

'I'd have died in that avalanche if Stefano hadn't come back for me, Valérie. Please, try to understand. You would do the same.'

She knew he was right. She had risked her life countless times for strangers, and she would do so again for Clara now too. And this was a friend of Philippe's —one of his own men. Nothing would stop him from trying to bring Stefano home safe, no matter how dangerous it was, no matter how much she pleaded.

Before she could speak, they heard a shout from the road-side and turned together to see Marianne wave from the gate.

'Can I come in?'

Marianne opened the gate and walked towards them, carrying a basket over one arm. In her tan trousers and jacket, with her dark curly hair shining, she looked healthy and full of life, more so than she had for a long time since her brother's death. She set the basket down on the table with a grin.

'I've brought something for your supper from my mother.'

Philippe lifted the cloth and looked inside the basket, then gave Marianne a hug.

'This looks lovely, please thank her for us.'

He got up to take the basket inside, but Marianne kept hold of the handle.

'It's all right. I'll take it. You love birds can stay outside.'

She grinned at them, whisked the basket off the table with a flourish and went inside.

'That's so kind of Madame Ducret,' said Valérie. 'She must have enough people to feed on their farm without helping anyone else.'

'Mmn...' Philippe frowned as he looked at the door slam-ming shut behind Marianne.

'What's the matter?'

He turned back to her, the frown deepening. 'How much is Marianne doing for the Resistance? Do you know?'

Valérie shrugged, thinking again about her close friend and the contacts she had in the Resistance. 'She's working at the telephone exchange, she passes on intelligence to the Allies. And she's been busy on the farm all summer, helping her mother. Why?'

'I think she's helping more refugees escape across the border... not just meeting them, but arranging for them to get further into Switzerland and organising their escape routes. I get the impression that the Resistance relies on her a lot more these days.'

He hesitated and then carried on. 'And I'm beginning to wonder if she's using this place to hide some of them.'

'You think your grandfather's involved?'

'I can't decide if he's actively involved or if he's just decided to turn a blind eye and let her use his outbuildings.'

'If he wants to help, then isn't that his decision?'

She saw the conflict in his face, admiration for the old man clouded by worry.

'I agree it is, but he's a sick old man, Valérie. He isn't fit enough to take on the border police, if they start harassing him. I'm worried he might have another heart attack.'

'What has your father said?'

'The same as me really; he's worried about another heart attack. And his job doesn't help. He's a senior police officer, how would his superiors react if they discovered his father was flouting the law only a few kilometres away? You know what the Swiss authorities are like, they don't hesitate to prosecute the people helping the refugees.'

'I know, but it's a long time since I've heard your father criticise people for helping the Resistance. I think he's changed, and I think he knows that this is more important than his job.'

He nodded. 'You're right, but we still worry that Grandfather's not fit enough.'

'What makes you think refugees are hiding here?'

'Well, I'm not sure, but Marianne's been coming over more often in the last few weeks and meeting him alone. What else would they be talking about? And he's developed this obsession with the barn and keeping it in order. It isn't like him.'

'Okay, but even if he is involved, it won't be for long. He can't stay here alone once you've gone back to Saint-Maurice. He'll go back to stay with your parents, won't he?'

'He can't stay here alone, that's for sure.' With an effort, he smiled across at her. 'I'm sorry. It's just that he worries me. You know what he's like, as determined as ever, ignoring the fact that he's been so ill and acting like he's thirty years younger than he is.'

They heard the door open and turned to see Marianne come back outside. She sat down at the table and turned to Valérie. 'How are things in town?'

Valérie leaned forward. 'I need your help,' she said. 'A woman spoke to me last night and asked me if I could help the Resistance get a young German girl out of France. She may be taken to one of the children's homes to protect her from the Gestapo. I don't know which one it is, but I thought of your friend Genevieve. She knows people there, doesn't she?'

'Yes. Genevieve works in one of the homes near Lyon, in a place called Izieu and she helps get children into Switzerland. I'll get a message to her and find out if your girl is there or in one of the other homes. What's her name?'

'She's called Clara, Clara Lieberman. She's only thirteen years old.'

Marianne nodded. 'Leave it with me and I'll let you know the plan for getting her across.'

'Thanks so much, Marianne. Maybe we could meet in the Café de Paris? Geraldine was asking when you're coming; it's ages since we've all been there together.'

Marianne sighed. 'I know. I'm sorry, but I've been avoiding it. I'm just not sure about Geraldine. She's always cosying up to the nearest man who's come into the café. And her last admirer almost got you both killed. You know how she lives in her own world.'

Valérie still thought Marianne was being too harsh. 'I'm sure if we needed her help, she'd be right behind us. We've known one another since we were small.'

Marianne took a piece of paper out of her pocket. 'This is

the latest information on German movements from one of the English agents operating near Annecy.'

'I'll pass it on. I'm seeing Bill Paterson from the Special Operations Executive later today.'

'Thanks,' said Marianne. 'Do you have any idea who the woman last night was?'

The memory of the fear in her eyes made Valérie shiver, despite the warmth of the pale sun. She swallowed a couple of times before replying. 'I only know her name – Isabelle. But she certainly knew me.'

'Did she say anything else?'

'Only that she was being followed by some Germans. She said she worked for the Resistance too.'

'They were spies then. Why were they following her?'

'There is something special about the child, Clara. She has information on her, and the Gestapo are looking for it.'

'So, she's in even more danger than most. Whatever the information is, it must be absolutely crucial to the Nazi side. We have to get her to safety as soon as possible.'

SEVEN
VALÉRIE

Geneva

It was late in the afternoon when Valérie reached the Place De-Grenus. She stood outside the familiar, tall apartment building overshadowed by the trees in the centre of the semi-circular square and rang the bell, glancing up at the first-floor window. There was no sign of life, an opaque curtain draped across the window. After hesitating for a few seconds, she pulled her bike away from the wall. But before she could move away, the large door opened and she heard the unmistakable voice of Bill Paterson, the bracing Scotsman who'd replaced Henry Grant, her previous Allied contact in the SOE Geneva office. The Special Operations Executive was the British organisation funding the French Resistance and organising espionage and sabotage against the Axis powers. Bill was older and shorter than Henry, habitually wore tweed and his red hair had faded to a sandy colour. He waved his plump hands towards her.

'Come away in...'

She wheeled her bike into the marbled hall and left it next to the ornate brass lift, before following him upstairs to the first floor. The dry, slightly musky smell of the apartment filled her nostrils as she walked through the hall to the living room, bare of all but the necessary furniture.

Bill waved in the general direction of the sofa and sat down opposite her, as she took out the watch part deliveries from her satchel and handed them over. Her deliveries all around the city for her father made it easy for her to hide her more clandestine activities in passing information between the Allies and the Resistance. Now that the safe house for the refugees from occupied France was Jacob's old apartment above the bookshop – today owned by the SOE – rather than her father's old workshop that she'd used in the past, she had another reason to keep in touch with Bill. He checked the papers and signed them with a flourish.

'This all seems in order,' said Bill. 'You'll have a drink?'

'Thank you.'

He stood up and poured whisky into two tumblers, added some water and handed her one. She'd got used to the whisky, but would have much preferred the tea and cakes she used to share with Henry.

'So, what news do you have for me?'

Valérie took out the paper Marianne had given her and passed it across.

'Marianne gave me this information on German activities north of Annecy.'

He scanned the note and frowned. 'The Maquis are being punished for the few successes they've achieved. German reprisals are hitting them hard.'

The Maquis were the Resistance fighters in the Haute Savoie region of France, who operated south of Geneva.

'I heard on the radio that the situation in Italy is worse.'

He nodded and his eyes were sharp in his round face. 'The Germans are flooding the north with troops to stop our advance. It's going to be a hard fight coming up from the south.'

She shivered. 'I thought things couldn't get any worse.'

'They'll get worse before they get better. What we must do is keep up the fight in our small corner and trust that we'll win in the end.'

She took a sip of her drink and the strong whisky burned her throat.

He beamed at her. 'I hear young Philippe is recovering well from his injuries.'

'Yes. He'll be away quite soon,' she replied quietly, unwilling to hear more about the dangers that might face him in Italy. She glanced at her basket and Isabelle's warning rang in her ears. 'Have you heard anything about new German spies in Geneva? Two men in particular.'

He shrugged. 'We can only keep track of a fraction of them. They're in and out of Switzerland on a regular basis, working in the consulate or for one of the international organisations, even in some of our foreign businesses. Most of the time we don't even come across them. Why?'

'I met a woman last night who said she was being followed.'

'Did she know why?'

Valérie frowned. 'It could be to do with a young girl we need to rescue from France, who has important information for the Allies. The woman also mentioned Jacob Steinberg, who owned the bookshop in the old town and lived in the apartment above it. He's connected to this girl and to her aunt Hannelore who is still missing...'

'The apartment above the bookshop that we're using as a safe house?'

'Yes.'

'They could be watching it,' said Bill, frowning at his empty glass. 'Could we stop using it for a while?'

'But I need it to hide French refugees. I don't have anywhere else.'

He sat in silence, pondering over her words, then spoke.

'Take extra care when you use it. I'll try to get some information about the active spies in Geneva currently, find out who they are and what they're looking for.'

'Thank you.' She put down her glass, barely touched, and left, worried more than ever that if the safe house was being watched, the French refugees she was trying so hard to help would be put into even more danger.

EIGHT

HANNELORE

Paris

Hannelore left the laundry later than usual that evening. It was part of the large Hôtel-Dieu building on the Île de la Cité, the oldest hospital in Paris. The hospital was so large and the laundry was right at the back of the building, which meant that she could be anonymous and keep hidden. She had worked there for months and no one knew she had tried to leave Paris. In the hospital she was close enough to the medical teams to feel at home but far enough away to avoid undue attention. She tried not to feel the familiar stab of resentment whenever she realised that her degree in medicine was never going to happen in wartime, the University of Frankfurt a distant memory. She just had to hope that she could start again when the war was over.

Shielded by the trees along the River Seine, she looked around her to check there weren't any German soldiers in the area picking up pedestrians. She had her yellow star burning a hole inside her pocket rather than being in full view. She would get into trouble if she was stopped. That was the last thing she needed when it was imperative to leave the city and find Clara, but she still concealed it whenever she could because she hated it so much.

She just had to accept the reality of life in occupied Paris, that she would always be afraid of being stopped by soldiers, not knowing what would happen to her if they decided to interrogate her. At the back of her mind the constant fear that the document she was hiding would never find its way to the Allies and she would fail to do the one thing her brother had asked of her.

The streets were unusually quiet as she crossed the bridge over the Seine in front of the magnificent Hotel de Ville and walked beneath the trees on the riverside, trying to keep as invisible as possible from the few army cars and trucks driving along the quayside. It had been raining and the paving stones concealed deep puddles that she tried to avoid, but splashed into as she walked, almost tripping on the uneven pavement. She stopped abruptly to cross to the other side and gazed up at the huge town hall building looming over the road. She saw two cars drive up the side of the building, with shadowy figures inside that must have been German officers, followed by three trucks. German soldiers got out of the trucks and fragments of their shouted orders floated towards her. But she didn't need to hear all the words to know what was happening. They were out to round up more poor souls to send to their deaths in the concentration camps. She had to get away.

She left the shelter of the trees and turned to cross the road, keeping her head low, looking away from the trucks. It was too late and her heart thudded in her chest when she heard a group of soldiers coming towards her shouting at her to stop. She started to run towards the back streets away from the Seine.

When she reached the Place Saint-Gervais she pressed herself against the wall, next to the bars on the bottom windows in the old building. Peering round the corner of the building she saw the three large trucks on the other side of the square with soldiers starting to push people inside. She looked around frantically for a means of escape from the soldiers surrounding her. If she got caught up in this she would never get back to Chantal's apartment.

Before she left her hiding place to run across the front of the cathedral she heard a whisper from the shadows in the alley next to the church. 'Come this way. I can hide you.'

Hannelore ran towards the voice and followed a shadowy figure through a side door into the church. She gazed up in wonder at the tall columns and stone buttresses stretching into darkness before she was bundled inside a small room at the side of the church. She heard the grating noise of a key turning in the lock and then only the sound of her own breathing in the small space. Her mind was in turmoil; was she being hidden for her safety or was it just another French person who would hand her over to the German occupiers? She looked all around her but could see nothing in the darkness.

Suddenly she heard the noise of someone banging on the main door of the church and she realised that her hiding place must be close to the front door. The door opened and a German voice shouted, 'Have you seen a woman come in here? I want to speak to her.'

A quiet voice answered, 'No one has come in here, the church is closed, monsieur. There isn't a soul here now but please search if you want.'

After a few moments' silence, Hannelore heard the noise of boots thudding on the stone floor, coming closer to her. She hung her head, terrified of making a noise and giving away that she was there. Suddenly the heavy door handle turned but the lock held fast. Hannelore held her breath, the presence of the German soldier on the other side of the door filling her with dread. She felt her nose twitch and she put up a hand to cover it, terrified that she would sneeze and give away her hiding place.

'Where is the key?' snarled the man at the other side of the door.

'We have lost it, monsieur,' replied the priest. 'It is a store cupboard and we can no longer use it.'

The door handle clattered in the lock again with more force, but held firm. The man cursed and, after a few tense seconds, she heard his heavy steps turn away.

'If we find evidence that you've been hiding someone in here, we'll be back.'

The front door of the church opened and closed again, followed by silence. Hannelore waited for what must have been ten minutes before she heard the noise of the key turning in the lock. She looked up as the door opened, half expecting to see a German soldier but instead there was a tall priest in a white robe and carrying a candle bending down towards her. He was young and looked as scared as she felt, his face white in the candlelight and the hand holding the candle shaking the small flame.

'You must go home,' he said. 'They've gone now but I think they'll be back.'

She nodded and touched his arm. 'Thank you. I hope you won't get into any trouble because of me. You saved my life.'

The young priest smiled. 'Follow me and I can take you out the back of the church away from the square. It's been raining again so take care going home.'

They walked down through the church, then the priest opened a small door and she stepped outside. She hugged the walls of the buildings as she walked briskly home, checking for German soldiers all the way. But no one was there to stop her this time and she reached Chantal's apartment block safely. Once inside she closed the door behind her and leaned her head on the heavy wood, her heart still racing. She had been lucky tonight but she wouldn't be lucky every time. She knew that the longer she stayed in Paris the more dangerous it would become. If she was ever going to get to Switzerland and hand over the document to the Allies then she would have to get away from here soon.

'Hannelore, is that you?' Chantal's voice came from the living room, bringing her back to the reason she had stayed. How could she leave Paris?

'Yes, it's me,' replied Hannelore. 'I was trying to get dry. I'll be inside in a moment.' She turned from the door and walked along the corridor to her friend.

NINE
VALÉRIE

Geneva

Valérie turned up the hill towards her father's watch workshop on the Rue de la Tertasse, at the edge of the old town. She pushed her bike into the courtyard at the back of the building and leaned it against the ancient stone wall. When she walked inside, she saw the familiar stooped back and thinning grey hair of Luca, their old storeman, bent over the boxes he was moving to the side of the well-ordered space. Her father had asked Luca to come back when he'd re-opened the workshop. Despite his age, he hadn't hesitated in accepting.

'Luca, how are you today?'

He nodded to her. 'I'm well, Mademoiselle Valérie. Almost finished in here.'

He gestured up the stairs and sniffed. 'Your father's not in. He's gone to see that German, the one helping with the export licences. Agathe's still tidying up, and the others are just leaving.'

Valérie glanced up the stairs and looked back at Luca's

wizened face. It was devoid of any expression but she knew he'd taken a dislike to Otto Hoffman.

'Thanks. I'll go up.'

She climbed up the wooden stairs to the main workshop. A thrill of pleasure lightened her step as she emerged into the bright room, the large windows letting the late afternoon sun stream into the space, the watchmaker's tools on the benches glinting in the light. It was no longer abandoned and derelict, but clean and fresh. Her father had only recently had the work-shop renovated after the fire which had almost destroyed their home, with financial support from the Allies who weren't prepared to see their supply of watch parts jeopardised, and the brightness of the space always lifted her spirits.

At the door she paused to let her father's assistants pass, nodding at Hélène. She had been the first watchmaker's assistant he'd asked to come back, just as she'd been the last he'd let go when the business contracted. The woman hadn't hesi-tated, despite the three young children at home. Her husband hadn't worked for months and the income she could earn was all they had to live on.

'Good to see you, Hélène,' said Valérie.

'It's good to be back, miss. To think of your poor father trying to keep the business going all on his own.' She shook her head, strands of her long dark hair flying across her face in the breeze flowing up the staircase. Her capable fingers smoothed the hair back into place.

A young girl, her short blonde hair glinting in the sunlight, stood behind her. She nodded shyly at Valérie, and Hélène smiled at her. 'Come on, we need to get home.'

At the side of the workshop, Valérie hugged Agathe and led her to one of the seats.

'I'm still working, Valérie, this place won't clean itself." She was breathing heavily, her cheeks red, and a few wisps of wiry grey hair had escaped from her bun. She waved a duster around in protest, but nothing could hide her pleasure at seeing Valérie. Agathe had made it her business to look after Valérie since her mother's death even though her fingers were now too bent from arthritis to do anything but ensure the house and workshop were tidy and cook their meals. Her father's longest-serving employee, she still saw it as her job to order everyone around.

'Agathe, I wanted to talk to you, it will only take a few minutes,' said Valérie, taking the duster from her. 'Let me help with that.'

The old lady's eyes were sharp in her wrinkled face, age taking away none of her acuity.

'What is it, my dear?'

'How much do you know about Jacob Steinberg?'

'Not much, really.' The old woman gazed at her, but Valérie had the impression she didn't see her, but someone from the past. 'He went away just before the war broke out. I don't know where, but I know he couldn't go back home to Germany. With everything that's happened he wouldn't go back there.'

'I don't want to ask Papa about him because he gets upset. Talking about Jacob reminds him of Maman's accident,' Valérie prompted gently.

'Well, Jacob was a man who liked people, all kinds of people. Jews like him who had been driven from their homes and places of work, Communists, artists, all sorts. He'd welcome all of them and give them coffee and cakes he'd bought at one of the patisseries in town. He wouldn't turn anyone away and he'd let them sit there for hours, just talking to him.'

Once she'd started, Agathe continued unprompted and Valérie gazed at her lined face, the reminiscences animating her features and making her seem much younger.

'I remember there were always lots of people there, meeting up with friends, discussing things together.'

Valérie could still remember a bohemian crowd, who wore colourful and stylish clothes and enjoyed intense conversations, the lack of formality clashing with a culture where formal politeness usually reigned. She couldn't see her father approving of the people Monsieur Steinberg surrounded himself with. His reluctance to talk about the past was probably as much to do with his unease about her mother's chosen companions before her death as about the accident itself.

'Papa said he'd been a banker in Frankfurt, not a bookseller.'

'Yes. Your mother said that, although he'd been a banker, he'd always loved books, so when he was forced to leave his job and come to Geneva, he decided to start the bookshop.'

'And did you ever meet a woman he knew, called Hannelore?' asked Valérie.

Agathe looked at her unblinkingly. 'Where did you hear that name? She was a great friend of your mother's for a few years. I always thought that Jacob was in love with her, that maybe he left Geneva to find her, but I don't know if he succeeded.'

Valérie took out the photograph of Thérèse and Hannelore. 'How old was she in this photograph? She seems younger than Maman.'

Agatha stared at the photograph and shrugged. 'She was quite a bit younger than your mother. She must be in her thirties by now.'

'Did you meet her?'

'Once or twice when she came by for your mother. She wasn't here very often, but every time she came to Geneva they were inseparable.'

'I didn't even know,' said Valérie quietly.

Agathe wasn't listening. 'Jacob was very fond of your mother. You were his family, he used to say. He was devastated when Thérèse died, said it was because of him. I don't know why he would say that, when it was a car accident.'

'I hadn't realised it affected him so much.'

'Well, your mother had been going to his shop for years,

helping out with the books. He used to give her the ones she was most fond of.'

'The foreign language books in my room.'

'Yes, they all came from him. If she picked one up and showed interest in it, the next day she'd be home with it.'

Agathe was frowning now, the memories bringing back a sense of unease and she glared at Valérie as if she was angry with her for stirring up unwelcome recollections from the past.

'There was something that worried your mother about the place towards the end, she didn't want to take you with her.'

'I thought you said she liked it there?'

'At the start she did, but it changed. I don't know what was going on, but before she died, I think your mother was scared of something... or of someone.'

Valérie knew she'd spent less time in the bookshop as she got older, being outdoors more often with her friends, but she hadn't realised there was any reason behind it. Her memories of that place were all happy ones, people laughing and talking, her mother smiling and kind Monsieur Steinberg handing her a book. She opened her mouth to ask another question but promptly shut it again when she heard the noise of footsteps on the stairs. Her father came into the workshop and stopped in surprise when he saw them.

'Hello, both of you,' said Albert. 'I didn't know there was anyone still here.'

His smile faded as he looked from one to the other and something of the atmosphere in the room reached him. His gaze rested on Valérie.

'Is something the matter?'

She scrambled to her feet.

'No, Papa. We were just chatting.'

Valérie pushed her bike back through the old town, pausing to catch her breath near Jacob's bookshop. What was Jacob involved in exactly, and how were her mother and Hannelore connected to it? Did it have something to do with the information Clara was carrying? And if she found Clara and reunited her with Hannelore and Jacob somehow, would she only be putting her in more danger?

As she stood at the end of the street, leaning against one of the old buildings, she saw two men in raincoats stop opposite the bookshop and stare up at the shutters on the first floor. Her heart pounding, she watched as they crossed the cobbled street and tried to open the front door, but it was firmly locked. Then the younger man pressed his face close to the glass window to look inside. After a few moments, the older man, thickset and red-faced, looked around them and pulled his companion away, shaking his head. She recognised them, having seen them recently with the younger man taking photographs of his surroundings.

They walked towards her, so Valérie bent down to adjust the chain on her bicycle, only standing up when they'd passed. Could they be the German spies who had been following Isabelle? Were they aware the bookshop was sometimes used as a safe house for refugees, or did this have something to do with Jacob? Whatever the reason, she was certain the locked door wasn't going to put them off for long.

TEN

PHILIPPE

Geneva

Philippe took the brush from the outhouse and started to sweep the dry, dead leaves to the side of the house. It was evening and he felt the cold November wind sweeping across the fields. He was lucky to have recovered so swiftly from the gunshot wound and to have been able to spend the summer with Valérie, but he was impatient to go in search of Stefano, even though he knew he had to get back to his unit and resume his job of defending the Alps. He didn't have much time left. He leaned on the brush and looked at the building he'd known from childhood, the low farmhouse with its sweeping roof and the outbuildings around the barn. He still didn't know what would happen to his grandfather, Guillaume, when he left, particularly since he hadn't told him yet about his plan to go to Italy, but time was running out and he couldn't wait much longer.

'Evening, Philippe.' A deep voice came from the gate. It was Thierry, their neighbour and the man who was working his grandfather's land.

Philippe went to shake his hand, smiling at the sturdy figure who had helped them so much at the beginning of the summer. Thierry was the first person he'd called when he came out of hospital and pushed his body too hard. He didn't like to think about how often he'd fallen at the start, but he'd recovered each time and had grown stronger and more confident day by day.

'How's your grandfather? I've got supper for you both here,' said Thierry, handing over the wicker basket, the delicious smell of stew wafting up.

'He's fine, thanks.' Philippe lifted the basket. 'And thanks for this, it smells wonderful. Grandfather had a nasty turn the other morning but he seems better now.'

As if Thierry could read Philippe's mind, he asked, 'How long do you plan on being here for? They must be wanting you back at the fort, the way the war is going.'

Philippe sighed. 'Yes, I'll need to go away quite soon.'

Thierry nodded. 'You know that we can help out, if you need us to. Dominique is in and out of your grandfather's house all the time and I'm never very far away.'

Philippe shook his head. 'We owe you both so much already. It's too much to ask.'

'You know very well that we only got so many internees to help on the farm because your grandfather told the authorities we were working his land as well as ours. It's made a huge difference to us. And anyway, we're fond of him and it's clearly good for him to be here, out in the countryside. If we can help him to be able to stay when you're gone, then we will. Dominique is used to cooking a couple of extra portions for our meals so we can bring food down to him.'

'That's very kind, Thierry, thank you. If you're sure. The longer he can stay here, the happier he'll be.' Philippe grinned. 'And if he's happy, everyone else will get a bit of peace and quiet.'

'When will you be going?'

'Very soon. Is that all right?'

'Of course, it's fine, Philippe. We'll take care of everything.'

'Thank you so much.'

Thierry gave a wave of his hand as he walked away, and Philippe went inside. He was setting the table when his grandfather wandered into the kitchen. 'We can have supper soon,' said Philippe.

'Who were you speaking to outside?'

'Thierry. He was just going home.'

'I need to talk to him about the nearside field. He'll have to rest that field for the next year, not try to grow more crops.'

'But you know it's important to grow as much food as possible.'

'Not if it affects the yield for the future, Philippe. We don't know how long this war is going to last and how much food we're going to need.'

They ate Dominique's rabbit stew in companionable silence but Philippe's grandfather looked up at the slightest noise, from a gust of wind to an animal's cry. When they both heard the distinct sound of a door closing, Philippe couldn't ignore it any longer.

'What's going on outside? Is there somebody out there?

His grandfather shook his head violently. 'Nothing's going on. I don't know what you mean.'

'You've been jumpy all evening. I'll find out anyway so you'd better just tell me.'

Before his grandfather could reply, a loud knock broke the silence and they jumped. Philippe went to open the door and found three Swiss border police officers, all of whom he knew. Two of them were decent enough but the sight of the third, a short, stocky man called Alain Pichon, made his heart race. This man was suspected of being a Nazi sympathiser. His presence meant danger.

Forcing himself to keep his voice steady, he greeted them. 'Hello Alain, is there a problem?'

'No, no. We're just going round checking the local farms along the border. We've had a tip-off that there are refugees being hidden somewhere nearby. I'm sure they aren't here but we have to check everywhere.'

'On you go, officers,' said Philippe's grandfather genially. Philippe stared at him, wondering why he sounded so confident. 'Search all the outbuildings. I'm sure there's nothing there.'

When the border guards moved off, Philippe wondered how he could get the truth out of his grandfather. He was sure he was hiding refugees on the farm, but he also knew that challenging his grandfather would be the wrong way to persuade him to stop doing it, so he bit his lip, waiting impatiently until the border guards came back.

'You're quite right, gentlemen,' said the guards when they came back. 'Nothing to find here, sorry to have bothered you.'

When they'd left, Philippe held his grandfather's gaze until the old man looked away.

'You're going to have to show me what's there. I'm not the enemy, Grandfather. You can trust me.'

The old man sighed heavily. 'I'm only doing what young Valérie has been doing all this time. We need to help those poor people escaping from the Germans. This is the least I can do.'

'I know, I understand. Will you show me?'

His grandfather got up and led Philippe out of the kitchen and into the backyard, then across to the outhouse. He opened the door and they looked inside but the small room was empty. Softly, Philippe's grandfather opened a panel of wood at the corner of the room. It slid back easily and, in the torchlight, Philippe could see a dark head turning towards them, a hand protecting his eyes from the bright beam of light.

In the cramped space behind the panel a strained voice

whispered. 'Have the police gone? I heard them come into the barn.'

Philippe's grandfather reached in and patted his shoulder. 'Yes. They don't know about the hidden room. You're safe now. Go back to sleep and someone will come for you soon.'

The young man nodded and pulled back from the door, lying down on the straw-covered ground and closing his eyes. Philippe shook his head when he saw such confidence and bravery. After going through so much, the young Frenchman still retained the ability to rise above his situation.

When they were back in the house Philippe turned to his grandfather. 'It's your decision what you do, and I'm proud you're doing this, but please do be careful. The border guards are suspicious and won't stop looking.'

'It will be fine. I can take care of myself, young man. You don't need to worry about me.'

All that evening Philippe expected to see Sébastien, a railway worker who lived on the neighbouring farm to Marianne and helped escaped refugees get across from France. When Philippe saw a shadow creep towards the outhouse he went outside. Sébastien jumped as Philippe touched his shoulder.

'What are you doing creeping around in the dark?' Sébastien hissed.

'I'm sorry, I didn't mean to give you a fright. Are you taking him away?'

'Yes. We need to get him out of Geneva. The border police are looking for escaped refugees. They were all over Marianne's farm earlier today.'

'I know, they came here too.'

Sébastien ran his hand through his dark hair with a frustrated gesture. 'They must be getting the information from somebody that we're hiding refugees. We're going to have to be more careful or the people we rescue will just get sent back to the Nazis.'

'Who is he?' Philippe asked as he walked with Sébastien into the outhouse, a torch lighting their way.

'He's been running from the Germans for a few months. They almost caught him but we got him out in time. The Swiss border police were alerted to look for him so we've got to get him out of Geneva as soon as we can.'

They walked into the room and Philippe opened the panel. The young man stretched out of the small space and smiled into the beam of light. 'They won't find that place in a hurry,' he said with a grin.

Philippe stared at him, finding his confident manner out of place in such a perilous situation. He watched the young refugee go outside, frowning after him, still not sure why he was worried. Then Sébastien's next words justified his qualms.

'You're right to be concerned,' said Sébastien calmly. 'We've been warned that German sympathisers are pretending to be escapees so they can tell the Swiss authorities the escape routes. Then the safe houses are raided by the border police.' He clapped Philippe's shoulder. 'Don't worry, I was told this man was genuine, but we'll have to be more careful in future. I don't want to get the old man caught up in it.'

'Thanks. I don't want that either.'

He was standing in the kitchen when his grandfather came downstairs.

'He's gone?' asked his grandfather.

'Yes, he's gone. And we're going to have to be more careful because the border police knew he was either here or at Marianne's farm. We won't be so lucky another time.'

Philippe frowned as he watched his grandfather go back

upstairs. He felt torn between needing to protect him and leaving to find Stefano. He was putting his life at risk by going into Italy and he might not come back, but Stefano had saved his life and he owed him a huge debt that he could now repay. The winter was closing in, and he knew that if he didn't go now, no one else would be able to save Stefano.

ELEVEN
VALÉRIE

Geneva

Late that evening, Valérie was drooping with tiredness when she let herself into the house and went into the parlour to find her father. He was with Nicolas Cherix, Philippe's father, who kissed her and sat back down.

'Nicolas is here on police business,' said her father. 'He needs our help. A woman has been reported missing. She might have been in the old town last night.'

'I wondered if you had seen her,' said Nicolas. 'I'm asking everybody in the area.'

'Who was it?' asked Valérie, sinking down onto the sofa.

'Her name is Isabelle Laurent,' said Nicolas. 'She's the daughter of a former bank manager. They live just south of here. She left after supper time and her father never saw her again.'

'I know her,' said Albert. 'Claude Laurent was my bank manager before he retired. I thought he was ill.'

'Yes, he's quite poorly.' said Nicolas. 'He is very worried

about his daughter, thinks something might have happened to her.'

Valérie could feel her father's eyes lingering on her face, but she shook her head. She wasn't going to tell the police that the woman had asked for her help, or what she'd said about Jacob.

'Do you have a photo of her? I was out in the old town last night and maybe I saw her,' asked Valérie.

He took a photograph out of his pocket and handed it to her. She saw the woman she'd met. At least she knew who she was.

'I might have seen her round the Café de Paris in the Place du Bourg-de-Four, but I don't know where she went after that.'

Nicolas Cherix waited. 'If you think of anything else, please get in touch.'

'Of course, I will, but I'm not sure if it was her.'

He nodded and took his leave.

Albert came back from the front door and sat beside her, the worry evident on his face.

'Why didn't you tell him you saw her? That she spoke to you?'

'You know why, Papa. Even though Monsieur Cherix is sympathetic, I don't often share Resistance secrets with him or anyone in the police force, it's too dangerous.'

There was silence in the room, as Valérie thought through her options.

'Do you still have the Laurents' address?'

'I think so, but what are you going to do? It's too late to see Claude now. He's an ill man.'

'I have to speak to him, Papa.'

Her father was twisting his hands together. Valérie reached out her own hand to still them.

'Give me the address, Papa. The sooner I go, the sooner I'll be back.'

Her father got up and went to his desk, pulling out the small book where he kept his addresses and phone numbers. He handed it to her.

'Rue Firmin-Massot,' he said. 'I don't think they've moved.'

Valérie grabbed her coat and went out into the hall. 'I shouldn't be too long. It isn't far.'

Going out of the old town round the Place de Neuve and along the old city wall to the Laurent house, Valérie asked herself why she hadn't told Philippe's father that she'd definitely seen Isabelle and why she felt so driven to find out more about her. It was the mention of Jacob that so intrigued her, because any mystery about Jacob might have something to do with her mother and what had happened to her. Valérie had to speak to Isabelle or to her father to find out more.

It was much cooler now and this late in the evening, the street was deserted. It would be December soon. It had been a lovely summer, hot and sunny, and the good weather had stretched right through the autumn, but the beginnings of winter were sneaking into Geneva. And you could feel it tonight.

By the time she got to Rue Firmin-Massot, it had started to rain heavily. The wind came in stronger gusts as she walked up to the front door, her hand stretched out in the darkness to knock, and she jumped when branches from the bushes around the door caught in her hair. When she rapped on the door it opened slightly and with a flash of unease, she realised it was unlocked. Pushing open the door, she saw the lock had been forced. She made herself go inside and pulled the door behind her to keep out the cold wind. Feeling her heart pounding in her chest, Valérie tried to banish the thought that she was walking into a trap.

She stood quietly, listening to the sounds of her own breathing. All was quiet and dark. Her heart thumping louder in the silence of the house, she moved quietly through the hall and looked into the dining room and the parlour. The house was furnished elegantly and expensively. It was also impeccably tidy, nothing out of place.

Turning towards the stairs, Valérie looked up to the first-floor landing. She certainly wasn't going to go up there. She looked down again and saw in front of her a dull glow coming from underneath the door to her right. She was rooted to the spot, hardly able to breathe. Urging herself to go forward, she forced her feet to go towards the door, when all they wanted to do was turn and run away. There was no noise coming from the room and Valérie paused for several long seconds in the hall. But hearing nothing over the insistent tapping of the rain on the windows, she crept up to the door.

Very slowly, she pushed the door open and looked inside. It was a study, with a large desk at the back facing towards the garden. The room was a scene of destruction, the office chair thrown on its side and the drawers pulled out from the desk, their contents scattered over the floor. The shutters had been pulled across the windows and the only light in the room came from the oil lamp on the desk facing the door. Checking that there was no one else in any of the corners of the room, she moved towards the light. The rain continued to pour outside, the only noise in the deserted house.

She looked around the room, wondering what someone had been searching for and whether they'd found it. The noise of tapping on the window made her take a step back, her heart pounding painfully in her chest. She thought she was going to faint and felt her knees start to buckle. She grasped the edge of the desk to steady herself and her foot crunched on the carpet. She looked down and, as she moved her foot, saw pieces of glass lying on the floor and glinting in the dull light. A broken picture frame was lying at a drunken angle below the desk and she picked it up. It was empty. She looked to see if there were any other clues that would tell her what had happened in that room, but there was nothing.

Then she heard a noise at the front of the house. They were coming back. She ran to the back door, scrabbling to open it, slipped outside into the garden and turned towards the wall running along the street, the small side door her escape.

When she reached the pavement safely, she saw a small group of people at the corner of the street, watching policemen entering the house. Her first instinct was to run in the opposite direction, but she shook her head and went to join them. She'd failed to find any clue to Isabelle's whereabouts that night and this might be a way to find her. Maybe the neighbours could tell her something.

Valérie came up behind the group of women who turned towards her.

'What's happening?'

'Who are you?' said one woman, older than the rest and instantly suspicious.

'I'm one of Isabelle's friends. I came to see her tonight but I don't think there's anyone here.'

The women stared at her. Then the one who had spoken visibly unbent, something about Valérie's worry for Isabelle overcoming her mistrust.

'There probably isn't anyone there. Claude often stays with his sister when Isabelle is working. She works at the Red Cross, so she often stays near there rather than coming all the way back here. I only saw her a few days ago, so she must be away.'

Valérie didn't dare to say anything else. Although the rain had stopped, she still felt damp and cold, disturbed by the feeling of violence lingering and spreading out from the deserted house.

'Thank you,' she said quickly and left them, disappearing into the darkness. Although it was late, she would go and see Nicolas Cherix at the police station. He was searching for Isabelle. Valérie shivered when she thought about the destruction in the house she'd left behind.

Valérie ran up towards the old town and past the Café de Paris to the police station on the Place du Bourg-de-Four. She could hardly breathe as the frosty air caught in her lungs, the fear of being discovered in the empty house still vivid in her mind. The square was dark this late in the evening, shutters all closed and only a few people still out. She headed down the side of the square towards the police station, the only building showing a faint light from inside, pressing herself against the building next to the trees to avoid a gang of youths running across the square. They were so intent on where they were going that they didn't even see her. The danger of being outside on her own this late at night suddenly hit her and she was filled with relief when she finally reached the safety of the police station.

She ran up the steps of the old building, pushed the heavy door open and went up to the reception desk. A middle-aged, balding police officer sat beside the low light on his desk, his head drooping. The noise of the door jerked him awake and he stared at her with a sleepy expression.

'I need to see Nicolas Cherix. Is he here?'

'He came in earlier. Who wants to see him?' The man yawned.

'Valérie Hallez. I have some information for him about the missing woman.'

Before the man could summon up enough energy to reply, Nicolas came in from the office behind reception. He looked exhausted and the lines on his face seemed deeper than ever. 'Valérie, what you are doing here?'

She came round to stand in front of him. 'I need to talk to you about Isabelle Laurent.'

He looked at her and then indicated that she should follow him into his office. The room was cold, the bare table and chairs the only furniture apart from an old desk in the corner, which was covered with papers. They sat down opposite one another at the table and immediately Valérie launched into her speech. 'I went to try to find Isabelle Laurent; my father remembered where they lived. The house was empty and the front door was unlocked. The study is a mess, everything's broken and lying on the floor. Somebody's been in there searching for something. I don't know who it was because they'd gone by the time I got there.'

He looked surprised for a moment at her news, then sighed deeply. 'I'm sorry, Valérie, but it's too late. One of my men just came in to say that Isabelle's body was found in the lake tonight. A fishermen who keeps his boat there heard a disturbance and called the police. He thought someone was stealing his boat but then found her body.'

Valérie sat back in her chair trying to take in his words. 'She's dead?' She shook her head, trying to work out if she could have done anything to stop it, but it had all happened too quickly. She felt that she'd failed the woman who'd asked her for help. 'Who did it? Their house was searched so that must have had something to do with it.'

He lifted his arms in a gesture of helplessness. 'I don't know yet. I need to go there now, and find any evidence of what happened and who may have been responsible.'

Valérie tried to think what might help, but knew that there was nothing she could do. Even if she told Nicolas about Isabelle trying to get her to rescue Clara, it wouldn't bring her back, nor would it help the young German girl. It was up to her now to make sure that Clara could escape from France. All she knew was that the men searching for Clara would stop at nothing to find her, even murder.

'Is there anything else you can tell me?' asked Nicolas. 'We will investigate her death, search the house for clues, but I doubt we can build a case if we don't find a culprit.'

'She told me that she was being followed by German spies,' Valérie burst out. 'I was worried about her so when you said she was missing I went to look for her. But I was too late,' she finished bitterly.

'We were all too late.' Nicolas replied quietly. He paused, considering her words. 'German spies, she said?'

Valérie nodded.

'I'll try to find out,' he carried on, 'but Geneva is full of different nationalities, from all sides in this war. Their activities don't often threaten us, but it's beginning to happen more often.'

Valérie held his gaze, his expression so like Philippe's in that moment, and knew that he was remembering the other Swiss citizens targeted by German spies. He turned to pick up his coat. 'I need to go and speak to her father now. At least he was staying with his sister. I need to tell him his daughter is dead.'

He kissed her cheek and she left him at the door to the police station. Maybe one day they would be able to prove what happened to Isabelle and bring her killers to justice but, until then, all they had was rumour and suspicion.

Valérie walked briskly home through the old town and didn't see anybody on her way. She was just at the corner of her street when a cat screeched from the side of the road. She jumped in shock, her heart pounding, and saw two cats fighting over a small dead animal. She ran home and flew through the front door, almost knocking over her father who was waiting for her in the hall.

'Isabelle's dead,' she sobbed. 'The police found her body in the lake.'

She hugged her father and breathed in the familiar smell of his favourite old jumper, comforted by his presence and his love.

TWELVE
CLARA

France

It was early afternoon and the light outside was already fading, the cold November day closing in around the school building. Clara was in one of the classrooms at the back, going through the new identity papers she'd been given by the Resistance. She knew that she had to memorise them so if anybody asked, she could talk as if she'd always been Claire rather than Clara.

'I can test you, if you like?' said the boy who'd been in the front seat of the car with her. She was surprised; he spoke as little as possible and hardly ever to her. All she really knew was that his name was Louis and that he had been brought up in Lyon.

'Yes, that would be good,' she replied. 'They said that we might have to leave at any time and I still can't remember it all without prompting.' She handed over her identity card and after a brief hesitation, he handed his across.

'Have they changed your name too?' she asked and he shook his head.

'Still Louis.' He smiled at her and she realised, with a small start, that it was the first time she'd ever seen him smile. She looked down at his identity card but before she could say anything, the door burst open and they looked up to see one of the younger teachers breathing heavily and struggling to speak, her dark hair falling over her face. She held out their coats that had been hanging outside the door from their earlier outing.

'There's a German car coming up to the house, they will be looking for Jewish children. You have to get out before they search the building. Even though you have false papers they mustn't find you because it's too risky.' She thrust the coats towards them and they quickly put them on, shoving their identity papers into their pockets.

'Where will we go?' asked Clara, fumbling with her coat as she tried to do up the buttons, her breath coming in short gasps.

'Go out the back and over the hill through the trees. There's an old farmhouse on the other side, you'll be safe there.'

Clara and Louis followed the teacher to the back of the school and out the door, the cold air hitting them as they went outside. The sound of a car screeching to a halt at the front of the building filled the air and Clara could feel her heart thumping in her chest. She glanced across at Louis, his face white and strained, and he looked at her, his brown eyes large and scared.

The teacher opened the gate and almost pushed them through. 'Good luck,' she hissed, hugging them both briefly before closing the gate behind them.

Without looking back, Clara and Louis ran away along the edge of the village, following the path up over the hill between the outcrops of rock. They stopped briefly at the top of the hill and looked back down at the school, seeing German soldiers all around the building. Ducking their heads, Clara and Louis ran down the other side and looked out for a farmhouse through the trees, thankful there was no snow to highlight their escape to the Germans.

They didn't stop running until they reached a solitary farm-house, where they caught their breath, staring at one another in relief. They knocked on the door, still breathing heavily. The door opened in an instant and the warmth of the house enveloped them. The smile on the face of the middle-aged woman made them feel safe and welcome.

'Come in, hurry!' said the woman at the door, closing it quickly behind them.

'Our teacher said to come here—' Clara started to say.

'I know what's happening,' the woman said in a comforting voice. 'You have to hide here until the Germans leave.'

She led them through the house and upstairs into one of the bedrooms. Opening the empty wardrobe, she pulled up a plank of wood in the back, waving them inside. 'Just stay in there until I come and get you. I know it's very small but you shouldn't be there for too long.'

'Thank you,' said Louis. The woman smiled at him and ruffled his hair, then put the plank back in place, plunging them into darkness.

They sat silently in the dark space, both listening intently. All they heard were domestic sounds coming from downstairs: plates in the kitchen sink, low conversation and the smell of baking. 'I hope we get some of that,' whispered Louis. Clara suppressed a giggle. It was a long time since she'd smelt home baking.

Her giggle died in her throat when she heard a loud knock on the front door. The sound of strange voices filtered upstairs as the door was opened and they heard heavy boots in the hall. She felt Louis grasp her hand and she clutched it like her life depended on it, struggling to breathe in the confined space. After a few minutes, the door to the bedroom was flung open and heavy steps came towards the wardrobe. Clara closed her eyes as she heard the wardrobe door open, the voices now much louder and closer.

'Niemand hier,' someone shouted. 'They aren't here.'

Then they heard the familiar voice of the farmer's wife. 'There's fresh baking downstairs, messieurs, some cakes you might like.'

'Come on, this is a waste of time,' said the soldier. 'The children must have gone somewhere else.' The wardrobe door was slammed shut and they heard the sound of footsteps retreating. Clara relaxed with a sigh, bending her head forward.

'They've gone,' said Louis. 'We're safe.'

'Maybe for now,' she replied.

A long while later they heard the noise of the wardrobe door opening and then the plank of wood was pulled up. A head appeared through the gap and Clara clutched Louis' arm, terrified who she would see.

'Are you all right in there?' said the farmer's wife. 'Come out now, they've gone. You need to get something to eat and then get some sleep.' The woman helped them out of the wardrobe and Clara stretched her stiff legs. They followed her downstairs to the warm kitchen. 'My husband will tell the Resistance where you are,' said the woman. 'You can't go back to the school, I'm afraid, they'll need to get you to Switzerland very soon. It isn't safe for you anymore in France.'

THIRTEEN
VALÉRIE

Geneva

The next day, Valérie was still haunted by the scene of destruction in the Laurent house and the shocking news that Isabelle had been found dead. Although it couldn't be proven, she knew that the woman's pursuers had caught up with her. What had she told them? Whatever had happened, she knew that Clara was in even more danger in France.

Unable to get the picture of Isabelle out of her mind, she walked to the Quai du Mont-Blanc and sat on the favourite bench that she and Philippe thought of as their own, looking out onto Lac Léman and trying to calm her thoughts. Today, the water was grey and the sky dull. There was no sunlight or warmth and she pulled her coat more tightly around her shoulders. She looked across at the Jet d'Eau and let her mind wander as she watched the tall fountain, sprays of water shooting down from its great height to splash into the lake.

She turned and saw Philippe striding towards her, a knapsack on his back, dressed in some of his old farm clothes. When he got closer, she knew before he spoke what he was going to say. Trying to keep her voice free from emotion, she pressed his hand as he sat down beside her.

'Your father said you might be here,' he said.

'You're going, aren't you?' she replied.

He nodded and put his arm around her, making her feel warm for the first time that morning.

'I can't miss the chance to go and find Stefano. His life is in danger if we don't find him soon. You know that the winter snow will be coming soon and if I can't get over the passes into Italy, I won't be able to get there until it's far too late.'

She turned her face into his shoulder. 'I know you're right, I just wish you didn't have to go.'

He squeezed her arm. 'I don't think I'll be more than a week. I'm going to take the train to Saint-Maurice and then meet Yves. From there we'll take the train through the Simplon tunnel to Italy and then the local train to Locarno. We're going to see Stefano's father there to get information about where in Italy he might have gone. If all goes well, we'll be crossing back into Italy over the hills the next morning.'

'I didn't think your Italian was that good.'

'Yves speaks Italian fluently. His mother is from Ticino. It's why he's coming with me. My Italian is quite basic, only good enough to get by. But with him, we should be fine. And he wants to come. With all that has happened, he's been determined to repay the Germans anyway he can.'

'I can see you have it all worked out. And I'm so glad Yves is going with you.'

But they both knew he would face a myriad of dangers in Italy, from the invading German army trying to stall the Allied offensive, to Italian fascists furious about Mussolini's fall from power as well as the partisans who hated anyone they suspected of being sympathetic to the fascists.

'Do you want me to come to the station with you?' asked Valérie.

'Better not. You know I don't like goodbyes at stations.'

'I just thought this time...'

'Don't think about it being any different. Only that this time, when I come back, we should get married.'

'Oh Philippe, I thought we agreed that we should wait until the war is over?'

He pulled her closer and kissed her hair.

'I've changed my mind. We could have spent all summer together as husband and wife but we didn't. And now I have to leave you again. Life is too short and unpredictable to wait, Valérie.'

They sat in silence as she snuggled into him, cherishing these last few precious moments together. Finally, he spoke. 'My father told me they found Isabelle Laurent's body last night. You were right to believe she was in real danger.'

'I was going to tell you, Philippe. She was so frightened when I saw her.' Valérie swallowed when she remembered their rushed conversation. 'We have to find the girl, Clara, before the Germans do.'

'Genevieve will find her.'

'I hope so.'

He tightened his hold.

'Take care, because the people who killed her might still be here.' He shook his head. 'My father said that no one saw what happened and they couldn't even be sure it wasn't an accident.'

'But I'm sure. And the same men are after Clara. I have to stop them.' She saw his worried expression and kissed him. 'I'll be careful, so long as you are careful too. Don't take risks, Philippe, please don't throw everything we have away.' She couldn't stop the tears coming then, however much she tried to be strong. She knew that she might never see him again, and her heart felt as though it were already bruised and torn apart. But she pushed away that thought and smiled through her tears.

They stood up and Philippe clutched Valérie close to him,

kissing her deeply one last time, as if he could imprint his body on hers. She returned his kiss but nothing could lighten the weight in her heart.

'I love you.'

'I love you too.'

Finally, Philippe turned his back and walked slowly away. This was the hardest parting they'd ever had. When she could no longer see him, she wiped away her tears roughly. She had to pull herself together, and summon the strength to find Clara, and maybe Hannelore too. Perhaps the information Clara had was so important it might help bring an end to this war, the war that kept threatening to tear her apart from Philippe. She sent out a silent prayer to a god she wasn't sure existed, that he would keep Philippe safe, that they would see each other again.

FOURTEEN

HANNELORE

Paris

Hannelore opened the door with shaking fingers, the woollen gloves hardly keeping out the cold of winter. It was still and dark when she got back from work these days and Paris was bitterly cold. She quickly closed the door behind her to keep out the freezing air but the temperature didn't improve. She glanced at the bucket in the lobby, the water in the bottom now frozen, and stamped her feet to try to get some feeling back into them. Hannelore opened the front door of the apartment, listening for the sound of any conversation, any sign that Marc had come home, but all was silent.

She went into the main room, eyes averted from the damp patches on the walls, and looked around for Chantal. Her friend was sitting at the table, bundled in the jumpers and blankets that Hannelore had left her with that morning. The stove in the grate was almost out and Hannelore ran towards it to resuscitate the only source of heat for the apartment. Then she sat next to Chantal and touched her shoulder. 'No news?' she asked.

Chantal shook her head. 'Monsieur Theroux came in today to see me, but said no one has heard anything.' She waved a hand listlessly towards the table. 'He brought some food for us from his wife.'

Hannelore pulled out a package from her bag. 'I went round to the charcuterie on my way back and he gave me some sausages. We can have them tonight. It will be a feast.'

Chantal smiled. 'You take good care of me. Everybody does, really.'

It was true that her neighbours did watch out for Chantal, knowing she was ill and needed to eat properly. None of them had very much and life was difficult for everyone in the Jewish community in Paris, but they looked out for one another and helped whenever they could.

Someone knocked at the door, the sudden noise making Hannelore jump. No one ventured outside at night these days. She went to the door and opened it a few centimetres. Standing outside was a young man and she realised it was Monsieur Theroux's son. Tall and thin, his handsome features had been lost to hunger and hardship. He looked nervously behind him and then back at Hannelore, leaning his dark head down towards her. 'My friends have left me some messages. Marc hasn't been sent away yet; he's still in Paris. That's all we know, but you need to take care. They said today in the hospital that the Germans are looking for a young woman who fits your description. I don't know why, only that you're in danger. I think you should leave Paris before they catch up with you.'

Hannelore clutched his arm, trying to take in the meaning of his warning, not knowing what she could do. 'I decided to go last week but I couldn't. Chantal needs me. You know she can't stay on her own and with Marc missing, I have no choice but to stay.'

The young man bent his head to one side and studied her. 'I

knew what you'd say but I had to tell you. I don't know what they're looking for but they think you have something they want. You just need to be careful when you're in the hospital, keep away from the German soldiers and don't draw attention to yourself.'

Hannelore thought back to her day at the laundry. She knew that the hospital wasn't supposed to employ Jews any longer, but they turned a blind eye to the regulars because they had no one else who would be prepared to do such hard work for such a low wage. But the little Hannelore could earn was all the money that Chantal had. It was the only thing that she could do to help her friend.

In that dark hallway she remembered the bright sunny days when they had first come over to Paris, days when she'd got to know Chantal, her sweet nature and her optimism about the world. The days when they would sit by the Seine and listen to music wafting from apartments nearby where Chantal used to work as a violin tutor. It seemed that those days would last forever. Sometimes, they would go to the Loire Valley, where Chantal and Marc came from. They would sit next to the broad river eating bread and cheese and drinking wine, talking of their lives and their dreams, trying to ignore the darkness that was all around them.

Hannelore heard movement from the apartment and turned back to the young man. 'Thank you for your warning and please thank your father for visiting today. Take care of yourselves.'

He stepped away from the door silently and she turned back into the apartment, locking the door behind her. She thought about Clara and leaned against the wall, unable to move from the sharp pain and worry burdening her. She hoped with all her heart that Clara had reached Switzerland safely. As long as her niece was safe, that was all that mattered. She closed her eyes and imagined her brother David's face, pushing away the thought of what he might be going through. She knew she had to follow Clara and leave Paris, but for now she had to keep focused, protect herself and Chantal if there was any chance that she would ever see her beloved niece again.

FIFTEEN

VALÉRIE

Geneva

Valérie made her deliveries quickly the next day because she wanted to check the bookshop to see if Clara would be able to stay there. The image of the two Germans looking through the window wouldn't fade from her mind, and she resolved to go and check it was undisturbed. If the Germans had managed to get inside then it wasn't safe any longer for refugees.

She stopped on the other side of the street opposite the bookshop. From there, it just looked the same, doors locked and shutters closed, but she had to be sure. She pushed her bicycle through the narrow lane to the back alley running behind the shops and left it against the wall. Unlocking the back door to the bookshop, she let herself inside. The small downstairs hall seemed the same and as she went through to the main space at the front, the usual mess of books and upturned bookshelves felt no different from before. Her nose twitched, smelling strong cigar smoke over the musty smell of the room. The windows were even filthier than before and she confidently walked across the room, stepping over the obstacles in front of her. No one would be able to see that anyone was inside.

She looked down at the broken desk her mother used to sit at, where she'd found her notebook all those months before. It all looked the same, but when she crouched down, she saw some large damp footprints on the papers lying on the floor. The room was cold, as cold as it was outside, and she shivered, knowing that someone had been there – the wet footprints evidence that it hadn't been long ago. She glanced over towards the lock in the front door and gasped when she saw that it was broken. It had been a new lock, strong enough to keep out any curious burglars, but someone had broken it and tried to make it look normal from the outside as if nothing was disturbed.

Valérie looked at the floor at the bottom of the door and saw a bundle of envelopes and papers that had been squashed and pushed to the side. It must be post that had been delivered to the bookshop, moved aside when the door was opened. Valérie picked them up, intending to check them later.

She turned away from the front door and went through the bookshop to the stairs. It was lucky that they hadn't been using the apartment upstairs to hide refugees for several days. She shuddered when she thought about the consequences of someone breaking in and finding Jews escaping from the Nazis.

She ran lightly up the stairs to the landing on the first floor. Everything looked undisturbed, the empty landing with closed doors leading to two bedrooms, the parlour, a kitchen and a bathroom. She pushed open the door of the parlour to find a scene of destruction. The sofa had been overturned, the small table where she used to leave food for the refugees upside down, one leg broken off. On the floor, the cushions from the sofa were strewn around and when she picked one up, the stuffing fell out through large rents in the fabric. The other rooms were also wrecked and she lifted a hand to her throat when she saw the mattress in the first bedroom slashed and destroyed. She knew it wasn't difficult to obtain more furniture for the apartment but whoever had destroyed it wanted to leave a message that no one should be given safe refuge there.

The cigar smell she had noticed downstairs was stronger here. She closed the bedroom door carefully and went to the other room, fearful of what she'd see. This was the room where Jacob's piano had remained. It had been played by some of the refugees – quietly so that no one outside could hear the sound coming from the apartment and give away their location. The top of the piano had been split in two by an axe or some other heavy tool and the keyboard destroyed, with keys scattered all over the floor. The furniture could be repaired but the piano was beyond all help.

She felt tears fill her eyes as she took in the wanton destruction in the apartment and what it told her about the men who had broken in. She didn't know what they'd been looking for, but the scene all around her spoke of their anger and frustration at not finding what they wanted. She ran back downstairs, suddenly scared that they might come back and find her there. In her rush to open the door she dropped the post she was still clutching in her hand. The envelopes and papers fell to the ground and when she bent to gather them up, she saw, among the advertisements and free papers, the edge of a postcard. The picture on the front was of Notre-Dame Cathedral in Paris and she felt a prickle of premonition as she turned over the postcard. It was addressed to the bookshop, with no name at the top. The message was short and simple.

I've stayed on here for a few days. Hope to join you soon.

H

The postmark was dated only a week before and Valérie turned the postcard over again, realising it must have come from Hannelore, which meant she was still in Paris. It was the only explanation. The bookshop had been deserted for years but it must have been the only address she had in Geneva. And the Germans had almost found it. She flicked the card against her hand, thinking about the possibilities it created and shivered. She let herself out of the bookshop, looking back at it, knowing that it was no longer a safe place, and picked up her bike.

She cycled across the Place de Bel-Air, hardly registering the people she passed, her mind full of the destruction she'd just witnessed. She went along the Rue des Etuves and arrived at the Place De-Grenus. Pressing on the bell for Bill Paterson, she knew she had to tell him that the German spies had destroyed the safe house. The door opened and Valérie pushed her bike into the hall, left it there and ran up the stairs to the first floor. Bill let her into the apartment and closed the door behind her. He took one look at her stormy face and his smile of welcome faded.

'What's the problem?'

'The bookshop has been vandalised. We can't use it as a safe house any longer.'

'Do you know who did it?' asked Bill.

'I think it was the German spies we were talking about the other day. I've seen them again.' Chilled by what they'd done, she leaned forward and spoke urgently. 'The woman who asked for my help has been found dead and I'm sure that they were the ones following her. They're after something that they're determined to find at any cost. Do you know who they are?'

He nodded, picked up a photograph from the pile of papers on his table and handed it to her. 'I found this in our files and one of our agents has identified the man.'

Valérie took the photograph and stared at the fleshy features. 'That's definitely one of the men I've seen.'

'We think they're agents from a special SS unit. The older man is called Hans Meyer, he's a bully and a sadist. The younger one is Klaus Werner, but I don't have a photograph of him.'

'Klaus Werner? But that's the name of the man Geraldine met! It couldn't be the same man, could it? Geraldine said he was a banker...'

'He probably is a banker and working for Meyer on the side, part of a special unit gathering funds for the Third Reich. You'd better tell your friend to keep clear of Werner.'

'I will, but what else was Jacob doing here?'

Bill leaned forward in his chair. 'This is all top-secret information. He'd been passing German secrets to the SOE in the years before the war. He came from Frankfurt. David Lieberman, one of his closest friends, worked in a chemical company there. The company was working on chemical weapons for the Nazis and Jacob got information from him to tell us what was happening. It was important information but the Nazis were becoming suspicious that someone was telling us what they were doing.'

'What happened?'

'The Lieberman family went on the run. They were Jewish too, so the danger was increasing for them and David couldn't work any longer for the company when the war started. He was a skilled scientist so managed to get work in companies which weren't working in such sensitive areas.'

'But why have the Germans come back here? What are they looking for?'

'That wasn't all that Jacob did in Geneva. He realised that all the money belonging to his friends would be stolen by the Nazis and banked safely in Switzerland for the Third Reich, so he started to divert that money, setting up accounts with false identities that would sit there safely until after the war was over. Then the money could be claimed by its rightful owners.'

'So, it's the money they're after?' asked Valérie.

'Partly, but there's something else,' replied Bill. 'There was one other thing, more valuable than all the money they're looking for. David stole a very secret document from the chemical company before he left. I don't know what was in it, because it disappeared, but I think this SS unit is looking for that document now. So Jacob is the link to all of it. I don't know how much Isabelle Laurent knew; we just have to hope she couldn't tell them anything. And given that this girl you're looking for in France is connected with Jacob somehow, I'm wondering if she might be David's daughter, and it's that very same document she has in her possession.'

'She is his daughter. Her name is Clara Lieberman. It must be the same document.' Valérie jumped up from her seat and paced the room, the threads from the past all beginning to draw together.

'Jacob's in England now,' said Bill. 'It was the safest place for him to go. I can try to get word to him about Clara, if she gets to Switzerland. But those spies are dangerous and determined, Valérie, so you must be careful.'

'And David's sister Hannelore was with them too,' added Valérie. 'She was my mother's friend.' She took out of her pocket the postcard of Paris she'd found in the bookshop and handed it to him. 'I think this is from her, so she must still be in Paris.'

'Let's just hope she hasn't got any part of the document then,' he said unemotionally. 'If she has, she'll be hunted just like Clara.' He took a step towards Valérie and handed the postcard back. 'Find Clara, do everything you can to get her to safety, and make sure you get that document to me. From what I hear, it could change everything. We mustn't let it slip away from us. If you need any help, you know where to come.'

She nodded, determination rising through her as she realised she had to thwart the Nazis' plans. She thought of

Clara being chased across France. She was a young girl, only thirteen years old, with no family around her, and she was being hunted down. She might not have family who could help, but she did have the Resistance on her side and Valérie would not rest until she'd found her.

SIXTEEN

VALÉRIE

Geneva

Her mind dwelling on the need to find Clara, she resolved to speak to Marianne before the day was over. She was so determined to act quickly that she hardly noticed anything around her, cycling fast to the PTT building where Marianne worked in the telephone exchange.

'Watch where you're going, mademoiselle!'

She stopped her bike in a screech of brakes, startled by the old woman's voice in front of her and the stick waving at the edge of her field of vision. She waited until the woman had crossed the road and took a deep breath. She continued to the Rue du Mont-Blanc, deep in her own thoughts, glancing up at the top floor of the imposing post office building across the road. Maybe Marianne was working today and she would have news.

'I thought it was you.'

Amélie, one of Marianne's friends who worked in the post office, walked towards her. She was a tall girl, with fine brown hair caught up in plaits wound round her head. She stared at Valérie through her thick glasses.

'I've just finished my break. I'm going back inside now, are you coming in?'

Valérie looked warily at the other girl, uncomfortably aware of her habit of finding out and dissecting everyone else's business. She was the most efficient teller in the whole building but she loved being the person who passed on the latest news to all her customers.

'Is Marianne working this afternoon? I need to speak to her urgently,' she asked quickly.

Amélie pursed her thin lips. 'She had to leave early. I can give her your message tomorrow if you like.'

'It's all right. I'm sure I'll see her soon.' Valérie waved as she got on her bike and rode away. Marianne might be at the Café de Paris. Re-invigorated now, she pedalled across the Place de Bel-Air, pushed her bike up the hill to the old town and parked it next to the Café de Paris in the Place du Bourg-de-Four. It was a cold day and she shivered as she walked to the front door, opening and closing it quickly to keep the warm air inside. The hum of conversation circulated round the café and she waved at Geraldine, who was standing behind the polished wooden bar, serving drinks to a group of off-duty soldiers, her blonde hair shining in the lights above the bar. The wooden tables all looked full and Valérie looked through to the back, past the crackling open fire, to see who was there.

'Valérie, we're over here!' Marianne was sitting with a petite, dark-haired girl she recognised, but wasn't sure where from. She weaved through the tables, hugged Marianne and shook the other girl's hand. 'This is Genevieve, I'm not sure you've met before,' said Marianne. Valérie suddenly remembered where she'd seen her before. 'No, we haven't met, but I've seen your photograph.'

Valérie sat down quickly. This was Marianne's friend who worked in the children's homes in France and who could give her information about Clara. 'What news do you have? Have you found Clara?'

Genevieve leaned forward and shook her head. 'I'm sorry. The children's home at Izieu was raided by German soldiers and some of the children were taken away.'

Valérie felt her heart jump. 'They didn't get her, did they?'

Genevieve stretched out her hand to calm Valérie's worries and clasped her hand. 'No, they didn't find her; she managed to get away with another boy. My Resistance contacts are trying to find out where they went. There are quite a few farmhouses nearby with sympathisers who would keep them safe, but we have to get them out of France urgently because the Germans are still looking for them.'

She paused, as if not sure how to say what she wanted. 'Our people in the children's home said that the Germans were looking for her in particular. They had her name when they were searching for her.'

'That's what I was afraid of,' said Valérie. 'They aren't just looking for any Jewish children. They know her name, it's her they want to capture.'

'Why is that, Valérie?' asked Marianne. 'How much do you know about her? What could she have been involved in that has come to their attention? She's just a child!'

Valérie sat back and thought about what she'd found out. 'She's thirteen, as I said, and the only relative she has left is her aunt, Hannelore. She was supposed to come to Switzerland too, but we think she is in Paris. It's all tied up with Jacob Steinberg, who owned the bookshop in the old town where my mother used to work. You must remember him. Jacob was involved in espionage for the Allies and managed to smuggle out secret, classified documents to them before the war. Clara's father worked with him and we think now that he gave Clara a document to pass onto the Allies – information so important that it could change the whole course of the war. Somehow, the

Gestapo knows that Clara has it and they...' Her voice broke as she thought of Isabelle and the danger facing Clara. 'I'm sorry. They are hunting her down. German spies are here in Geneva who won't stop until they find her.'

Genevieve listened carefully. 'No wonder they knew her name. We need to get her into Switzerland and away from the border before the Swiss authorities send them back.'

Even at the end of 1943, when the world could no longer deny what the Germans were doing in the concentration camps, they all knew that the Swiss authorities still sent Jewish refugees back to occupied France if they found them less than ten kilometres from the border.

'Once they have the children in Annemasse,' Genevieve carried on, 'the Resistance will get them across by taking groups for exercise and games in the sports field right next to the border. The fact that fewer children go home from the field than came to the sessions still means it's a good way to get them across,' she explained. 'The Germans don't seem to look too closely.'

'We'll get them out of France and arrange to meet you to hand them over,' Marianne carried on.

Valérie bit her lip. She wanted to be more involved, to do all she could to save Clara, but one glance at Marianne's face stilled her words. She knew that Marianne had been more involved in helping the Resistance over the summer and couldn't question her friend's commitment or ability. She also knew that the more people involved, the more dangerous any rescue would be. In the end, she just nodded. 'Very well then. Leave me a message and I'll come and meet you. Just let me know when they're coming across and I'll get them to safety.' She grasped Marianne's arm. 'Remember not to use the hiding place at Philippe's grandfather's farm,' she said quickly. 'The border guards know about it and have searched it already.'

Marianne's features clouded over and she shook her head.

'It's impossible these days even to trust that the refugees are real.' She shrugged her shoulders. 'Sébastien said that Philippe was suspicious about one of them.'

'And watch out for that policeman, Alain Pichon,' added Valérie. 'He's becoming more involved in the border police raids and is dangerous.' Valérie felt the suspicions swirling round them; the ground seemed to move under her feet, with nothing solid to count on. She knew that they had to be more careful than ever, and to trust no one until they'd proved their worth.

'I need to go now,' said Genevieve, standing up. 'I'll go back into France and find out what's happened to the children who escaped the raid. We need to get them to the border as quickly as we can, so you can get them to safety.'

Marianne stood up too and they exchanged brief hugs, before the two women left.

Valérie looked around the familiar wood-panelled café, the heavy glass partition at the door and the dark green canopy outside the window, not seeing the people sitting around her, but only the dangers facing Clara and all the other young refugees. It was a dangerous existence and they couldn't hide for long.

Her eyes found Geraldine, who was sitting with a young man she recognised at a table in front of the bar. It was Klaus Werner, the youngest of the two German spies. She averted her gaze, not wanting to stare too obviously at him. When she looked again, he'd got up from the table and was leaving. Geraldine closed the door behind him but when she turned back, her smile was gone and she looked worried. Valérie waved to attract Geraldine's attention and she came briskly up to the table and sat down.

'What's the matter?' asked Valérie. 'Isn't he the man you mentioned? I thought you liked him.'

Geraldine shivered. 'He scares me. There's something about him that's cruel. I thought he was a banker but he doesn't seem to spend much time at the bank. All he wants to do is ask me about the people here, the shops, who owns them and who used to own them. He started asking me about Jacob Steinberg and got angry when I said I didn't know him.'

She leaned forward and clutched Valérie's arm. 'You have to be careful. If he's asking about the bookshop, I'm scared he'll start to ask about your mother and you.'

It was the first time that Geraldine had ever warned Valérie so seriously about one of her admirers.

'He's not a banker, Geraldine. If he's the man I think he is, then he's a German spy, working with an older man called Hans Meyer. I've seen them together. The SOE have warned me about them. I think you should keep being friendly with him if you can, just don't tell him anything.'

Geraldine looked around the familiar café as if she no longer recognised it. 'All he wants is information,' she said sadly. 'He's just like all the others, isn't he? They don't really want to spend time with me, they just want to use me to get information.'

Valérie felt a pang of pity for her friend and held her hand with both of hers. 'That's not true, Geraldine. They aren't all the same, it's just that some of them have their own agendas and getting information about their enemies makes them forget everything else.'

'You can't ignore it, can you? I mean this war. I've tried to ignore it, to meet new people and keep the café going, but I don't look at anyone in the same way now. Too much has happened, too many people have died and things only seem to be getting worse.'

Before she could say anything else, Geraldine was interrupted by the radio which had been turned on at the side of the bar, the latest news about the Allied advances in the south of Italy stilling the voices in the café.

'It may not be better soon, but it will end, Geraldine. We

just need to keep going until then,' said Valérie. It was all she could come up with to comfort her friend. She swallowed and looked away, the agonising worry she felt about Philippe and what he might be facing in Italy flooding back.

The radio continued inexorably. *'There are reports of German atrocities north of Milan committed against Italian civilians... the Allied bombing of Turin continued last night...'*

Geraldine's eyes widened. 'Philippe will be all right, Valérie.' Before she could say anything else, her father tapped her on the shoulder and pointed towards a group of young people waiting for their table. 'Back to work, young lady,' he said and smiled at Valérie.

Outside the café, Valérie picked up her bike and stood at the edge of the Place du Bourg-de-Four, watching the thinning crowd walk quickly home, their collars turned up against the cold. She looked beyond them to a figure further down the square, his face obscured by a camera. She recognised Klaus Werner, the young German spy, and her hands tightened on the handlebars when she saw the camera flash. She couldn't see where he was aiming the lens, but she turned her bike away from him and left the square.

As she rode home, her breath coming out in freezing clouds, she thought again about what Geraldine had said about trying to ignore the war. It was true; it could not be ignored. So many people were in danger – Philippe, in Italy, her friends risking their lives to help refugees and of course all the children. It was all around them and it would affect every decision they made and every step they took until it was over.

SEVENTEEN

PHILIPPE

Switzerland to Italy

Philippe walked to the station in Geneva, his steps feeling heavier the farther he was from Valérie. They'd spent all summer together and it was the first time they had been apart since his shooting. It made him realise how strange a life they were living during this war and how much happier he was when they were together. He felt flurries of snow in the bitter cold wind, which quickened his steps. He was all too aware it was late in the year for him to go across the mountains into Italy.

He walked into the large entrance hall in the main Geneva Cornavin station and towards the platforms, running to catch the first train around the north bank of the lake towards Saint-Maurice. He breathed a sigh of relief when the train left the station within a few minutes. He was aware of a few people glancing at him curiously, looking at his casual clothes among the uniforms of the Swiss soldiers returning to the forts around Saint-Maurice. He averted his eyes and looked out of the window. The stares didn't last for long; too many young men had been demobilised from the army and were now working on the land, so he didn't feel too strange. He glanced at the soldiers, hoping he wouldn't recognise anyone. He didn't have time to explain what he was doing, knowing that he was risking his return to his unit.

The flurries of snow continued as the train wound its way round Lac Léman and the sky was grey. He looked at the pale body of water that stretched across to France, so close, but life there was so different. Valérie had told him about the desperate refugees she'd helped to save. The huge numbers who never managed to escape weighed heavily on both of their minds.

The train turned into Villeneuve at the end of the lake and he looked out of the window to see the Rhône Valley stretch out before him, the mountain tops on each side heavy with snow. He frowned when he saw how low the snow line was, not quite on the valley floor but only a few hundred meters above. He just had to hope that there were no heavy snow showers in the next few days that would make his journey more difficult.

At Saint-Maurice station, he picked up his knapsack and jumped off the train, keeping his head low and avoiding the trucks that were waiting to pick up soldiers and take them back to the fort. It wasn't just Fort de Dailly the soldiers were heading for, but the other forts on both sides of the valley that formed the Saint-Maurice Fortress. Now that German soldiers had flooded through the north of Italy, the forts would all be on high alert in case the Nazis invaded Switzerland.

Philippe walked through the town. He knew he had just enough time to visit someone important before he met Yves in the Café de la Gare. Max's wife, Sofia, had known Valérie and Philippe since they were children and they'd seen her often when they went to Max's shooting range. She was now very ill. He told himself it might be the last time he ever saw her, and didn't dwell on the thought that it might be him who didn't come back.

He walked up to the back door of the familiar house, the old wooden chalet building only a few hundred metres from Max's shooting range, the back door hidden from the soldiers at the range. He'd been there too often with his unit to want to get too close. If his senior officers knew that he was well enough to leave Geneva, they would insist he returned to his unit. Philippe pushed open the wooden door and looked into the familiar kitchen with the wooden pine table and pictures on the wall, the traditional Swiss paper cuttings showing scenes of farming life that had been there ever since he was small.

'Hello, is there anybody in?' he called, as he always had.

He heard a faint shout from the parlour and closed the back door behind him, walking towards the voice. He went into the room and saw Sofia sitting in a chair next to the large window that looked out onto the shooting range, the bustle of activity as cars and trucks came in and out of the car park injecting life into the quiet room.

She stretched out her hand and he came across to her, sitting directly opposite. He smiled, trying not to let the shock of her pale face and the dark circles under her eyes show in his expression. Her luxurious grey hair was the only thing that hadn't changed, the locks held back from her face by a hairband, only a few wisps escaping onto her thin cheeks.

'It's so good to see you,' said Sofia, pressing his hand. 'When I heard about the shooting, I was so worried about you. How the army could let such an accident happen, I don't know. You should have heard Max talking about it.'

'I'm fine now, Sofia. I was very lucky that the bullet missed my spine. I'm back to normal now, thank goodness.'

'So, are you going back to the fort?' She looked him up and down. 'Why aren't you in uniform?'

Before he could answer, they both heard the back door open and then Max entered the room. He came up and enveloped Philippe in a fierce bear hug. 'I'm glad to see you safe and well,' he said, then looked down at his wife. 'I told you he was all right,' he said gruffly. She leaned her head back on the cushion and closed her eyes.

'She's tired,' said Max. 'Let's go through.'

Philippe bent down and kissed Sofia on the cheek then followed Max through to the kitchen, shaking his head at the offer of coffee. 'I can't stay.'

'What are you going to do now?' asked Max. 'You don't look like you're going back to the fort anytime soon.'

'Not yet. You know that Stefano has gone missing in Italy?'

Max nodded.

'I'm going to find him if I can. It's very dangerous down there and I need to get him out.'

'You're going on your own?'

'No, Yves Masson is coming with me. We're going today, to try to get there before the worst snow. We're going first to see Stefano's father to find out as much as we can about what he was trying to do, then follow the route he took.' Philippe leaned forward. 'Have you heard anything about what's going on in Italy near Locarno?'

'I've heard from some people who came across to Switzerland in the last few days,' replied Max. 'The Germans are guarding all the borders and hunting down the partisan groups. All I can say is, be very careful, you won't know who any of the Italians are working for and whether they're friendly or not.'

'I wanted to ask you to look out for Valérie. If anything happens to me, could you make sure that she stays safe? She's got involved with someone who's being chased by Nazi spies in Geneva. I don't know what they want, but they're looking for something connected to the man who owned the book-shop where Valérie's mother worked and where Valérie hid refugees. If you hear anything, could you tell my father? I've asked him to look out for her too, but you have your ear to the ground and might hear something about what's going on.'

'Anything I can do.'

Philippe hugged Max and left the house. As he walked across the fields towards the bridge over the Rhône River, he pulled his knapsack tighter on his back. He didn't know if he would see Max and Sofia again, if his goodbyes would be forever.

Shrugging off his gloomy thoughts, Philippe entered the small town and walked briskly towards the Café de la Gare. He let himself inside the warm space and saw Christophe and Yves at one of the tables.

They greeted one another and Philippe sat down, pleased to see that Christophe looked more like his former cheerful self, blue eyes flashing as he smiled, blond hair curling in protest at the military haircut. Yves was a more solid and placid character, his hair more straw than golden. Philippe felt his spirits rise in their company. They ordered food and then discussed what Philippe and Yves planned to do.

'I have Stefano's father's address,' said Yves. 'He lives in the centre of town, still in the house where Stefano was brought up. My mother knows the family, or at least used to.'

Philippe nodded and turned to Christophe. 'What did Stefano tell you about where he was going?'

'Not much. He'd heard that his cousins and their friends had left home to join the partisans. His cousin Luigi had been in the Italian army and when the army changed its allegiance from Germany to the Allies, lots of men returned home, unsure which side they were fighting for or against. Like many others, he took his weapons and joined the partisans in the north. Stefano was more worried about one of the girls, a friend from the area called Francesca who had left home to join the partisan group in the mountains above Cannobio and then disappeared. He wanted to find her.'

'Where did he plan to start looking?' asked Philippe.

'He was going to cross the border to Italy and head for the

countryside above Cannobio. It's the last place he heard there was trouble with the partisans. But then he went missing and we've heard nothing else.'

Philippe and Yves shared a glance. 'We'll start with Stefano's father and find out who went with him,' said Philippe, 'then try and follow his route.'

Christophe put out his hand. 'I'm sorry I don't have better information. We only know he is missing because one of the other lads from Ticino came back from leave and said everyone was talking about it in the town.'

Philippe looked out of the café window, seeing the dark clouds hanging over the town.

'You might not get to Locarno today if you don't leave soon. It will be dark when you arrive, even though you're taking the quicker route through Italy,' said Christophe, pulling out a piece of paper from his pocket. 'This is Walter's home address in Brig. He said that if it got too dark you should stop there today and carry on to Locarno tomorrow. He told his wife about you and you can stay there.'

Walter had been one of the men in Philippe's first unit, a farmer whose land was on the outskirts of Brig, the town where the train line split, with one line going southeast through the Simplon tunnel, emerging in Italy only twenty kilometres away, before going back into Switzerland and arriving at Locarno. There was a much safer route staying completely in Switzerland through the Gotthard tunnel, but it was a longer way around and Philippe knew they had to risk the quicker route.

'Let's see how we get on,' said Philippe, knowing that the sooner they left, the more chance they would have of reaching Locarno in good time.

Yves checked the clock on the wall. 'If we go now, we will get the next train.'

Christophe paid the bill, waving away Philippe's protests. 'Just make sure you come back safely,' he said, as they left, walking across the wide road to the station platform. Philippe pulled his jacket more tightly around his shoulders. It was going to be a cold night. A few minutes later, the train that ran through the Rhône Valley came into the station and they climbed aboard, passing the soldiers who were all getting off at Saint-Maurice. Philippe looked at them enviously as they walked across to the trucks on the other side of the square waiting to pick them up, laughing and joking as they walked. It didn't seem long ago that they were all so carefree and young, but their responsibilities were now a matter of life and death. As the train left the station and sped up through the outskirts of the town, he thought about Valérie, understanding more than ever why she took the risks she did. He was about to go into enemy territory, just like she had. He had no doubts anymore that Italy was an enemy territory and knew that Switzerland's neutrality would give them very little protection.

The train went south to Martigny, the Roman town leading up to the Great St. Bernard Pass into Italy, and then turned northeast following the river up the valley, the mountains on each side stretching ahead of them. As the train went through the valley, Philippe looked at the small farms and chalets next to the railway line, at a farmer moving his cattle along a footpath at the side of the track to a woman feeding another herd of cows further along the line. He glanced at Yves, who was trying to sleep, and then at the other passengers, people going about their daily lives, mothers and children, businessmen and country people.

He didn't know this part of Switzerland very well, but the names they passed were familiar, from the medieval Castle of Saillon, its ancient towers rising above the town on a rocky outcrop in the middle of the valley, to the airport at Sion, its gates guarded by soldiers protecting a hive of activity. The Rhône Valley widened at this point and the rocky cliff sides stretched up above the train line. As they passed through Leuk and into German-speaking Switzerland, Philippe could hear the number of French voices diminish all around him. Like most Swiss, he was fluent in both French and German but he still felt strange as he travelled further away from Saint-Maurice and the French language gave way to German.

They reached Brig in the middle of the afternoon. Although the light was fading when they arrived at the station in the town, Philippe shook his head wordlessly. He wasn't going to get off now; it might be getting dark but it was still only the afternoon and they couldn't waste any more time. Before the train left the station for the Simplon tunnel the Swiss border police went through the carriages checking identity papers. Their checks were cursory for trains travelling in this direction, but they saw a train coming in from Italy that was taken off to a special siding, with Swiss border guards waiting to board. Even from this distance, it was apparent the Swiss were taking much more care checking passengers coming into Switzerland. Pulling out of Brig station, they left the other train behind, knowing that anybody turned back at the border would be following them on the next train to Italy. Philippe looked ahead out of the window and in the dull light of the afternoon saw the stone entrance to the tunnel, surrounded by fir trees, leading into darkness.

The tunnel was just under twenty kilometres long and they came out to see the Italian mountains, scenery very like the Alps they'd left in Switzerland. But at the first station in Italy, Iselle, the difference was stark. As they pulled into the station, the platform was crowded with German soldiers, and swastika signs were hanging from the eaves down the walls of the station building. The atmosphere was no longer calm and business-like but tense and fearful, violence just under the surface. German soldiers boarded the train, and as at Brig, quickly checked the papers of the passengers.

When they got to the town of Domodossola, they got off the

train to change onto the line for Locarno, standing in the queue
to show their papers. To the right, in one of the sidings at the
station, they saw groups of people being herded onto closed
carriages. As they waited, they watched them being ordered
onto the train. Philippe felt cold, not only because of the
freezing wind but because of what was happening to the people
so close to him. Suddenly there was a shout and one figure
started to run away from the crowd waiting to get on the train.
He was a young man, only a boy really. He was trying to escape
into the streets of the town, weaving round the groups of people
watching him, but then there was a shot and the boy collapsed
onto to the ground. Philippe started at the noise and instinctively moved away from the line, but Yves grasped his arm and
hissed, 'Don't make a scene, you can't do anything about it.
We'll be sent straight back to Switzerland if you complain.'

'But he's just a boy! They shot him!' He felt helpless,
desperate to do something and tried to push ahead past Yves.
The worst thing was that the people all around simply turned
and continued to get onto the train carriages, seemingly oblivious to the violent scene that had just taken place. No one did
anything about the boy, whose body was still lying on the
ground, the blood pooling around him, until two German
guards came and dragged it away. Philippe was breathing heavily, straining against Yves' grip, his hands curled into fists. But
he knew that Yves was right and there was nothing he could do.

They got to the front of the queue and Philippe handed
over his papers. The German guard looked over them. 'Why
have you come to Italy?' he asked. Philippe couldn't speak, the
lump in his throat making him feel sick.

'We're going straight back into Switzerland, to Locarno,'
answered Yves. 'We're visiting some family there for a few days.'

The guard nodded and waved them on. Yves still kept hold
of Philippe's arm as he marched them down the steps to the
other platform for the train to Locarno.

'I'm all right now,' muttered Philippe. 'Thanks. I won't react again.' He clenched his jaw as he waited for the smaller train. He knew he'd have to get used to this casual violence or he'd ruin the whole plan. He'd seen enough of Nazi methods and their warped sense of justice to have no doubt of their capacity for cruelty, but seeing it on such a big scale, affecting a whole population rather than a few individuals, was still shocking. Focus on the job at hand, he kept repeating to himself, *get in, find Stefano and get them all out*.

EIGHTEEN

PHILIPPE

Switzerland and Italy

They boarded the smaller train that ran through the mountains towards Locarno. It wasn't very far in terms of distance but the train weaved through the mountains and around outcrops of rock in the darkness, stopping at small stations and villages along the way, until Philippe was confused and tired. On the border to go back into Switzerland, the train stopped for over an hour, until the German soldiers had gone through it again, making sure that no one was escaping into neutral territory.

Finally, they arrived in Locarno and they stumbled off the train in the darkness. At least it wasn't as cold as it had been in the mountains. Even though it was late evening, the warmer temperature coming from the lake didn't feel like early December.

'Where are we going?' asked Philippe.

Yves started walking down towards the lakeside through the old town, past houses that had been there for hundreds of years, but which now looked tired and worn. They stopped outside one house in a narrow street, the ground floor of which was some kind of shop, its shutters closed. Yves rang the bell and they waited, hearing nothing apart from the rumbling sound of Philippe's empty stomach. They had taken some bread with them for the train, but that had been eaten hours ago and they were both ravenous again.

After a moment, a man opened the door. He moved like an old man, but when Philippe took a proper look, he realised that he was just thin and the resemblance to Stefano left him in no doubt but this was his father.

'Signore Novelli?' asked Yves.

'Who wants to know?' the man growled, his hand already starting to close the door.

'Monsieur,' burst out Philippe in French. 'My name is Philippe Cherix. I'm a friend of Stefano, we're in the army together. I've come to find him.'

The man leaned forward. 'You're Philippe? Stefano told me about you, how you gave him a second chance. But you can't help. He's gone to Italy and he hasn't come back. The border mountains are too dangerous these days. You'd better just go back to the fort.'

Philippe hadn't come this far to give up now. He put his foot in the door and leaned forward. 'Stefano saved my life. I'm not going to leave him now.'

The man stared at him silently and then his shoulders seemed to crumble and he nodded. 'All right, you'd better come in. My name is Massimo.'

They went inside and through to the back of the house, to a simple kitchen with a small table and chairs, a small, old stove in the corner. Despite the stove, the house was dank and cold, colder than the temperature outside and Philippe pulled his jacket collar up around his neck.

'Have you eaten?' asked Massimo, pushing some stale bread across the table. When they shook their heads and hungrily picked up the bread, he went to the stove and heated up a small pan. After a few minutes, he poured some cassoulet into two bowls, filled two glasses with water, and put everything on the table in front of them. They said nothing until they'd finished eating.

'Thank you,' said Philippe finally, the food reviving him and reminding him why they were there.

'We want to follow Stefano's route and find him. Can you tell us exactly where he went?'

Massimo put some cups of coffee on the table. 'He went across the border over the mountains. One of the boys we know, Alessandro, took him the safest way. He was going to the hills above Cannobio. There's a church up there that the partisans are using as their base for attacks on the Germans. Stefano thought that his friend Francesca was there and he was desperate to find her. We've heard nothing else from him.'

He went over to the small dresser at the side of the room and picked out some photographs, before coming back to the table and handing the top one to Philippe, pointing at a pretty dark-haired girl laughing at the camera. 'This is Francesca.' He passed over the second one. 'And this is Luigi. He was in the Italian army but he left when Italy changed sides. He was supposed to be making his way to Cannobio to fight for the partisans against the Germans.' He heaved a big sigh. 'My nephew had rebelled against his father, who was always sympathetic towards the fascists. He told his father not to come after him. All this trouble has split the family apart...' He shook his head. 'Even if they're still alive, the family is broken. My poor wife's sister is devastated.' He went and picked up a photograph in a frame from the top of the dresser. 'This is myself and my wife, before she got ill, with her sister and her sister's husband. We were good friends, they came out here to Cannobio every summer from their home in Milan. Even when my wife died, they would come up and take Stefano for the whole summer. He loved it with them, that's why he went to find his cousins and their friends. He couldn't bear it if something happened to them.'

'Thank you,' said Philippe. 'That's where we'll start, then. Where do we find Alessandro? If he could take us, that will help.'

'I'll speak to him early tomorrow and ask him to take you.' He looked back down at the photograph and Philippe saw a young Stefano peering out from behind his mother's skirts. 'Stefano is all I have left, he's my only boy. We never had any other children. If something happens to him...' His voice broke.

Philippe reached out and clasped his shoulder. 'We'll find him, sir. I promise.'

Massimo shook himself and stood up. 'You need to get some sleep.' He led them back into the parlour, the room holding only two mattresses rather than the usual pieces of furniture.

'Alessandro helps people come across from Italy. This is a place that they can stay before moving on safely.'

Philippe nodded but was too tired to say anything. It wasn't just in Geneva on the border with France that Swiss citizens were helping people to escape, here too on the border with Italy others were playing the same role. When would it all end? he wondered, as he lay down under the thin blanket. For how much longer would there be thousands of desperate people fleeing Nazi persecution?

The next morning, Massimo came through very early to wake them up, accompanied by a young boy who must have been no more than twelve years old. He was short and thin, with a shock of dark hair, but he looked fit and strong.

'This is Alessandro. He takes people in and out of Italy,' said Massimo.

Yves spoke slowly in Italian so Philippe could follow the conversation. 'Will you take us to where you left Stefano?'

The boy shook his head.

Philippe stared at him in confusion and then at Massimo. Why would the old man go and get this boy who wasn't prepared to help them? But before he could protest the boy said, 'I can take you but not today.'

'Why not?' said Philippe quickly in French, forgetting for a moment where he was. But the boy understood and shook his head firmly.

'Today I must go to Bellinzona, east of here, to the railway that leads into the Gotthard tunnel. We have information from the partisans across the border in Italy that a train of Italian civilians will be taken to Germany and sent to Nazi concentration camps there. It's stopping at Bellinzona and waiting until nightfall so there will be less people to see it travelling through Switzerland. We are going to try and stop them.'

Yves stopped Philippe from answering by placing a restraining hand on his arm. He spoke in Italian, slowly so Philippe could understand. 'But we didn't think that this was allowed – Italians to be taken through Switzerland like this. It was agreed before the war that only necessary supplies would be carried by train through our country, not civilians or slave workers or prisoners of war.'

Alessandro threw up his hands. 'All I know is that the Nazis are doing it, breaking the rules any time they think they won't be caught. They take trains of cattle carriages and force people to go inside, then they travel through the Gotthard tunnel under the Alps and onwards into Germany. They either kill them or make them work for the Third Reich. I help to get some of the people out in Switzerland if we can.'

Philippe was torn, feeling he should insist that they find Stefano immediately, but then an image of Valérie came into his mind and he was in no doubt about what she would do, faced with the thought of all the people she might be able to save. He remembered with a sharp stab of pain the boy who had tried to run away and been shot in the station at Domodossola. It wouldn't be much of a delay and if he could help to save more people, then he had to do it. 'All right, we'll come with you and help you if you promise to come back and take us to find Stefano.'

Yves nodded his agreement. Alessandro smiled for the first time and stuck out his hand. 'I agree. You help me and then I help you.'

NINETEEN
VALÉRIE

Geneva

Valérie went inside the workshop and waved at Luca, who was packing up boxes in the corner of the storeroom. She ran up the wooden staircase and past Hélène and the other women working on the benches in the bright sunshine streaming through the tall windows. She touched Hélène's shoulder on the way past and sat in front of her father, who was gathering packages together on his table. He gave her the smaller, more valuable packets to put in her satchel and stacked up larger parcels to take downstairs.

'I'll help you with those,' he said, picking up some boxes and heading for the stairs. 'There's quite a lot today,' he added. 'You need to send them off from the post office.'

'I want to see if Marianne is there anyway,' she answered.

'And you need to deliver some watch mechanisms to Universal on the Rue du Rhône,' he added. 'They're selling more of their luxury watches to German customers and they want to use our mechanisms.'

She didn't react, knowing that this was the price he had to

pay to keep in business. She thought about the general manager of Universal who was a Nazi sympathiser and expected them to be the same. 'I'll try to behave myself,' she said with a grimace. 'I know he's an important customer, but he seems to be getting worse. Every time I go there, he's entertaining someone from the German consulate. I've probably been introduced to them all by now.'

He helped her load her basket. 'I know, mignonne, but at least the war seems to be turning against the Germans. Just you wait, he'll be criticising them next, once he sees his business disappearing.'

Valérie kissed him on the cheek and left, pushing her bike across the cobbles in the old town. She decided to go to the post office first, because she wanted to ask Marianne whether she had any news of Clara. It was a few days now since they'd spoken, surely enough time to find her.

She rode across the Rue du Mont-Blanc towards the grand post office building, leaving her bike next to the entrance and picking up the parcels to be sent off. She ran up the flight of steps and waved to Amélie at the counter, before joining the long queue, the low tones of conversation of those waiting bubbling round the large room.

When she finally got the head of the queue, she piled the parcels on the desk.

'Hello, how are you?' she greeted Amélie in a bright voice. The other girl blinked a couple of times behind her thick glasses and gave a wan smile in response, as she automatically gathered the parcels and started to stamp them.

'Is Marianne working in the telephone exchange today?' asked Valérie.

'Yes, she's come in, so she'll probably have a break soon.' Amélie always knew everybody's movements in the building, and liked to pass on the latest news to her customers but there was no bright voice this morning. She sniffed as Valérie paid for the postage and her eyes filled with tears.

'Are you all right?' asked Valérie.

'We're just having a difficult time at home. My mother's not been well and it's costing so much every time we have to call the doctor out. We never seem to have enough money.'

Valérie reached out and clasped her hand, stung by the girl's misery. Everyone was struggling to get enough food and fuel, far less pay medical bills. 'Maybe you could get some extra hours here. Have you asked?'

Amélie wiped her eyes. 'I keep meaning to, but my boss isn't that easy to talk to, so I haven't mentioned it yet.'

'There's no time like the present.' Valérie looked behind her. 'It's quieter now so we can get someone to sit in for you. Go and ask him.'

'Oh Valérie, I'm not sure I can.'

'Of course, you can.'

She ushered Amélie upstairs, hoping that the girl would receive a sympathetic hearing. Once she'd disappeared from view, Valérie went out to meet Marianne, impatient to see her friend.

She walked briskly to the seat in the paved area between the post office and the English church where she usually met Marianne. She didn't have to wait very long before she saw her friend coming towards her, leaving the group of girls who had all come out of the imposing building at the same time, putting on their coats against the cold wind.

Marianne gave her a hug and sat down next to her on the seat, leaning forward and speaking urgently. 'We're getting some teenagers out tonight. Clara should be one of them. If everything goes well, they should be at our farm by late afternoon. We'll give them something to eat and take them into Geneva late tonight. Can you wait at the normal place beyond the Jardin d'Anglais at eleven o'clock and take them to a safe house?'

'I'm so relieved you found her,' said Valérie. 'I can take her to the SOE immediately. I'll leave them a message to expect me tonight.' Then she shook her head, unable to let it go at that. 'Can't I come with you? This waiting for news is worse than anything. I know it's what we usually do, but it feels different this time. Clara isn't some anonymous refugee; the German border guards will be watching for her.'

Marianne clasped her hand. 'I know you want to be there and make sure she gets out safely but she'll be fine. We've done this hundreds of times. You're an important part of the network here in Geneva. The fewer people at the border the better, because it's much more dangerous.'

'If you're sure,' Valérie replied uncertainly.

'We should stick to the plan,' said Marianne firmly. 'If we start changing it now, we risk making mistakes.'

'How many children do you need me to take?'

'Two. Clara and a boy.' Marianne stood up. 'I need to go back now, but just be at the handover point next to the Jardin d'Anglais at eleven.'

They embraced and parted, Valérie pushing away the disappointment that she couldn't help more, wondering why she felt that this wasn't like their usual operation, no matter what her friend said.

She continued to make her deliveries across the city, the next call being to the Universal watch factory on the Rue du Rhône. She sat in the large art deco building missing the friendly presence of the old manager, Monsieur Levy, so different from the pompous self-important man who had engineered his removal. She waited for a longer time than usual because the new manager was occupied with an important customer. She saw the plump figure through the door to his office, hands gesticulating energetically before two tall men, their black coats similar to those of the Gestapo.

Valérie shook her head to clear away the thought. The Gestapo didn't walk around openly in independent Switzerland. They operated in the shadows, like the spies who'd killed Isabelle and were hunting Clara. At least she now had a plan for saving the girl. By the end of the night Clara should be safely in Switzerland and with the SOE. Valérie couldn't contemplate any other outcome.

TWENTY

CLARA

France-Switzerland Border

Clara and Louis joined the other children and young people, all kicking a ball between one another and doing some exercises together, led by Jean, who had recovered from his injuries. The laughter was loud in the field at the edge of Annemasse, though to Clara it sounded false. They'd never met the other children before and Jean had told them to act as if they'd always been together. It was harder than it seemed and Clara stayed close to Louis, terrified that they would be split apart and she would lose the one person that she knew.

Jean had reassured them that the Germans never suspected anything unusual about the groups of children who went to play in the field next to the border, nor did they notice that fewer children came back than had set off.

It was late in the afternoon and the light was fading when Jean told them to come to the edge of the field nearest the border, but before they could carry out the plan they heard the sound of marching boots on one of the roads coming towards them.

'Go back,' hissed Jean. 'Back to the safe house! They're coming from the other direction.'

He looked around quickly and then pushed them towards the town. 'Run to the house you came from and stay there until I come for you. Be careful of any German soldiers and keep going, whatever you hear.'

Clara bent down low and ran for her life, Louis at her heels, his breathing growing heavier as they ran. At the gate to the field, they ran back to the house they'd only left a few hours before and through the open door held by a sturdy woman who helped Clara inside before she fell over.

'You're safe. They haven't followed you,' said the woman, leading Louis into the kitchen. Clara sank down onto a chair in the warm room, her heart still racing from the sudden failure of their escape. She gazed at the woman's tense features.

After a few moments of silence, Jean came inside and caught his breath before he could speak. 'They need to stay here another night and we'll try again tomorrow. There were too many soldiers snooping around. I don't want them realising what we're doing here. It's too valuable to lose this escape route.'

The woman nodded. 'They can stay here for another night.'

'It may be longer. We'll only try again when it's clear,' answered Jean before turning to leave.

A dark-haired girl came into the kitchen and stared at Clara and Louis. 'I thought they were going today.' She glanced at the window, shutters closed against the cold. 'I've told you before, Maman, this is too dangerous. There were German soldiers all over town today, patrolling this area. They must have been tipped off about the escape.'

'I know what I'm doing, Monique. Just get on with supper.' The woman turned back to Clara and Louis, her features softening when she looked at them. 'Come on, let's get you something to eat and then you can sleep tonight. Jean will get you across when it's safer.'

After they'd eaten, Clara stood at the door to the backyard, listening to the sounds of the night, the quietness only broken by the rush of the wind and the occasional noise of a car on the road outside. Louis came up towards her. 'You should sleep. Why are you still up? What are you doing?'

She shook her head, still feeling a desire to run. 'I just don't want to stay. We need to keep moving and we're stuck here.'

'No, we can't do anything and we have a chance to rest.'

She pulled her jacket around her shoulders, the cold of the night creeping into the house. 'I don't want to stay here,' she said finally. 'I don't like it.'

He grabbed her arm, trying to pull her away from the door. 'What are you talking about? They said they'll take us into Geneva tomorrow. Don't you trust them?'

'I'm not sure I trust anybody,' she replied. 'I know the address of a place in Geneva my father said was safe. He told me I should go there.'

'You always think you know best,' said Louis with a deep sigh.

'Will you come with me?' she replied.

He looked at her in the darkness, the sincerity of her question filling the air between them.

'We escaped from the children's home, didn't we?' she continued.

'I know we did, but this time is different. The best chance we have of getting to Geneva is with these people. You saw the German soldiers. We'd never get past them on our own. Give Jean a few more days and if we don't get out then we'll try on our own.'

She bent her head, knowing he was right. It was a strange feeling to trust someone else to take decisions for her. It was normally she who determined what she did, but things were changing now.

Clara sighed deeply. 'All right then.' She paused and then added, 'You're my friend, the only person I trust in the whole world. Of course, I'll stay.'

TWENTY-ONE

VALÉRIE

Geneva

Valérie went home for supper and found Agathe in the dining room at the long table polishing a silver cup, breathing heavily as she rubbed vigorously. Agathe pushed her wiry grey hair away from her red cheeks, before placing the cup down with the others, then picked up the last one, grasping the stained handle between her gnarled fingers.

The smell of silver polish was overpowering. Valérie dropped her packages on to the table and ran to catch the cup before it slid to the floor. 'Why are you bothering with this? It's my job to clean the cups.'

Agathe grunted a response. 'I'm bothering, young lady, because I'm ashamed by the state of the silver in this house. It might be your job, but when was the last time you did it?'

Valérie felt herself flush, immediately taken back to being the naughty little girl who avoided housework to escape outside to meet her friends. 'I'm sorry. I know I should have done it, but I've been so busy making the deliveries.'

Agathe's wrinkled face softened as she looked up. 'Well,

now you're here, you can put the silver away in the dresser for me. You know I can't reach the top shelf.'

Obediently, Valérie arranged the cups in the dresser. She paused as she placed the largest in pride of place and stroked the curved handle. 'This is the cup I won in the last competition at Veyrier before the war.' She moved it closer to the framed photograph of herself smiling up at Philippe and holding the cup. She touched his face and felt a wave of longing and fear almost overwhelm her. He was in a perilous place and she'd heard nothing from him since he'd left. Even though he'd only just gone, she wished with all her heart that she could see his familiar figure walk towards her and pull her into his arms.

She turned away from the dresser and came to sit next to Agathe.

'When's Papa coming home?'

Agathe folded her arms across her faded patterned apron. 'He'll be back for supper,' she said before she waddled through to the kitchen.

After they'd eaten Agathe's rabbit stew and Agathe had set off home, Valérie cleared up and after ten o'clock, she went to get her coat. 'I might be a long time tonight,' she said to her father, kissing his cheek.

He looked up at her and shook his head. 'I'm not sure I'll ever get used to this life. Worrying about who's watching, wondering what you're doing every time you're out and who you're seeing.'

She pushed away the unanswerable questions and hugged her father. 'Don't be worried, Papa. I'll be fine.'

Valérie opened the door carefully, looking up and down the street before venturing outside. All her senses were alert. She could smell cooking wafting through the air and there were people moving around in the houses along the street. She passed by the edge of the Place du Bourg-de-Four, her eyes looking straight ahead. It still wasn't too late for a few people to be out in the small square, on their way home or heading to a nearby bar. The Café de Paris was busy inside, laughter bursting out when the door opened so she made sure she stayed in the shadows.

Valérie went down out of the old town and crossed the Rue du Rhône, reaching the edge of the Jardin d'Anglais a few moments later. She looked up and down the dark boulevard, seeing only a few figures scurrying home this late in the evening. A cold wind was blowing through the city and Valérie pulled her coat tight around her and stuck her hands deeper in her pockets. She stood in the agreed place and leaned on one of the trees lining the boulevard. As she waited, her thoughts moved to Philippe and where he might be. She was desperate to get news from him but realised that it would be too dangerous for him to get in touch with her, even if he could.

She stamped her feet to try to keep the circulation going and blew on her hands in her woollen mittens before sticking them back into her pockets. She glanced at her watch and realised that the meeting time was long past, then looked again up and down the boulevard, hoping to see someone coming towards her.

A solitary car came down the boulevard and slowed down in front of her. The petrol shortages meant there were very few cars on the road and those there were didn't stop without a reason. Despite that, she purposely turned away, her heart beating louder. But then she heard laughter and someone shouted at her, before the car sped up and left her behind. The occupants of the car didn't care why she was there. She breathed a sigh of relief and moved behind the tree. It wasn't very safe in the gardens this late at night; she looked too obvious waiting in the December cold. The next car might not be young lads enjoying themselves, but the Swiss border police, or others looking for people escaping from France.

She looked at her watch again and saw that it was almost midnight. What had happened to them? She knew there must have been some problem. She'd waited in this very spot many times, but Marianne had never been so late. She stamped her feet again. There was no choice; she would just have to wait until she came.

Although the ground was cold, Valérie sat down on the roots of one of the trees, not knowing how long she would have to wait. She looked down the boulevard, hoping to see a figure appearing to meet her, imagining all kinds of horrors that might have befallen them. There were no cars any longer and, as the night drew on, she began to wonder what she should do. If it got too late, her father would be out looking for her before too long.

Then she heard the sound of running footsteps and struggled to her feet. In the darkness, she recognised Marianne and hurried towards her. 'What happened? You're so late.'

Marianne shook her head. 'They had to put off the escape. There were too many German soldiers in the town and Jean took the children back. We don't know when he'll try again.'

The disappointment in Marianne's voice struck Valérie like a physical blow. 'You're sure Clara was there?'

'I don't know. We heard the children in the field but they had to go back. I'm sorry, Valérie, but she's not safe yet.' She swallowed.

Valérie knew what she couldn't bring herself to say. If the Germans caught Clara with the document, she would be killed. Then they would never find her, far less get her safely to Switzerland.

'My contact said she was the one they were looking for,' said Marianne. 'They are desperate to get the document she's carrying.'

Valérie heard the noise of another car coming towards them. 'You'd better get back home. It isn't safe to be out so late.'

They embraced, cold and aching with their heartbreaking disappointment, and Marianne left. Valérie crossed back over the Rue du Rhône and walked home, the failure to get Clara to safety bitter and overwhelming. She wondered if she'd ever feel warm again, her breath freezing in the air in front of her. Back at home, as she locked the door behind her, she felt something inside her harden into steel. All was not lost. It couldn't be. She would get Clara back.

TWENTY-TWO

PHILIPPE

Switzerland and Italy

For all of that day Philippe had to wait. He was restless, haunted by the conviction that delaying their search by even one day would risk losing Stefano in Italy, but Alessandro was insistent they wait until the afternoon before they went to Bellinzona, where the train full of Italian prisoners would be standing in one of the many sidings at the station. He could understand that it was important to have the cover of darkness to raid the train, but he was impatient as the hours passed and the weather was cold, despite the warmer temperature from Lake Maggiore. It looked like snow was coming, even as low as the lakeside.

They had received clear instructions from Alessandro to wait inside and Philippe realised that this was a major operation. The intelligence about the train seemed legitimate and groups from all over the area planned to take part.

Knowing how well guarded the train was likely to be, and how many German soldiers would be there, he had asked Alessandro how he expected to open the carriages.

'That's part of the plan,' said Alessandro. 'We hit the train when the senior Germans are speaking to the Swiss railway workers, the ones who take money and let them wait there.' He spat on the ground at the back of the Novelli house, where they were waiting until the van came to pick them up. 'We have decided to let them continue taking bribes, because then we find out what the Germans are doing at the station.'

'But they must leave some guards on the train?' asked Philippe. 'What do we do about them?'

'There aren't many. We make sure they can't stop us and then we need to be quick before the others come back.'

'What do they do when they come back and find the refugees gone?'

'There is little that they can do, because they know that they are breaking the law. There is no one to tell. The train will need to go back into Italy; it can't proceed through Switzerland.' He sighed deeply. 'We know that this does not save many lives, there are only a few carriages in these trains, but at least we are doing something. We have also found that it is important to get the people out before the train goes much further. They haven't been in it for long as they start from the north of Italy, so they are still quite strong and can escape. Later on, they've been in these carriages for many hours, even days, with no food or water so they are in a much worse condition and cannot run away, particularly the old ones.'

'How many trains have you raided like this?' asked Yves.

'Only two so far,' replied Alessandro. 'But we think there will be many more in future, now that the Germans are occupying the north of Italy and they are no longer our allies. The British are still in the south of the country and may take months to get up here. The Germans are transporting people to the concentration camps and also men to work in their factories.' He got up to leave. 'A van will come here and pick you up at five o'clock. We will drive to the woods at the Bellinzona siding and wait there until it gets fully dark, then we wait for the signal to run to the train. Our job is to break into the carriages and get all the people out. They should run into the woods and away from the station and the town. There are many houses where they can seek sanctuary. We will concentrate on opening the carriages and getting them out while others will lead them into the woods.'

Finally, it was late afternoon and a battered old van stopped in front of the house. Philippe and Yves clambered into the back, nodding to the men already inside. The van looked like an old ambulance or delivery van, with makeshift seats on each side facing the middle and small windows high up.

The men shuffled along to give Philippe and Yves some space and muttered greetings. They drove out of Locarno to the east and Philippe couldn't help feeling that they were driving away from his objective to find his friend, but one look at the faces around him made him realise how serious these men were, how determined to save the Italians trapped in the train. He looked out of the small window on the other side of the van and, in the dim light, he saw the white tops of the Ticino mountains glowing against the dusky sky. They passed a few houses with dim lights shining out of the windows. They seemed old and rundown, as if they'd been there for centuries. The whole land-scape looked ancient and it was only when they came into the outskirts of Bellinzona that more modern buildings emerged from the darkness.

They turned abruptly onto a rougher track, the men grip-ping the benches to hang on as the vehicle swayed from side to side on its twisting route through a forest trail, tree branches slapping on the sides of the van. Philippe grabbed the side of the van as the back slewed sharply sideways on one of the tight corners down the narrow track and he lost his grip on the seat.

The wheels skidded on the surface, tyres crunching the gravel at the side. As the van lurched violently, the men gripped on to anything fixed to the inside of the vehicle to avoid being thrown to the floor. Philippe held his breath and hung on. Just as he thought they were going to slide off the track, the driver recovered control and the wheels regained their grip. The men exchanged some nervous smiles and a few muttered comments.

Suddenly, the van came to a halt, and the driver turned round and ordered, 'No guns, we need to keep quiet. Follow me and wait for the signal. We jump down the embankment to the train, wait for the all-clear and then break the locks of the carriages. Take one of the heavy tools from the back of the van and wait for me outside.'

Philippe and Yves got out first and waited for the other men to clear the way for them to pick up one of the assorted hammers, crowbars and other tools in a box fixed on to the floor beneath the bench seats. Then they followed the others, trying not to trip up on the rough ground, the smell of the fir trees all around them. They jumped down the embankment at the side of the railway lines, crouched in the tall grass and waited. They could see the outline of train carriages a few tracks over and in the silence could hear shouts and cries from the carriages, but there was no one else around to hear the desperate pleas of the people locked in the cargo vans.

Philippe felt a burst of anger rise in his body as he looked down at the windowless carriages. He heard a noise at the back of the train and saw the head of a German guard briefly visible as he lit a cigarette. His resentment at being forced to come on this mission evaporated as the German guard stood there, oblivious to the suffering next to him. Philippe looked up and down the train to see if there were any other guards but he could only see the one. Suddenly the burning cigarette was thrown away in a cloud of sparks and he heard the crunch of the ballast as something heavy hit the ground. Shortly afterwards he heard the call of a barn owl and the van driver at the front of their group hissed, 'That's our signal. Come on, follow me.'

They got up and followed behind the man to the back of the train, another group emerging from the woods at the front. They spread out along the side of the carriages and attacked the locks on the doors. With a deafening crash, the lock on the carriage door broke. Philippe pulled open the door and jumped backed when a man fell out of the carriage onto the tracks in front of him. A wave of the smell of humanity, bodies crammed together in a small space, filled the air. Philippe bent down to help the man up, but Yves grabbed his arm to stop him. 'He's dead, you can't help him. Help me lift him out of the way.' As they moved the body other people were jumping out of the carriage to safety, helped by Alessandro.

When Philippe stood up, he looked into the carriage and saw in the torchlight terrified faces staring down at him, unable to move, not knowing what was happening. 'Come on, you're free, get out quickly, now!' He spoke in French but the people inside understood his meaning, finally came to life and jumped down from the compartment. He helped them down and pointed towards the forest and the men and women waiting to lead them to safety. Philippe helped children, young people, parents and old people from the train, the whole of civilisation in one carriage. One young mother was holding her baby as she jumped down and she stopped to steady herself and hold onto his arm. She looked the same age as Valérie. 'Grazie...' she whispered as her husband took her arm and they ran into the forest.

When he looked up the train Philippe saw that there was one carriage in the middle that hadn't been opened and he could hear the desperate screams of the people inside, who must have known something was going on. Freedom was so close, but no one was helping them.

'Come on, we have to get these others out.' Philippe ran towards the middle carriage, but Yves grabbed his arm and pointed to the front of the train, where they could see torchlight advancing towards them. 'We can't wait much longer, the Germans are coming back.'

Philippe shook off his hand, picked up a heavy hammer from the ground and ran on ahead. Reaching the carriage, he attacked the lock savagely with the hammer. He could hear the pleas and shouts of the people inside and nothing was going to stop him before he got the door open, not even the approaching Germans. The sound of shouting from behind him was getting louder and hands were trying to pull him away from the door. He refused to move and finally the lock gave way and he pulled the door open wide. Men, women and children burst outside and ran past him, some falling down in their desperate rush for safety. They were picked up and helped on their way as Philippe looked after them, breathing heavily.

The sound of a gun going off made them all duck down and he followed the other men running away from the railway line towards the van, parked on the track up from the sidings. There were no other shots, but he could hear the sound of running feet coming towards them so he ran for his life, climbing up the embankment of the railway line and heading for the open door of the van. He was the last man to get inside and the vehicle moved off almost before the door was shut. Everyone inside hung onto their seats as the van swerved round country lanes, branches slapping the sides when it went too close to the edge. His heart thumping in his chest, Philippe almost ducked his head every time the branches crashed against the van, as if he was outside and unprotected, feeling as vulnerable as the people in the train must have felt.

They slowed down when they reached the main road around Bellinzona and drove towards Locarno. Philippe looked at Alessandro, now sitting in the back with them. He was surprised when the boy smiled broadly at him. 'Good job,' he said in French. 'We saved most of them.'

'What will the Germans do?' asked Philippe. 'I thought there would be more shooting when they saw what was happening.'

Alessandro shook his head. 'They can't afford to make too much of a fuss, they're not supposed to be there anyway. This happened last time and they had to take back the empty train to Italy. We'll have to speak to our informants to find out if they choose a different station next time.'

'Or if they have more guards on the train,' added Yves. 'They didn't have enough men tonight.'

'Won't they try to find you?' asked Philippe.

'No. They have no right to do anything in Switzerland and they know that. Nobody here likes the Germans; we see too much of what they're doing across the border. And the railway workers who helped them tonight will be much more reluctant to take their money again.'

Philippe tried to dislodge the picture of the desperate young couple and their child, of the gruesome sight of the dead man who had fallen out of the carriage. 'Where will these people go?'

'They'll be taken in,' replied Alessandro confidently. 'Many families in Ticino will take them in.'

Philippe felt a wave of exhaustion overcome him and all he wanted was to lay his head down on a comfortable bed. No one else spoke and they drove directly to Massimo's house. Philippe and Yves stumbled down from the van and Alessandro came out to shake their hands. 'That was a good night's work. You'd better get some sleep now. I'll be back early tomorrow morning and we can go into Italy.'

They nodded and went into the house. Massimo offered them some food but they shook their heads, wanting only to lie down on the mattresses and sleep. As Philippe lay down, the images of the night and the desperation etched on the faces of the people locked in the train filled his mind. Only then did he realise how close they had been to discovery. The failure to rescue the people from the train would have condemned them to certain death. Philippe could still see the terrified faces of the children as they jumped from the train. Despite being exhausted, it took him a long time to get to sleep.

TWENTY-THREE

PHILIPPE

Switzerland and Italy

Philippe felt a new energy surge through his body the next morning: it was finally time to track down Stefano and bring his friend safely home. Before they left, Philippe tried to get as much information as he could from Alessandro about Stefano's journey into Italy. He knew they'd have to find the people Stefano had gone to meet, probably a group of partisans active in the mountains up from Cannobio. They'd just have to hope the partisan group would be in the same place and wouldn't see them as an enemy.

'He wouldn't let me come very far with him, not after he met the others,' said Alessandro. 'They told me to leave them and come home.'

'Who did he meet?' asked Yves.

The boy lifted his shoulders. 'I don't know who they were, but he seemed to know where to find them.'

Knowing they had a long walk across the mountains into Italy, they got ready to leave as soon as they could. When

Massimo handed them food and water, he waved away their thanks. 'Just find Stefano safe,' he said. 'That's all I need.'

They left him at the door, standing tall and upright now, rather than hunched. The prospect of action to find his son had given him new life and they left him opening the shutters of his shop for the new day.

West of Locarno, they skirted the centre of Ascona before climbing up into the hills. Alessandro avoided the main roads and picked up a well-trodden footpath through the trees at the outskirts of the town. Once in the trees, they were completely out of sight from the road and only now and again they heard the noise of a truck or car below them. They walked past old houses as they forged deeper into the forest and Alessandro carefully avoided any sign of life. It was a cold morning, but quite still, so Philippe grew warm as they started to climb steadily. The sweet, fresh smell of the forest and trees surrounded them, the only sound now the regular tramping of their footsteps. Now and again, they heard the sound of a bird calling and the rustling noise of a small animal in the undergrowth.

As they walked closer to the border with Italy, Alessandro stopped more frequently and held his hand up for complete silence. Each time he didn't seem to hear anything untoward, so they continued on their way, avoiding the open areas. Philippe didn't know exactly when they crossed the border, although from a certain point Alessandro kept to the thickest forest. Whenever it looked like they were coming into a clearing or towards a small mountain village, he veered off into deeper cover.

When they stopped after a few hours following a steep ridge, the sun shone down on them and Philippe turned his face up to the warmth. Despite it being early December, the lack of wind and warmer lakeside climate made it feel pleasant.

Alessandro indicated that they should sit down and eat. He didn't seem to want to say anything and they sat in silence. Finally, Philippe asked, 'How much longer is there?'

Alessandro answered in French. 'We've come about half-way, but we need to be more careful now. There are soldiers and partisans everywhere around here. The Germans are hostile and the partisans might be too. I'll take you to the church where I left Stefano and you can find out where he went from there. Ask the priest, he will know.'

Philippe nodded and they left to continue their journey. The mountain landscape was very similar to the lower slopes of Switzerland but the houses were all run down, if not deserted and in ruins. They saw smoke coming out of one chimney but no other sign of life. As he walked, Philippe thought about Valérie and how much he missed her. He put his hand out and trailed it along the leaves of the trees, wondering what she was doing. She would have loved this walk – perhaps not the dangers they were facing, but the simple pleasure of being outside in nature.

Alessandro grabbed his arm, almost pulling him off his feet and dragged him behind a tree, Yves close behind them. He hadn't heard any noise, but the sound of voices growing louder was coming towards them. Alessandro put his finger to his lips and they all crouched down in their hiding place. Behind the leaves, Philippe saw four men walking towards them, all dressed in worn country clothes, carrying rifles over their shoulders. As if suddenly aware of a presence near them, the men stopped and pulled their guns off their backs, ready to respond to the unseen danger. Nothing moved and a few minutes later, their leader shook his head. They continued walking, their guns still at the ready. Alessandro waited until they were completely gone before he started back onto the path.

Yves touched his arm. 'Who were they?'

'I didn't know them, so it was safer to let them pass,' Alessandro answered.

They didn't see anyone else on the way, though they once heard the faint noise of cars from the nearby roads and German voices raised in anger. That time Alessandro ran lightly into the trees, moving like a shadow and making no sound.

Later in the afternoon, when the light was fading and the sun no longer held any warmth, they reached a country road that led towards a church, overlooking a small lake. Alessandro looked in all directions before he jumped down onto the road and they all walked up to the church. It was an old building, with ancient gravestones all around it, enclosed by a stone wall. Alessandro let himself into the church and the others followed. As soon as they entered they were greeted by a priest in white robes, middle-aged with greying hair. He walked towards them, his eyes full of sorrow and understanding.

'How can I help you?' he asked, spreading his arms wide.

Yves stepped forward. 'We're here to find our friend, Stefano Novelli. He came here a few weeks ago, but he never came home. Do you know where he is?'

Before he could reply, a group of men and women, all young and carrying rifles, stepped out of the shadows at the back of the church and surrounded them. Philippe could feel the waves of hostility and suspicion coming from them, especially the man in front who must have been their leader. Philippe looked at them, hoping to find somebody who looked sympathetic and might help them. One of the younger women at the side of the group had an elfin face that he felt he'd seen before, but he didn't know where.

He stared at the small features, the short dark hair and slim body, and then he realised where he'd seen her before. The photograph of Stefano's friend Francesca! He didn't understand it. His friend had been looking for her; he'd come all the way here thinking he would find her, but he was the one who was missing. The young woman went across to their leader and whispered urgently to him.

After a few moments, the man in charge set down his gun. 'Can you shoot?'

'Yes,' answered Philippe.

'If you want to find your friend, you can come with us and help fight to get him back.'

Philippe felt a rush of excitement. Stefano must still be alive. The man's next words punctured his excitement. 'He's being held by the Germans in a house near here along with some of our comrades and they're going to execute them all tomorrow. We have a plan to try to get them out, but we don't have much time. We came here to get some rest before we go.' He touched the priest's sleeve. 'He has lookouts all around here to make sure we're safe.'

'Tell us about your plan and how we can help,' said Yves.

The man nodded and they all sat down at the back of the church. He put out his hand, 'I'm Carlo,' he said. He took out a piece of paper, unfolded it and held it in front of one of the candles. It was a map; the drawing in charcoal showing the church and the road leading down to the house where the partisans were being held. 'There is another house in a small village close by where the Germans are living. When we start to attack the house, they'll send out reinforcements. We need some men to be waiting on the road to stop them from getting through. Our men are not sharpshooters, so we need people to stop the truck before it gets to the house.' On the map he pointed at the road leading up from the village. 'You should wait there in the trees next to this bend so you can attack when the truck's going slow and they don't expect it.'

'What guns do you have?' Philippe asked in his halting Italian. One of the men came up and put three rifles down in front of them. Philippe picked one up, making sure that it was in working order. He handed it to Yves, checked the second and gave it to Alessandro, and then checked his own. He looked through the box of bullets the man had also produced. 'We won't be able to keep them back for long,' he said. 'Are there no more bullets?'

Carlos shook his head and pointed towards the explosive charges some of the other men were checking. 'Our explosives are also quite old, so I'm praying they'll all work. If the attack fails then just get out of there quickly. There is only one chance to save our men, but it is risky as the Germans are on high alert across the whole area.'

He stopped talking when some old women came into the church with food for the partisans.

'We eat now,' said the priest. After putting down the food, the women left quickly, disappearing into the night. Philippe could see how the small country community was coming together to support the group of young men and women.

'Anyone who can leave won't stay here after tomorrow,' said the priest as he handed out the bowls of pasta. 'There will be terrible retribution against our people after the attack. The Germans will kill ten Italians for every man they lose, so no one here will be safe.'

Philippe tried to swallow his pasta, but what the man had said filled him with horror. 'And you still do this? You still try to fight them?'

The priest nodded. 'It is hard, but we must always fight against evil.'

After they ate, Philippe searched for Francesca, wanting to hear about Stefano's disappearance, wondering how she could be safe and he'd been captured. He saw her in the corner of the church alone and went over to sit next to her. She looked up as he approached and surprised him by speaking first in fluent French.

'You're Philippe Cherix, aren't you? Stefano told me about you, he said how you helped him when he was threatened in

Saint-Maurice. It's why I told our leader he had to believe you weren't an enemy. It is difficult in Italy now to know which side someone is on and whether you can trust them. Two men turning up that no one knows are often never seen again.'

'Thank you,' replied Philippe. 'I wasn't sure earlier this year about Stefano's loyalties but they're very clear now. What I don't understand is that he was coming here to find you but now he's the one who's been captured. How did that happen?'

Francesca took a deep breath and shook her head as if she'd gone over the whole story so many times that she could no longer believe it. 'He was looking for me. I was with a group who were working west of here, trying to blow up a German arms depot. Some of my group had split off from the rest of us to make a separate attack and they were captured. I managed to escape before the Germans attacked and a few of us got back here. By the time I arrived I was told that Stefano had come to look for me and the other men who had been captured but he ran into a German patrol and was taken too.' She lifted her hands up in despair. 'It's impossible sometimes to get messages through safely, half the time we're working blind in this fight.'

'I'm sorry, I'll help you to find him. It's why Yves and I are here.'

She gazed at him, her eyes filling with tears. 'If anything happened to him because of me I couldn't bear it. That's why I have to go after him. If they kill him, they might as well kill me too.'

There was nothing else that Philippe could say; her torment was written all over her face. They might be childhood friends, he thought, but it wasn't a child's love Francesca showed. It wasn't only Massimo who was pleading with Philippe for Stefano's life.

They slept on the benches in the church, covered by blankets the priest gave them. It seemed like only an hour or two when Philippe was woken by Carlo at first light.

'It's time. You need to get into position.'

They picked up their rifles, and two younger men joined them. They all set off, thanking the priest in turn as they went out of the door. He blessed each of them. Although Philippe had gone to church with his parents and with Valérie since he was small, the emotion of that simple blessing made the tears come to his eyes and he kissed the priest's hand before he left.

It was a misty, cold morning, and the men walked down the road without a word. After a short walk, they approached the house where the partisans were imprisoned – an old stone building with barns and outhouses around it. Most of the group split off to surround it while Philippe and the others crept past it and on down the road to the bend. From their hiding place, Philippe and Yves watched some of the partisans run towards the house and outbuildings to plant their explosives.

After a few minutes Philippe saw the partisans running back to the trees, then the sound of explosions ripped through the air, smoke billowing out from the buildings. German soldiers came running out of the house, shouting in alarm and firing wildly into the mist. More gunshots erupted as the partisans returned fire and some of the German soldiers dropped to the ground. The shooting continued as the partisans closed in and entered the house, the sound of more shouts and explosions coming from inside.

Over the noise, they heard a truck grinding up the hill from the village. Philippe pulled his rifle into place and waited for the truck to come round the corner, glancing at the others around him to check they were in position and ready. As the truck emerged round the corner, he took aim at the driver. He could hear the others already shooting at the truck and saw the windscreen shatter. He pulled the trigger and the truck lurched across the road. Quickly reloading, he fired at the front tyre and the truck veered towards the barrier at the side of the road, crashed through the flimsy metal, tipped over and rolled down the steep hillside.

He and the others emerged from their hiding places, shocked by the suddenness of the crash and the sound of screams coming from further down the hillside. Another explosion from the house jerked them into action and they ran back up the road. They stopped in front of the house, the door swinging open amid a scene of chaos, smoke from the explosives still filling the air and dead bodies all around, Germans and partisans together in death.

Philippe could see partisans being led up the hill at the back of the house. Then he saw two Germans coming out of one of the outhouses and going round to cut off their escape. 'We have to stop them getting round,' he shouted to the others and ran up the slope to try to catch them. Heart thumping in his chest, he fired at the Germans, who returned fire and he ducked behind a tree, shots flying past his head. Carlo emerged at the back door, as another explosion rocked the old building. They must have cleared the house, he thought suddenly, his heart lifting in relief. But one of the Germans shot Carlo and he collapsed to the ground. Without a moment's thought, Philippe shot both Germans who fell in the rubble next to the house. Drained of energy, he looked at the bloody scene, the dead men lying all around.

Someone grasped his arm. 'Come on, it's done,' shouted Yves, his face dirty and scratched. 'We have to get out of here now before more Germans appear.'

They both turned to follow the others when a hissing sound made Philippe look behind him. He saw a small plume of smoke in the stones at their feet and realised in horror that one of the bombs thrown by the partisans had not exploded and had landed right next to them. He pointed at it wildly and, understanding the danger instantly, Yves' boots scrabbled in the loose stones as they tried to put some distance between themselves and the weapon. But before they could take more than a few steps, a loud explosion filled the air behind them and caught them in the blast. A huge white light filled Philippe's vision and he felt himself flying through the air before crashing to earth and then—

Nothing.

TWENTY-FOUR

HANNELORE

Paris

Leaving the Hôtel-Dieu hospital after finishing work in the evening, Hannelore looked over her shoulder back down the long, dim corridor, checking that no one was following her. German soldiers had come into the laundry the day before searching for Jewish people and she had turned the other way, desperate not to attract their attention. The woman who ran the laundry was glad to have a strong worker and was prepared to give her employment without asking too many questions. But she knew it wouldn't last for ever and then she'd have to leave.

She came out of the huge stone building, occupying a whole block in the Île de la Cité, glancing back up Rue d'Arcole at Notre-Dame Cathedral, her favourite place in the city. The blackout lighting in Paris made it difficult to see the beautiful stone carvings on the façade of the cathedral but she could still make out the looming mass of the building, which had looked down on this part of Paris for centuries. Although she could not see it properly, its beauty was apparent even in the darkness, almost glowing in the evening sky. It was still early so there were people around the hospital going about their business, walking home from a day's work or, for the lucky few, going out to sample the delights of Parisian nightlife.

Hannelore didn't wait for long, but crossed the Pont d'Arcole towards the Marais, looking down at the dark waters of the Seine. As she passed the Saint-Gervais church where the young priest had helped her, she saw an old woman sitting on the steps outside. She may as well have been invisible for all she was noticed by people walking by. She looked confused and lost and Hannelore bent down, touching her shoulder.

'Are you all right, madame? Can I help you?' She glanced down at the small bag of belongings next to the old woman and then looked more closely at the thin features surrounded by wispy white hair, the yellow J sign prominently displayed on her chest and visible in the dim light.

The women clutched her arm. 'I have nowhere to go. I thought I might walk to the hospital, maybe they will find me somewhere to sleep.' She looked behind Hannelore in the direction of the hospital and gasped when she saw a group of soldiers coming towards them. 'You must go now. It isn't safe to stay here,' urged the old woman.

Hannelore saw the soldiers stop a few metres away, lighting cigarettes and chatting with one another. They didn't look at the two women on the steps but Hannelore knew that they were there to control the area. She recognised some of them who had come into the hospital laundry searching for Jews. She looked down at the old woman, pity filling her heart when she saw that she had so little in the world. She couldn't leave her there alone to face the soldiers. She grasped the small bag and helped the woman stand up. 'Come with me, you can't stay here alone,' said Hannelore.

They walked together along the street, Hannelore wondering where she could take the old woman to be safe. They crossed the wide Rue de Rivoli and then the woman stopped. 'Thank you, my dear, I have remembered now. This is where I live. It's just across here.' She pointed towards a narrow street leading north from the boulevard.

'Do you know the address?' asked Hannelore.

'I don't remember the address but I know the apartment. My son and his wife live there with me, but I got confused when they didn't come back tonight and I left to look for them.'

'Let's see if they're there now,' replied Hannelore and let herself be led to the front door of one of the old buildings on the Rue Ferdinand Duval, the shutters worn and dilapidated and the metal balustrades discoloured with rust. The old woman knocked on the window next to the door and they waited. A few seconds later, the door opened and a balding man stood behind it.

'Mother, where have you been? We've been so worried. Come inside now, it's not safe out.'

The old woman let herself be led through the door into the apartment but before she had taken more than a step she turned back to Hannelore.

'This young woman helped me get home. You must say thank you to her.' She gave a vague smile and then disappeared inside.

The man turned to Hannelore. 'Thank you for helping her get home. My mother gets very confused. This is the third time she's walked away from the house without knowing where she was going.' He scratched his bald head. 'I think we're going to have to leave the city. She's going to get picked up one of these days and get into trouble. And then where will she end up?'

Hannelore nodded, handing over the old woman's bag and the door closed in front of her. She sighed as she turned to go home, the weight of another family dealing with illness and old age slowing her stride. They were so vulnerable at a time when weakness and infirmity could easily lead to danger and death. She still felt burdened when she reached Chantal's front door.

She'd only been with Chantal a few days but it seemed an even more impossible task to get to Switzerland than it had before. She knew she couldn't leave her friend alone, but the longer she stayed in Paris, the more dangerous it became for her. If she wasn't careful, she'd be stopped by German soldiers and the vital information she was carrying for the Allies would be lost forever. She would never see Clara again.

She came into the main room of the apartment and smiled at Chantal, who had managed to keep the stove going so the room didn't feel so damp and cold. She started to speak but then heard the noise of the front door open and close with a crash.

'Did someone follow you?' asked Chantal in a panicky voice. 'You've been so long.'

Hannelore couldn't reply, her breath coming in short gasps as she watched the door to the room slowly open. Her mind was full of dread as she stared, transfixed at the door. She shouldn't have taken a detour to help the old woman. Maybe the German soldiers had followed them and had finally caught up with her. She cursed herself for not having locked the outside door properly. Then they heard a familiar voice.

'Chantal, help me. I'm hurt.'

They saw with horror a hand covered in bloodstains grasp the edge of the door and then Chantal's husband, Marc, staggered into the room. They both ran to help him to a chair and sit down. His dark hair was plastered against his head and there was a bloodstained bandage on his arm. His clothes were filthy and he bent his head on Chantal's shoulder.

'Thank God you're here. You're alive!' said Chantal. 'I thought I'd lost you. Where have you been?'

Hannelore went to fetch a glass of water and handed it to him. He gulped it down as if he hadn't seen clean water for days.

'The Germans held me captive; they thought I was someone else and kept asking me questions. Every time I denied knowing anything about their accusations, they just hit me harder.' He shuddered, as if the memory of the last few days was impossible to forget. Then he looked up, wonder and bewilderment etched on his face. 'They'd mistaken me for someone else. This afternoon, they picked up the right man and they just let me go.' He shivered. 'I hate to think what will happen to him.'

'The poor man, but at least you're safe,' said Chantal.

He looked at Hannelore. 'And you came back to stay with us. I was so worried about Chantal being on her own. Thank you for being here.'

Hannelore's mind was racing. 'I saw them take you so I knew that Chantal would be on her own and couldn't leave her. But now you're back I can go.'

Chantal put out her arm. 'Please stay until Marc is better.'

Her husband nodded. 'I need to get my strength up but that won't take long. Then I think we should all leave Paris. It's too dangerous now. Nothing will protect us any longer and we can't work because of all the checks. The Germans are rounding up more people in the Marais so we won't be safe here.' He turned back to Chantal. 'We should go home to Saumur. We have family there who can help look after you. I might be picked up again at any time. We were lucky I got away and that Hannelore was here, but we can't be lucky all the time.'

'We can leave together,' said Hannelore. 'You go to the Loire Valley and I'll go south.'

'But not yet,' insisted Chantal. 'We only need a few days to get ready.'

TWENTY-FIVE

VALÉRIE

Geneva

Valérie didn't hear anything more about Clara for the next few days and was deeply worried about her safety, desperate for any news of Resistance plans to bring her across to Switzerland. Nor did she see Marianne again, even though she'd gone to all the places she usually met her friend in Geneva.

When she came back home after asking for Marianne at the PTT, Valérie entered the parlour and saw her father on one chair and Nicolas Cherix on the other, both sitting silently in the dim light from a single oil lamp. They turned to look at her as she entered and she stopped in the doorway, scared by the shocked expressions on their faces. Her father got up and came towards her, walking like an old man, and grasped her arm. Valérie shivered with cold and with the tense atmosphere in the room.

'Sit down, Valérie,' said Nicolas.

She sat on the sofa with her father. Nicolas looked down, not meeting her gaze, then cleared his throat and looked back up at her, his eyes filled with tears.

'I'm sorry, but we have bad news about Philippe. He's dead. He won't be back... Nothing will ever be the same again.' His voice cracked and he couldn't go on.

She made a sound of protest and tried to pull away from her father. She couldn't stop the words bursting out. 'No, no! I don't believe you. He must be coming back, he's got to come back.' She felt icily cold, the shock of his words clutching at her heart. 'Tell me what happened,' she said. 'You have to tell me everything.'

Nicolas started to speak, his voice fractured. 'Philippe joined up with a group of partisans to free Stefano and other members of their group. They attacked a house where the Germans were holding them and managed to get them out, but as they were leaving, Philippe and Yves were caught in an explosion.' He looked down, his eyes filled with bitter tears. 'They saw them lying on the ground covered in blood. There was nothing they could do.'

'They just left them?'

'They had to. It was too dangerous to go back and get them. They expected more Germans to appear at any moment.'

'So, he saved Stefano?'

'Yes, it was Stefano who came back to the fort and told them there what had happened. They spoke to me earlier today.'

She bent her head, her body numb with shock, trying to take in the enormity of what he was saying, while wanting to scream that he must be wrong. Philippe couldn't be dead. All her hopes for the future and her happiness had been torn away in one single moment. She'd known that the scheme to go into Italy was dangerous but she'd always believed he would survive whatever he faced. She had been so confident that he would come back to her, but she couldn't believe that any longer.

Nicolas got up and came over. She stood up and clutched at him, not wanting to let go; he was so like Philippe. 'I need to go back to Philippe's mother,' he said. 'I'm sorry, Valérie.' He shook

Albert's hand, and then they embraced, as if they both needed the comfort.

Valérie sank down on the sofa again, her mind whirling. Philippe had been taken from her. Her father turned to her, but she put out her hands and ran from the room up the stairs to her bedroom. It was then that she couldn't hold the emotion back, sobbing uncontrollably as she sat on the side of the bed, her arms clutched around herself as if she had to hold her body together. After a long while, she crept under the covers and just lay there numbly, wishing she too could be dead, together with Philippe. How could she go on without him? How could he really be gone? It didn't seem real, it couldn't be.

The next day, Valérie woke up with a heavy weight pressing down on her, not knowing for a moment why she felt like that. Suddenly, it all came flooding back and she felt tears sting her eyes as the pain hit her like a physical blow. She couldn't face the day ahead, couldn't bear the reality of Philippe's death. How could she live her life now? Her pain made it impossible to stay in bed and she threw on some clothes unsteadily and went out of her room. As she walked shakily into the kitchen, both her father and Agathe looked up, their faces pained and sympathetic.

'Have some hot chocolate, chérie,' said Agatha, pulling out a wooden chair and guiding her into it. Agathe placed a cup in front of her and sat down next to her. 'I'm so sorry, Valérie,' she said quietly.

Valérie nodded, words sticking in her throat. She drank the sweet chocolate, but hardly tasted it.

She let herself be steered to the sofa, where Agathe pulled a blanket around her shoulders. Her father had left the fire burning but she was still bitterly cold. She felt a deep lassitude weighing down her spirits and leaned back against the sofa, her mind trying, bit by bit, to accept her new reality. She looked up at the mantelpiece above the fire, at the photographs of happier times, Philippe so full of life and laughing down at her. Through the sorrow and the pain she began to feel the stirrings of deep anger. Anger that he'd gone away, and that he'd been taken from her. Her fingers curled into claws when she thought about what the Nazis had done to their hopes and dreams.

Wrapped up in her own thoughts, Valérie jumped when she heard someone knocking at the front door and the low voices from the hall. Marianne came into the parlour and ran towards her.

'I heard about Philippe at the telephone exchange, is it true?' Tears were falling down her cheeks as she looked at Valérie, desperate for someone to say it wasn't.

'Philippe is dead, Marianne. Word came back to the fort that he and Yves were caught up in an explosion. They didn't get away with the others.' She leaned her head on to Marianne's shoulder, too exhausted to cry anymore.

After a few moments Valérie lifted her head, the anger still burning inside. 'They killed him. The Germans killed him.'

Marianne wiped her eyes and sat back, still holding Valérie's hand. 'What will you do?'

'Do? I'll fight even harder. It's the only thing I can do.' She squeezed Marianne's hands. 'I want to help the Resistance as much as I can. Anything I can do to beat the Germans, I'll do. Have you heard anything else about Clara? I've been so worried about her. We have to stop them capturing her.'

Marianne sat back in the chair. 'The Resistance are going to get the children out tomorrow morning, but we can deal with it. I thought it was too soon after Philippe for you to be involved.'

'Nothing's too soon. I want to do it. I want to help get the children out.'

'Are you sure that you'll be able to...' Her friend couldn't finish the sentence, unable to pretend that she thought Valérie could play her part.

'I'm sure, Marianne. You've got to believe me. It's the only thing left for me to do.' A new and indescribably strong sensation had come over Valérie. She'd been determined before, she'd been fierce before, but nothing like this. Fury was exploding inside her, a white-hot rage towards the Nazi machine that had taken away the man she loved, destroying her future with him. She was going to fight back, whatever it took. Her life didn't matter now; all that mattered was ending the war. If she could rescue Clara and get the information to the Allies, she might have a hope of doing just that. Clara might already be in the Nazis' clutches, but she wasn't going to let that stop her. Nothing would get in her way, not anymore.

'All right,' replied Marianne. 'I won't stand in your way. Come to the farm at ten tomorrow morning. They're going to try and get the children across in the morning this time. We think there will be fewer patrols than in the afternoon. If we fail again, we'll have to try something else.'

'We won't fail,' said Valérie. 'We can't afford to fail, not if Clara really is carrying something that will affect the course of the war. We need to get it to the Allies if we have any hope of stopping the Germans.'

After Marianne had left, Valérie pulled the blanket around her shoulders again. She still felt empty, bereft in a strange world, but she knew now she wouldn't stop fighting for what was right. She would just have to get used to fighting alone.

TWENTY-SIX

VALÉRIE

Geneva

Valérie cycled to Marianne's farm early the next day. It was a cold frosty morning, the fields were empty and she felt like she was the only person left in the world. As she went further south from Geneva and towards France, she turned to take the road towards Presinge, away from Philippe's grandfather's house in Vessy. A sharp wave of despair flooded across her as she remembered Philippe in the summer, growing stronger and recovering from the wound he received when he'd saved her life. After all they'd been through and the dangers they'd faced, she couldn't believe that he was gone and he would never come back. For a moment she stopped at the side of the road, unable to go on.

'No, no. I won't let this beat me.' The sound of her voice was loud in the silence and she heard a bird flying away, startled by her outburst. She watched as the bird disappeared into the low misty clouds rolling in from the hills to the south of Annemasse. Feeling stronger now, she knew that the only way she could avenge Philippe's death was to rob the Germans of their victory in every way she could. If she could get Clara out of their clutches and hand over the secret document to the Allies then she could play her part. Bill had said the document could change the course of the war. She hoped that he was right.

Arriving at the farm, Valérie leaned her bike against the house and waved at Marianne's mother who was feeding the hens on the other side of the farmyard. Marianne must have been watching for her because she came outside immediately and took Valérie's arm.

'Come inside and get warm.' She looked down at Valérie's trousers and her warm woollen jacket, tied right up to the neck. 'At least you're dressed for the weather. It will be cold waiting for the children today.'

They went inside and Marianne handed her a cup of hot chocolate. Her features clouded over as she watched Valérie warm her hands on the cup. 'Are you sure you want to do this?' she asked quietly. 'After what's happened.'

'Yes.' Valérie's voice was flat and determined. 'I want to do it myself.' She reached over and squeezed Marianne's arm gently. 'It's the only thing that will keep me going. If I don't continue to help refugees escape and try to make a difference, I'll give up completely.'

Marianne nodded and glanced up at the clock above the stove in the kitchen. 'I'll take you to the border. Come back here when you get Clara. I've got the van and we can drive you into the city.'

'Yes, I need to get her away from the border as soon as possible and hand her over to the protection of the SOE. We can't afford to lose her again.'

They made their way out of the house and down the track between the fields towards Annemasse and the border. Instinctively, they kept to the few trees and hedges that surrounded the fields, trying to keep out of sight as much as possible. When there were no trees to shield them, they bent down and ran across the frozen ground quickly. There was nothing growing in the fields, no crops or animals to keep them hidden from the German border guards. They ran without speaking, knowing that in the cold morning their voices would carry and give them away.

After a few minutes they got to the clump of trees at the far end of the farm on the Swiss border. To the south of the trees were some low buildings on the edge of the sports field. Valérie looked to her right and saw the barbed wire of the border stretching into the distance. At this particular place the barbed wire fence was broken but the break was hidden by one of the low buildings. The rear of this building was almost falling down and she could see where the Resistance had opened a large hole in the wall to allow people to escape quickly across the border. She shook her head, unable to believe that the Germans hadn't realised the Resistance were using the building as an escape route.

Right up against the fence she saw Sébastien, with another man behind him. They were crouched down, waiting for someone to come through the fence.

'Sébastien will take the younger children. He knows you're here for Clara. We've been told that there will be two older children coming through, a boy and a girl,' Marianne told her in a low voice. 'Be careful, Valérie. Make sure you stay on this side of the border or you'll be caught by the German guards if they find out what's happening.' Then her friend was gone. Valérie crouched down next to the tree and stared across at the gap in the fence. She felt her heart pounding in her chest and tried to breathe slowly to calm her nerves. There had been so many false starts to this rescue that she couldn't believe it was actually going to happen this time.

Then they heard the noise of children playing in the sports field on the other side of the building. They waited for a few moments and then she saw two young children climb through the wall and run to the fence. They must have been about eight or nine years old and Sébastien immediately stepped forward and guided them away with him. Valérie could hear nothing apart from the laughter and shouts from the children on the other side of the border. Then there was a scrambling noise and an older boy appeared through the gap in the wall, looking behind him for someone.

'Clara, where are you? You have to come now,' he hissed fiercely into the building, then turned as if he was going to run back the way he had come.

Valérie didn't hesitate, terrified that she would lose them again. She flew out of her hiding place and ran up to grasp his arm. He turned and looked at her, his brown hair falling over his face.

'Come on, you have to get out,' she urged in a fierce whisper.

'I have to go back and get her. I don't know what's happened.'

Valérie heard some scuffling noises from inside the building and they both squeezed through the wall and ran towards the noise, shoes slipping on the rubble in their haste. Inside the building Valérie saw two people struggling, a girl trying to pull away from a young man who was dragging her towards the front of the building, back out to the sports field.

She knew immediately what was happening and ran to grab the girl. The boy got there first and tried to pull Clara away but the young man wasn't letting go so easily and shoved him away so strongly that the boy lost his footing and fell down onto the ground, stunned by the heavy fall. Valérie jumped forward and put herself between the girl and the young man. She knew she mustn't get caught and pulled further into France. At best, she would be interrogated and at worst, she would disappear just like so many other people had disappeared.

The assailant was only about sixteen but he was strong and his face was full of desperation, his dark eyes flashing with anger. She tried to push him away but he was winning and slowly pulling them both towards the doorway at the front of the building. The sounds of the children laughing and playing had gone now and Valérie expected to see German soldiers at any moment.

She had to do something or they would lose Clara for ever and she wasn't going to let that happen. She had to fight before it was too late. Instinctively, she pulled the knife out from her belt and thrust the fierce-looking blade at the arm clutching Clara, pulling it across his flesh, the blood oozing out of the wound. He jumped back, letting go of Clara and clutching his arm, shocked at the sight of his own blood. Valérie pulled Clara away, still holding the knife out.

'Come on, move.' Valérie and Clara backed away from the man. He opened his mouth to shout. She knew who he was going to shout for but before he could utter a sound, the boy on the ground swung a piece of rubble, hitting the man on the shin, knocking him to the ground. Without hesitation, the boy swung the rock back and hit the man's head. He lay on the ground, unmoving.

Valérie grabbed Clara and they ran for the back of the building, squeezing out through the hole and bursting into the daylight. They looked behind them to check that the boy was following and then ran to safety.

Once they reached the farmhouse, they slowed down to catch their breath. Valérie looked at the girl standing next to her, her straight dark hair framing the thin face and at the boy, who was still looking a bit dazed.

'You both saved me. He was German, that man who was trying to stop me leaving,' panted Clara. 'He was one of the people in the Resistance and he betrayed us. He's working for the Germans. You must tell your friends.'

Marianne came out of the farmhouse and ushered them inside. 'You were a long time. What happened?' she gasped.

Valérie glanced at the door closing behind her, half expecting to see German border guards chasing after them. 'I need to warn you about what happened but then we must get these two away from here. They won't be safe until we can get them to the SOE.'

Marianne took them into the warm kitchen and the two children stood over the stove trying to warm up their chilled bodies. Valérie and Marianne sat down at the table.

'We almost didn't get away,' said Valérie. 'There was a young man who was trying to stop Clara from going across the border. She said he was German, posing as someone else trying to escape. He must have been another one trying to infiltrate our escape routes.'

Clara turned around from the stove. 'He started insulting me in German and then he grabbed me to stop me from leaving.' She clutched her shoulders, reliving the moment of terror. 'Anyone helping the Resistance will need to be careful because you can't know who the people you are trying to save really work for.'

Marianne started putting on her gloves and turned around to get her jacket, then stood up and looked down at Valérie. 'We know; it's happening all around us. We've had to stop hiding refugees here. Even Sébastien's farm has been searched and we're now using an old barn in a field between our farms so there's no connection to anyone's house. We're also making sure that the refugees we do get out don't stay here, but are taken into Geneva as soon as possible.' She shrugged her shoulders. 'It's all we can do.'

She pointed at the bread and cheese on the table. 'You should eat and I'll go and get the car out of the shed. We need to get you away from here.'

Clara and Louis sat down at the table and started to eat. Marianne indicated that Valérie should follow her outside. At the door, she pointed at the farmyard. 'I have workmen watching all the entrances. They'll tell you if somebody comes up to the house before I get the car.' She shook her head. 'The border police and the Germans are making this much more difficult. The Swiss police even took Philippe's grandfather into the police station to interrogate him and warn him not to hide any refugees in future. They're just trying to pressurise him not to get involved.'

Valérie stared at her, thinking of the proud old man being treated as a criminal. 'They've taken Philippe's grandfather? How long did they keep him for?'

'I don't know, but it's made us all nervous. He's staying at Philippe's parents' place in Geneva. He hasn't gone back to Vessy.'

As Marianne went to get the car, Valérie remembered the happy days they'd spent in Vessy, Philippe's grandfather's affection and spirit always making her feel so welcome. After losing Philippe and now being taken into the police station for questioning, he'd be suffering; she resolved to see the old man as soon as she could.

She turned to go back inside, looking all around the farm-yard for potential threats, and glimpsed one of the farm labourers disappear round the side of the barn. She shivered, wondering if these men could be trusted to alert them to danger. She had come so close to getting Clara to safety that nothing could be allowed to stop them now.

TWENTY-SEVEN

VALÉRIE

Geneva

Valérie went back into the kitchen and the two teenagers looked up at her, chewing bread and cheese mechanically, their eyes full of fear. The girl was tall and thin with short dark hair and deep brown eyes, her gaze nervously darting around the kitchen as if she was still looking to escape. The boy was about the same age, no longer a youngster but not yet a man, with tousled sandy hair and light brown eyes. Valérie checked the yard and then sat down on the edge of a chair, ready to move quickly if they had to flee.

Clara looked at Valérie. 'I'm sorry... I don't even know your name and you almost died for me.'

'Valérie. My name is Valérie. I've been trying to find you and get you out of France for days.'

'I'm Clara and this is Louis. We escaped from the children's home together.'

'You have no idea how pleased I am to meet you both,' Valérie said with a smile.

Excitement and relief swept across her as she stared at the

girl, hardly daring to believe that she'd got her to Switzerland safely, knowing how close she'd been to failure. The terrible news about Philippe had pushed her on, fighting all the obstacles in her way, but a dark cloud settled over her excitement as she assessed their situation. They were still too unprotected this close to the border, particularly with such a dangerous document in their possession.

'Please tell me that you still have the document your father gave you?' asked Valérie.

Clara paused for a moment, as if she was weighing up how much she should say, then answered, 'I suppose the Resistance told you about it, but my father said I should only give it to the Allies. He insisted I shouldn't trust anyone else.'

'We're taking you to the Allies now,' said Valérie. 'I don't want to see the document, I just want to know you still have it safe.'

Clara glanced at Louis, who got up from the table and stood next to her protectively. He shook his head. 'Don't say anything,' he muttered.

'You can trust me,' said Valérie, a flash of inspiration quickening her movements. She reached into her inside pocket, pulling out the photograph of her mother and Hannelore and handed it to Clara. The transformation in the girl's face was instant, her expression changing from uncertainty to surprised excitement and she looked up at Valérie, her brown eyes huge in her pale face.

'Where did you get this? It's my aunt, Hannelore. Who is she with?'

'That's my mother, Thérèse. They were friends before the war here in Geneva.'

'Is your mother still here? Can I see her?'

Valérie's smile faded. 'That's impossible, I'm afraid. My mother died before the war, just after this picture was taken.' She gave herself a shake and reached into her pocket. 'I have this for you too.' She handed over the postcard she'd found in the bookshop. 'I think this is from Hannelore to tell you that she's still in Paris.'

Clara turned over the postcard and read the message, then looked up at Valérie. 'Yes, it's my aunt's handwriting. And she always signs her notes with an "H".' She took in a deep breath. 'But she left Paris before us that day. I thought she'd be in Switzerland by now. Something must have happened to make her stay in Paris. I don't understand what it could be.'

'I don't know either, Clara, but she's still there.'

'Can I keep this?' asked Clara. Valérie nodded and watched her gently put away the precious link to the only family she still had left in the whole world.

At that moment, Marianne came back into the kitchen. 'We can go now. Sébastien says he'll drive us. Hurry! We must be quick.'

They all went to the door, but Valérie stopped them before going outside. 'We need to do this quickly in case someone's watching.' They all nodded and Valérie could see the tension in Clara and Louis' faces. They were used to moving around at night in the darkness, but this would be the morning in the centre of Geneva, the winter sun shining into every corner and the watchful eyes of neighbours at every turn. Marianne looked right and left outside the door, before venturing across the yard and opening the back door of the van. She kept the door open and waved at the two young refugees to come outside. Clara went first with Louis following and then Valérie went last, closing the door behind her.

Sébastien drove carefully into Geneva, his dependable bulk and practical good sense as reliable as ever, reminding Valérie of how often his quiet confidence could calm any fraught situation. Out of the back window of the van Valérie could see that no one took any particular notice of them as they drove through the city streets and she avoided the casual glances of the people walking along the pavements who did look in their direction. 'Stay out of sight,' she ordered Clara and Louis. 'We don't want to attract any attention.'

When they left the Jardin d'Anglais and crossed the Pont du Mont-Blanc, Valérie looked out of the back window again but no one was following. It wasn't far to the SOE apartment on the Place De-Grenus but she knew that it might be under surveillance. The closer they got, the more it felt to Valérie that every eye was on them, every car was following them. She looked down to see her nails had dug into the palms of her hands and felt her heart beat faster as they turned into the square. She hoped that Bill Paterson would be there and they could get Clara and Louis safely inside. She knew that if the apartment was empty then they would have to turn back and go through the centre of the city to the SOE manor house over-looking the lake, exposing them to yet more risk.

TWENTY-EIGHT

VALÉRIE

Geneva

Sébastien stopped outside the apartment in the Place De-Grenus. The elegant square was quiet and Marianne jumped out to ring the bell next to the main entrance, leaving the van door slightly open. In the back, Valérie put her finger to her lips and Clara and Louis nodded obediently. She watched as Marianne waited for a few moments before trying again, looking around her to check that no one was studying them too closely. She was about to come back into the van when Bill Paterson's red hair and bulky figure appeared at the door. 'Marianne, to what do I owe this pleasure?' he said loudly.

'We have people who need to see you, they're in the van. Valérie will explain everything when they get inside,' she hissed.

Bill opened the door wider, her urgency wiping the welcoming smile off his face.

Valérie threw open the back door and Clara and Louis ran across the pavement and inside. She followed them.

'Thank you,' she said to Marianne at the door. 'We'll be fine now.' She went inside and closed the door firmly behind her, brushing the dirt off her clothes, realising suddenly how grubby they all looked. Clara and Louis were gaping around the elegant marble hall with open mouths and they both jumped when they heard the noise of the ornate lift moving back upstairs.

'Come on, all of you, before somebody else comes down,' said Bill as he led them upstairs and opened the apartment door. He took them into the parlour and encouraged the children to sit on the sofa. Valérie went to the window and looked outside, but nobody was paying attention to the apartment, nor could she see anybody she recognised. The noise of the parlour door opening made her turn around and she gasped when she saw the man who had come in. 'Henry, you're back in Geneva?'

Ignoring everyone else in the room, Henry Grant walked towards her and held her hands. 'I'm so sorry about Philippe, Valérie. We heard from Swiss Intelligence what happened.'

She gazed into his dark eyes, the old affection undimmed, and her own filled with tears. The realisation of what had happened to Philippe came flooding back and she tried to regain command of herself. She looked at Clara, and when she saw the girl's face she remembered why they were there, and moved away from Henry, raising her voice. 'This is Clara Lieberman, she has something for you.' Valérie could see both SOE agents react to the name. 'You know that it was Clara's father who gave Jacob Steinberg the intelligence about chemical weapons before the war, the information Jacob passed to you. We helped Clara to escape from France and she has a document to give you.' She turned to Clara. 'These men are the ones you've been looking for. They can help you now.'

Clara stared at Bill and Henry, then nodded to herself. She took off her jacket, turned it inside out and pulled apart the stitching of the lining at the shoulder, all the time watched by the others. Bill took a few steps towards her.

'So that's why you wouldn't take your jacket off,' said Louis.

'It was hidden in there.'

'It was cold as well,' retorted Clara with a smile, as if a huge weight had been lifted from her shoulders.

Henry perched on the edge of the table at the side of the room and both he and Bill watched carefully as Clara pulled out some papers from the lining. She held the papers for a moment and then handed them to Bill.

'Thank you,' he said. 'That was a very brave thing you did.' Bill took the papers to the table and spread them out. Both men bent down to examine the document.

'It's some of the document,' said Clara quickly. 'I only have part of it. We have to find the other half, the part that's with my aunt. She's still in terrible danger, someone has to find her.'

Valérie sank down on to a chair and stared at her in disbelief. Her job was only half done and the second part was even more dangerous than the first.

Into the silence, Bill exclaimed, excitement vibrating through his voice: 'This document could change everything! It's a list of high-ranking people on our side who are Nazi sympathisers. I don't recognise some of the names, but others I know. They're all in senior positions in the government or in the industries working on the war effort.

'This document talks about what they're doing, from conspiring to overthrow Winston Churchill's government to assisting the Germans during an invasion. It also describes the scientific secrets they've already divulged. These people have to be stopped before they do any more damage. It could make all the difference in this war. We have to get this to London, firstly the transcript, but then the original to convince them it's real. Once they've seen it written down with all the details of the people and where they work, together with the information they could give to the Germans, it makes it irrefutable.'

Valérie shook her head when she realised what was in the document. It was more than a list of names that had risked

Philippe's life before. This would fundamentally alter the course of the war, and they only had part of it.

'So, the rest is with your aunt?' Henry asked Clara.

'Yes,' replied Clara. 'We split up in France because my father thought it would be safer to divide the document.'

'Do you know where she is?' he went on.

Clara shook her head. 'I thought she was coming here too but she's still in Paris.'

'Do you have any idea where she could be in Paris, Clara?' asked Valérie. 'If she's still there I need to go and get her and I need somewhere to start.'

As she said what she'd resolved to do, she looked at the hope and longing on Clara's face. The young girl had probably lost her parents, had no family left apart from her aunt and was now split from her. And Valérie could not deny that she wanted to meet Hannelore for herself too. This was a woman who had laughed with her mother, who might be able to talk to Valérie about her. She looked at Henry and could tell exactly what he was thinking. It was too dangerous for her to go back into France; the Nazis had her name from her work with the Resistance. But the SOE needed the rest of the document. They couldn't risk any of the traitors getting any warning that their true loyalties were being uncovered. She addressed Bill and Henry directly. 'If I find Hannelore and the other part of the secret document, will you promise to take them all back to England with you?' She gestured towards Clara and Louis, who were looking between them.

'You can't go back into France, Valérie,' said Henry. 'It's too dangerous because they know who you are now and what you've done with the Resistance.'

'But we need the other part of the document,' Bill countered. 'If the names on the other half are like the first ones, we have to find it. We think that these traitors are part of a secret network and we can't afford to lose any of them. Rather than

Valérie go into France, we could notify our contacts to look for Hannelore but this would take too long. Valérie's plan is the only real way.'

Henry pushed his hand through his hair, the frustration clear on his face. 'If you do go, I'll need to get you new identity documents. My friend Robert in Evian could do it for me. I just need to speak to him.'

Valérie shook her head. 'It will take too long. I'll just have to take the chance, find Hannelore and somehow get her back across the border. There is no point discussing it any further.' The others could hear in her voice that she'd made up her mind and she turned back to Clara. 'Is there anything you can tell me, any clues as to where she might be?'

Clara took Hannelore's postcard from her pocket and held it out to Valérie. 'She must have sent me this picture for a reason.'

Valérie looked at the postcard, the familiar picture of Notre-Dame Cathedral and its surroundings. She stared at the buildings in the photograph, running her fingers over the picture. She felt a raised bump in the card and suddenly realised it corresponded exactly with one of the buildings at the edge of the picture. She looked up at Clara. 'What's this building? It seems to be raised, it isn't flat like the rest of the scene.'

Clara took the postcard back and studied it. 'I never noticed that. It's the side of the Hôtel-Dieu hospital, where my aunt used to work. Maybe it means she is still there.'

'That's good enough for me,' said Valérie. 'She must have marked the building for a reason so that's where I'll go. Could you give it to me so I can take it with me to prove to Hannelore who I am?'

Clara nodded reluctantly.

'I promise I'll give it back.' Valérie turned over the postcard and read the message again. 'What was she doing in the hospital?'

'She always worked in hospitals,' Clara replied. 'Any job she could get. She was training to be a doctor in Frankfurt before the war but had to stop when the university would no longer take on students from the Jewish community. She said that she would be a doctor one day and until then she would do all she could to learn about hospitals and medicine.'

'So that's where she must be,' said Valérie.

'The last job she had before we split up was in the laundry attached to the hospital. It was the only job she could get.' Clara leaned forward, her dark eyes lit up with excitement. 'She must have gone back to work there. That's where you'll find her.'

'I think we should take you both to the SOE manor house at the lake,' Bill announced. 'It will be safer there and we need to photograph the document and send it to London. We must keep you safe until we can get Hannelore here too and then we can get you all out of danger.'

'I need to go now,' said Valérie. She embraced Clara. 'I promise I'll find her for you.' Then Henry accompanied her to the door and went downstairs with her.

'I'll contact Robert to get some new identification for you,' he said as they stood in the downstairs hall. 'But I have the impression you're not likely to wait for me.'

Valérie didn't answer, kissed him briefly on the cheek and let herself out. She walked quickly back across the river into the Place de Bel-Air and climbed uphill to the old town. At the door to their tall townhouse, her hand on the doorknob, Valérie suddenly felt that she wasn't alone and turned sharply to look behind her. At the edge of her vision she saw a figure disappear into the alley down from the house. It looked like Otto Hoffman, the consulate official who was being so helpful with her father. What was he doing skulking around the house in the middle of the afternoon? She shook her head to chase away the unwelcome thoughts. She was seeing enemies everywhere, even where they didn't exist.

Her father came running out of the parlour. 'Valérie, where have you been? You've been hours. What have you been doing?'

'It's all right, Papa, I'm fine.' She took his arm and they went back into the parlour, sitting down on the sofa in front of the crackling fire, which she knew he had lit for her. 'I'll never get used to Philippe not being here, but there are still important things I can do.'

He held onto her hand, rubbing and warming it in front of the fire. 'I'm glad you feel that, mignonne, but it will take time for you to adapt to your new life so just take it slowly.'

She nodded and reached into her bag. 'There's something I want to tell you. This postcard from Paris has told me I need to go there to find Maman's friend Hannelore.' She turned the postcard over. 'Look, it's from her.' She usually didn't say much to her father when she went across the border to France, because he worried about her, but this time it was different; he needed to know that she might go there and struggle to get back.

He took the postcard from her and glanced up warily. 'It's from "H" but how do you know it's Hannelore?'

'Her niece said it was from her. I got the girl out of France but Hannelore is still there and I need to get her out too. There are lots of reasons why we need to find her, she's in real danger and is the only family the girl has left. It's for my sake too, I want to speak to Maman's friend.'

Albert lowered the postcard and his face looked troubled, the lines on his forehead more marked than before. 'I don't think it makes any difference to ask you not to become involved with them. But everything was fine with your mother until she got tied up with Jacob, Hannelore and the rest of them.'

'I'm sorry, Papa, but I have to do it. Don't you see that Maman would have done it if she'd been here?'

'That's what I'm worried about,' he said finally. 'You're very like your mother, and I worry about losing you just like I lost her.'

She pressed his hand, knowing that there was nothing she could say to make him feel better. 'I'll be careful, you know that. I won't take any unnecessary risks.'

'Going in the first place is an unnecessary risk, ma fille,' he answered.

'But will you help me? Tell me where you used to stay. You used to go there a lot.'

Reluctantly, he got up to get something from the dresser, coming over with an old map of Paris. He spread it out onto the low wooden carved table in front of them and pointed to the area around the Gare de Lyon. 'There's a small hotel across from the station where I used to stay. As far as I know, the owners are still there and they know me so if you go there you should be safe. Their name is Vernier.'

Valérie put the postcard back into her bag and gave him a hug. 'Hannelore's niece said she was working in the Hôtel-Dieu hospital opposite Notre-Dame so that's where I'm going to look.'

'When are you going?' asked her father.

'As soon as I can. I don't have much time.' She didn't say anything about the Germans who might recognise her name or how difficult it would be to get Hannelore out of France. That was something she would have to work out herself.

She went upstairs to change out of her dirty clothes, her mind turning over how she might achieve it. Her best option seemed to be to wait for Henry to get her false documents from Robert, but she was anxious that this would take too long. She picked up the photograph of her mother and stared at the beloved face, speaking to her as if she were still there. 'I have to find Hannelore to get the document to the Allies. She also might be able to tell me more about what happened to you and what was going on in the bookshop before the war.' Agathe's words came back to her. 'And what might have scared you so much.'

TWENTY-NINE

VALÉRIE

Geneva

Valérie couldn't settle that afternoon, desperate to go in search of Hannelore, but knowing she needed to give Henry at least a day to get the false documents. There was one person she could see before she left. Ever since Marianne had told Valérie that Philippe's grandfather had been questioned by the Swiss police, she was desperate to check he was all right. With Philippe gone, she felt even more responsibility towards him. A law-abiding citizen for all his life, with a son who was one of the senior officers in the Geneva police force, it seemed so wrong that he was being treated as a law breaker by the authorities who were always trying to stop Swiss citizens from helping their French neighbours. Other people probably wouldn't worry about the stigma but Philippe's grandfather was different and he would take it to heart. She knew going back to Philippe's parents' apartment would bring back lots of painful memories but she wanted to see his family because, after all these years, she loved them as her own.

Valérie walked across the old town past the columns and

steps of the Cathédrale Saint-Pierre towards the Rue du Vieux-Collège where Philippe had always lived with his parents. She paused when the sound of beautiful music flowed into the square from the cathedral. Although it was a cold evening, it was clear and frosty so she sat on one of the benches in the square and let the music flow over her, the soaring voices lifting her spirits. When it stopped, she sighed at the loss of such beauty and got up to carry on her way.

She reached Philippe's home on the Rue du Vieux-Collège and looked back at the Madeleine church. She remembered the area of town so well, where she used to sit talking with Philippe. The emptiness of her life without him struck her again and she forced herself to walk more quickly and ring the bell to the apartment. Before the bell was answered she heard a voice behind her.

'Valérie, you've come to see us.' It was Philippe's mother, Annette, and Valérie turned into her embrace. They stood there for a few moments and Valérie could feel the other woman shake with emotion. She had never felt very close to Philippe's mother until that moment when they shared the same grief and loss. A shout on the street made them pull apart, interrupting the moment, and Valérie pulled away from her warm embrace, shocked to see the new lines on Annette's pale face.

'It's been so awful,' said Annette. 'Nicolas has tried to find out more about what happened but it's all very confused. He went to the fort to speak to Stefano but he could add nothing. And we just have to get on with our lives as well as we can. It's very hard.'

Valérie nodded, unable to speak and Annette's eyes filled with tears. 'Come inside,' she said as she put the key in the door. Valérie followed her through the heavy wooden door and up the stone staircase to their large apartment on the first floor. Inside, Annette led her through to the main parlour, warm from the fire in the hearth. Philippe's grandfather was sitting on the sofa facing the fire as if he could soak up all the warmth before it could escape. Nicolas was sitting on the chair next to him and looked up as they entered. Valérie was shaken to see how gaunt he was and glanced down at Guillaume, but the old man seemed just the same as always.

She took a step forward and hugged them both. 'I had to come and see how you were. It's not just about what happened to Philippe. Marianne told me that the police questioned you. I was so worried about you.'

Guillaume snorted in derision. 'That's kind of you, my dear, but no need to be worried. The standard of policing in this town these days is beyond terrible.' He wagged his finger at his son. 'Nicolas knows it, but he won't admit it.'

Nicolas shook his head at his father's accusation. 'The police have apologised to you, Father. They were only doing their job. What else do you expect them to do?'

'I expect them not to interfere when honest citizens are just trying to help people in need,' Guillaume snapped. 'You know my feelings on this.' Valérie breathed a sigh of relief. The old man had lost none of his spirit. She felt as much a part of this family as she ever had and realised how important this was for her. Philippe might have gone but they all had to live together without him. She turned towards Nicolas, who was gazing up at her.

He smiled. 'I've decided that you and Philippe were right. We're going to have to take sides in this war and not try to please everyone. So, as well as being a policeman, I'm now working for the Swiss Secret Service. They agree with me that we can't allow Swiss citizens to be terrorised by the Axis powers in our own country.'

Valérie returned the smile, seeing the change in him as if a weight had been lifted from his shoulders, his grief hardening his resolve.

'I'm glad,' she said.

'About time, son. Maybe you'll help me now, rather than trying to stop me,' said Guillaume, staring into the fire. 'And believe me when I say that Philippe might not have died.'

'Father, we've already gone through this,' said Nicolas wearily. 'Everybody who was there said that Philippe was caught in the explosion. He never came back to Locarno and he wasn't found by the partisans who went back to look for him. You have to accept it. I know it's difficult, it's the most difficult thing I've ever had to accept, but Philippe has gone and isn't coming back. If you keep talking about the possibility that he's still alive then it makes it more difficult for everyone. You know we can't go down there and find out ourselves, you know how dangerous it is. Stefano said that their guide had gone back and wasn't able to find him or speak to anyone who knew what happened to him. The Germans carried out reprisals on the local population after that they lost their men. If Philippe was still alive from the explosion, then they would have killed him.' Nicolas bent his head.

Philippe's mother turned away as if she couldn't bear to hear any more and Valérie stood up, knowing that she couldn't say anything to help. She'd done what she had come to do. Philippe's grandfather was still the argumentative old man that he'd always been. She bent down to kiss his cheek. 'I'll see you again soon, I promise.'

Nicolas came with her to the door. 'I'm sorry about my father, he refuses to accept Philippe's death and we're all struggling to deal with it. His way is to refuse to believe it without proof.'

'That's all right. It's difficult for everyone.' She took a deep breath and then continued. 'I didn't say anything in there but I'm going away for a few days. I just wanted you to know.'

He frowned. 'Where are you going?'

'To Paris. I need to go and find someone there and bring them back.'

He looked thoughtful. 'You know how risky it is to go that far into France, especially Paris.'

'I know, but I have to do it.'

Nicolas looked down at her, his eyes glistening with tears. 'You sound very like Philippe before he went into Italy.'

She kissed his cheek. 'You know we were very alike.'

'I won't try to dissuade you, but we're getting reports of a lot of attacks on trains, in particular on those trains that are transporting German troops and armaments, even close to the Swiss border. The Resistance are targeting passenger trains less but you could be caught up in some of their operations. There are almost no trains coming into Geneva from France at the moment so you'll need to be careful about how you get back. Don't drop your guard any time, Valérie, because that might be the moment you could get caught up in the fight. It looks as though the Germans are going to lose this war but that will make them even more desperate and dangerous.'

'I'll be careful, I promise,' Valérie reassured him. 'And when I'm back, I'll come and see you all again.'

She walked away from the apartment and up the hill towards the Place du Bourg-de-Four. The square was quiet as she headed towards the Café de Paris. She would go and see Geraldine and ask her to keep an eye on her father in her absence. At the door to the café, she waited for a group of soldiers to leave, their grey uniforms reminding her of Philippe. She didn't respond to the smile of the last soldier as he held open the door for her. Inside the café, she was greeted by the warmth of the fire crackling in the corner and a few old men looked up from the bar.

She looked around for Geraldine and saw her friend at the back table next to Bernard's stocky figure, her blonde hair shining under the lights of the bar. They didn't look up and seemed engrossed in one another. Valérie smiled. The breakout of peace had been a long time coming. They had squabbled since they were small and Valérie had always suspected that the loud battles covered up a deep affection. Perhaps they had finally seen the truth that everyone else suspected. She walked towards them and sat down at the table.

Geraldine returned her smile and Bernard sat back, looking a little sheepish, but still kept hold of Geraldine's hand.

'How are you both?' asked Valérie.

'We're fine now,' replied Geraldine. 'But I needed some help yesterday.'

'I had to come across to the café,' explained Bernard. 'Geraldine was being bothered by that young German who's been hanging around for days, the one who says he works for the bank. He was asking her lots of questions about the area and he started asking her about the bookshop and Jacob Steinberg.'

'I know you warned me about him, but this time he wouldn't leave me alone.' Geraldine screwed up her face.

Bernard puffed up his chest. 'I got rid of him eventually, but I've promised to keep an eye on Geraldine in future. The sooner we get rid of these German bankers, the better. The old one was there too. He didn't say much but he was watching everything.'

Valérie was becoming more concerned as he talked. 'Have you told the police? Nicolas Cherix should know about this.'

Bernard shrugged. 'I could do, but one of his men was with the Germans the other day. They seemed the best of friends. You know what the police are like, doing everything to keep the Germans sweet.'

'I still think you should tell him,' said Valérie. 'His priority is to protect all of us, he's certainly not going to allow the Germans free rein in Geneva.'

'I will, then,' he said, then carried on awkwardly, 'We're so sorry about Philippe.'

'I couldn't believe it.' Geraldine stretched out her hand to Valérie. 'Bernard told me and then stayed with me.'

Valérie looked at her friends. 'I'm glad you were together. If there's something to take from such an awful thing it's that you have to take care of the people you love.'

Geraldine and Bernard nodded.

'Can I ask you for a favour?' said Valérie.

'Anything,' replied Geraldine.

I'm going away for a few days. Could you keep an eye on my father? He should be fine in the workshop and with Agathe but I would be happier if I knew that you would help him if he had a problem.'

'Of course, Valérie,' replied Bernard.

She left them sitting together contentedly and closed the door behind her, remembering all the arguments they'd had over the years when she'd doubted that they would ever end up together. She just hoped that Geraldine's mercurial nature and love of drama didn't blow them off course.

Walking home, Valérie was unable to forget Philippe's grandfather's words and his hope that Philippe might yet be alive. She couldn't help but be attracted by the idea of this wonderful world where he would come home to her – but she knew it wasn't true. Trying to take her mind off hard reality, she looked down one of the alleys leading towards the lake as she turned towards her street. She stopped when she saw the door to the Moulins' apartment swing closed. It was odd that there was no light leaking out from around the shutters in the apartment. Monsieur Moulin was a constant presence in his wheelchair and was always there in the evening. She turned abruptly towards the apartment door, her heart beating faster.

Pushing it open, she paused for a moment. There was no sound coming from inside the apartment so she stepped into the hall and looked into the front room where Monsieur Moulin was always sitting. As her eyes grew accustomed to the darkness, she saw his figure sitting to the side of the window, which was slightly open behind the shutter. She saw the old man turn towards her, his finger pressed against his lips and he beckoned her over, indicating that she should close the front door behind her.

When she reached him, she whispered, 'Are you all right? I thought something had happened to you.'

'No, I'm fine,' he replied in a low voice. 'My wife has just gone out to meet my son. I often sit in darkness with the window slightly open at this time of year. It isn't that cold and it's surprising how much you hear from the people passing outside.' He indicated towards the seat next to the window and she sat down.

'What kind of things do you hear?' she asked.

'People walk down this alley, making deals. Cigarettes, stockings, all kinds of things. People helping the French Resistance meet up here, spies from the consulate share information, a snapshot of the whole world in these mad times.' He turned his head and looked directly at her and she saw the sparkle in his eyes. 'Those Germans you asked about have been here a few times and I've heard them discussing their nasty secrets.'

Before she could reply, she heard footsteps and then the noise of matches striking outside the window. She breathed lightly, trying to make no sound. She looked at Monsieur Moulin in surprise as they heard a voice speaking German.

'What do we do now? We're running out of time. That woman told us nothing we didn't know already.'

An older man gave a humourless laugh. 'You probably didn't apply enough pressure.'

'Maybe not.'

The same distinctive cigar smoke that she'd smelt in the destroyed bookshop wafted into the apartment, proof that the same men had been responsible for the destruction she'd found there. Valérie felt sick when she heard the prosaic tone of their voices as they confirmed what had happened to Isabelle. They could have been discussing the weather.

'We know what Steinberg was doing here. Everything he was up to.'

'All the money he spirited away from the bank.'

The older man cursed his companion. 'It isn't the money, you fool. It's the girl we want to find. The document she is hiding is much more important than the money. You heard our superior officer. Whatever it takes, we have to recover it.'

'They're checking the border, aren't they? That usually works to get the people we need.'

Suddenly there was a scuffle in the alley below the window. Valérie pulled away from the opening and backed further against the wall, hoping they wouldn't come and investigate. But their next words filled her with dread.

'What was that?'

'It sounded like it was coming from in there.'

Valérie looked up, terrified to see their faces at the window. She waited.

'That's what it was.'

She heard another scuffle, further down the alley this time, and bowed her head in relief.

'It was only a rat.'

'Let's get out of here. There's someone coming.'

She heard them grind their heels into the pavement and then the sound of their steps walking away.

A few moments later, two figures entered the apartment and shone their torches into the room.

'What are you doing in the dark?' said Madame Moulin, turning to light the oil lamp on a side table. The room was flooded with a dull yellow glow and Valérie blinked her eyes to get used to the light.

'We were just sitting chatting, my dear,' said her husband. 'I didn't realise it had got so dark.'

'I need to go now, madame,' said Valérie. She turned to

Monsieur Moulin. 'Thank you for everything. You have no idea how important it was for me to hear that conversation.'

The old woman squeezed her arm. 'You take care of yourself, chérie. You are a sweet girl, very like your mother. I would hate it if something happened to you too.'

Touched by her words, Valérie instinctively hugged her and then left, disturbed by what she'd heard. The Germans' words, the reality of what they had done and their determination to find Clara filled her mind. They'd killed Isabelle and searched the bookshop to find any evidence of where Clara and the document could be. Valérie knew that she had little time left to find Hannelore and bring her to safety with the other half of the document.

THIRTY

VALÉRIE

Geneva

The next day Valérie made her father's most urgent deliveries, her mind still turning over how she quickly she could obtain false identity papers for herself and Hannelore. Her initial reaction, just to leave without anything and take her chances in France that they wouldn't be stopped, had been tempered by her experience of working with the Resistance and the efficient brutality of the Nazis.

She tried to see Marianne in the post office but her friend wasn't working. It was a cold winter's day, the cloud hanging low over the city and a bitter wind sweeping round the streets as the inhabitants moved quickly, wrapped in warm coats and hats.

Late in the afternoon, Valérie went to the edge of the lake, drawn to the bench she and Philippe had made their own. A battle was raging within her, one side telling her not to go there because it would be too painful, the other yearning to go back to the place where she had been so happy, and somehow connect with him there before she left for France. Sitting down, she looked out onto that familiar view of the lake, the water from the Jet d'Eau rising up into the air on the other side, like an old friend. Despite the cold, people were walking briskly along the lakefront, carrying parcels and packages, laughter bubbling up from couples walking together. Valérie averted her eyes, the happiness of others making her own sadness seem so much worse.

A voice broke into her gloomy thoughts. 'Can I sit here with you?'

She looked up in surprise and saw Elsa Bauer, an Austrian woman who had met her mother at Jacob's bookshop. Valérie didn't really want company, but she moved along the bench and tried to smile. As always, Elsa was smartly dressed in a thick woollen coat and her blonde hair was perfectly arranged. Her blue eyes seemed dull today, with no sunlight or bright blue lake to reflect their colour. She looked strangely hesitant, as if she was battling with herself about what she should say.

'I'm sorry about your Philippe. I saw Henry last night and he told me about what had happened. Your fiancé was a brave man, saving his friend like that. When I lost my husband, Anton, I thought that my world had come to an end, but even though you don't think it now, life does go on and it's not always bad. There are other things that can give you joy, although it doesn't seem like that at the beginning.'

Valérie nodded, unable to say anything in reply. She felt like jumping up from the seat and running away, but Elsa reached out and held her arm as if she could read her mind. 'He also told me that you wanted to go into France and that it would be very dangerous for you.' Elsa looked behind her as if she expected somebody to be listening, then turned back. 'Henry would be furious if he knew I'd come to see you, and what I wanted to say, but I knew I could help so I had no choice.'

Curious now, Valérie asked, 'How can you help?'

'You must know by now what Jacob was doing in Geneva.

He was passing valuable information to the Allies from the middle of the 1930s, and he was also setting up bank accounts and safety deposit boxes to hide his friends' money and valuables. It started with his concern about Hannelore and how she and her brother were going to lose everything when they left Frankfurt. He knew that the Germans were stealing from the Jewish community right across Europe and thought that he had to find a way for people to get back what belonged to them once the war was over. From what he'd seen before he left Frankfurt, the Swiss banks were all too happy to take money from anybody, irrespective of where that money came from. And Hannelore's brother, David, he was a great friend of Jacob's. When Jacob moved to Geneva, Hannelore would come and visit him, smuggling information for the Allies.'

'Did you ever meet Hannelore?' asked Valérie.

'Yes, once or twice in the bookshop when she visited Jacob. I remember her clearly, she was great friends with your mother. One day in the bookshop an old man collapsed. No one knew what to do except for Hannelore, she went running up to him and checked his breathing and pulse. She asked Jacob to get an ambulance to take him to hospital. Hannelore kept calm through the whole thing and insisted on going with him. It was as if he was her patient.'

'And was the old man all right?'

'Yes, she came back and told us. She was a natural carer of people who were sick or vulnerable. That's one of the reasons Jacob loved her so much, I think; she had such a sweet nature.' She paused for a moment. 'But that isn't what I came to tell you. Jacob hatched a plan with his friend Claude Laurent to set up bank accounts, and obtained fake identities for people to use to access their money if they managed to get to Geneva.'

She now had Valérie's complete attention. 'So where are these false identities?' Valérie asked. Her mind was racing through where they could be and whether she and Hannelore could use them. 'They aren't in the bookshop, I've already searched there. And at home, there are only the books Jacob gave my mother. If there was a novel that she liked, she would come home with it the next day. I have a bookshelf full of books that came from Jacob.' She looked up at Elsa, 'My mother said that Jacob used to hide things when he didn't want anybody to find out about them. He had a mischievous streak, and would often tease her with secrets. It must be the books; they must contain the documents! For all this time, there have been hidden documents in my room and I never realised! It's the only possibility.'

'Keep your voice down,' Elsa hissed. 'Jacob took a lot of effort to hide what he was doing. It's why I think he was followed towards the end, why he had to leave Geneva.'

'How long after my mother's death did he leave?'

'Not long. I don't know what she was doing that night but he blamed himself for her death. Then he went to see Hannelore and something happened between them and he came back alone. I don't remember much of that time because my husband was very ill, but he left very quickly and didn't tell anybody where he was going.'

Valérie could hardly listen to what she was hearing, desperate to go home and find out what was there. 'Thank you, Elsa,' she said, abruptly standing up.

'I'm leaving Geneva,' said Elsa, standing up too. 'I think I'm being followed here and I don't feel safe any longer. I don't know when this war will end but sometimes I feel like it never will. As the Germans get more desperate, life, even here in a neutral country, will become more dangerous.'

Valérie embraced her. 'Thank you for telling me about Jacob and my mother.'

She picked up her bike and pushed it away, heart beating with excitement, hoping she would find papers that she could use to get Hannelore to safety. Jumping off her bike to push it up the cobbled streets towards her house, she heard a few greetings as she got closer, but she was too intent on her mission to do more than smile briefly at her neighbours.

Valérie reached the front door of the townhouse and let herself inside, leaving the bike in the hall. She ran upstairs into her bedroom, but on hearing some noises from the kitchen, she stopped at her bedroom door and leaned back over the banister to shout down, 'I'm back, Agathe. I just have to look for something in my room and then I'll come down.' She heard an acknowledgement from downstairs and turned back into her bedroom, closing the door, satisfied that Agathe wouldn't come and check on her. Throwing off her coat, she lit the oil lamp and sat down cross-legged on the floor in front of the bookshelf.

She looked closely at the book titles, wondering if she was right, whether Jacob had hidden the false identity papers in the books. She looked around the bedroom, trying to see where else something could be hidden, whether there was anything else that she had from her mother or from the bookshop, but she could see nothing. She turned back to the bookshelves, knowing that she would have to look through all of them before being satisfied.

One by one, she pulled out the books and flicked through them, starting at the bottom shelf. Some of the books she recognised and had read before, but there were others, in English or Russian, she'd never opened. She was surprised to see that there were German books there too, the classic texts, Goethe and Schiller. In a burst of enthusiasm, she pulled out all the German books, wondering if Jacob had played some joke, hiding the false identity documents in the German texts. But they were all empty and she sneezed as the dust floated up from the pages. She was almost halfway through the bookshelf and had found nothing. She felt her heart drop in disappointment; she'd been so sure she would find something.

Valérie moved from German to Russian to English texts.

She knew she'd read some of these books, so didn't think there would be anything there. But the second book she opened, Charles Dickens' *Bleak House*, had an old cover over the book. She flicked through the pages and nothing fell out. Then she looked at the back cover that snugly fitted over the book. Impatient now, pessimistic about finding anything, she pulled off the cover of the book and something fell out of it onto her skirt. She looked down and saw a folded piece of card. When she turned it over and opened it, she saw that it was a Swiss identity document, the photograph inside of a man she didn't know and the name Pierre Lebrun, she had never heard before. She stared at the identity document and then started to pull out the other English books feverishly, more Charles Dickens, Emily Bronte and other classics, putting on one side the ones with covers. A few books later, another identity card dropped out of Emily Bronte's *Wuthering Heights*.

This time when she turned it over, she gasped. The photograph was of her mother but it could have been her. The name was Thérèse Lavigne. She felt growing excitement as she realised that this was her ticket in and out of France. She carried on looking and in a copy of Charlotte Bronte's *Jane Eyre* she found another card. This one had Hannelore's picture on it with the name Véronique Martin. She put both cards in front of her and realised that this was all she needed. She carefully got up, pulled her small suitcase down from the top of the heavy wooden wardrobe and opened it, then slotted the new identity cards into the top pocket. She glanced at the sky outside her window and saw that it was getting dark. She would pack and go the next morning.

By the time she'd checked all the books to see what else she could find, she'd found eight identity documents, all in English books. Then, in one of the Swiss novels, she found a small piece of paper with names and numbers written on it, the key to Jacob's accounts. She stood up, stretching her stiff legs and went to get her mother's notebook, the one she'd found in the book-shop all those months ago. She flicked through it, studying carefully the notes and numbers and saw that some of them were the same as on the paper she'd found. On other pages, her mother's scribbles showed that she was playing around with names and numbers. Valérie realised when she looked at the notebook how much her mother must have been involved in the whole plan, helping Jacob to protect money and valuables from the Nazis.

She replaced everything exactly where she'd found them except for the two identity cards she would take with her to France. She started to pack her bag, only planning to be away for one night or two at the most. As she walked around her room, gathering what she needed, she glanced at the photograph of Philippe and went over to pick it up, deep sadness overcoming her new sense of excitement. She took the photograph carefully out of the frame and put it with the identity cards in her suitcase. She would take him with her because it was all she had left of him. The she opened the jewellery case on her dressing table and put on Philippe's engagement ring. It was the first time she been able to look at it since she'd heard the awful news. 'If anything happens to me now,' she said quietly, 'you'll be with me.'

THIRTY-ONE
VALÉRIE

Geneva

Valérie could not delay for another day, but there was one place she had to go first. Early the next morning, she rode through the centre of town on her bicycle towards the north bank of the lake and the SOE manor house, watching people trying to stock up for Christmas. In the past few years of the war, the lights in the town were much diminished because of the blackout restrictions but some shopkeepers still tried to generate Christmas spirit by creating festive window displays and stocking the bright wrapping paper in their stores.

It was a cold, dull day, the dampness all around seeping into her bones, so she sped up for warmth. But by the time she turned into the Rue de Lausanne and towards the gate of the manor house in the park looking down onto Lac Léman, she was desperate to get inside, feeling no warmer than she had at the beginning of her journey, despite her efforts.

She reached the gates of the manor house and looked up the drive towards the familiar cream-coloured stone façade. Two men came out from behind the trees and walked towards the gate, blocking her way. She didn't recognise them and felt a shiver of concern as she came off her bike and pushed it towards them.

'I'm here to see Bill Paterson,' she said loudly. 'Please let me pass.'

The older man narrowed his eyes. 'And you are?'

'My name is Valérie Hallez. You must know me, I've been coming here for months.'

The man nodded and they moved back to let her pass. 'Just making sure, mademoiselle. We've had a few people trying to get in lately so we've been told not to take any chances with strangers claiming to be visitors.'

This was a new development. The SOE had increased its security and she looked behind her suddenly, expecting to see someone following her, then turned back to him, trying to smile. 'I didn't realise you had to take such measures.'

The men didn't reply and she continued up the drive pushing her bicycle in front of her. They were right to guard this place more carefully if they thought that Clara was in danger. It meant that it was even more important for her to go and get Hannelore and bring her into a safe place. She rang the doorbell and heard steps from inside coming towards the door. She looked up at the windows on the first floor and knew that she was being watched.

The heavy wooden door opened and Bill Paterson thrust out his hand.

'Come away in, Valérie, you look cold. Come and get warm inside.'

She left her bike beside the front door and followed him inside, the warmth of the house a welcome change from the dampness outside. They went into a parlour at the back of the house, looking out onto the grass and the trees bordering the lake and she walked quickly to one of the chairs in front of the fire, holding out her hands towards it. Bill sat in the other chair.

'Can I get you something?' he offered. 'A hot drink, perhaps?'

'Yes, but I can't stay for long.' She indicated to the back of the house. 'Has anything happened? You have guards outside now. Clara is safe here, isn't she?'

He frowned and then replied, 'Yes, she and Louis are both safe here, but we had an intruder in the garden last night so we've had to increase our security on the building. They're a lot safer here than anywhere else, but we need to make sure the place is guarded.' He leaned forward. 'Our people in London have started to investigate the names in Clara's part of the document and have taken action on the most dangerous people identified. There are people in that document who could tell the enemy about our bombing plans, any invasion plans we might have and the state of our weapons capability. It's perhaps the most important document that they've ever seen and acting on it will make a monumental difference to the outcome of the war. We really have to get hold of the other half of the document, the part that Hannelore has with her. It's more important than ever to get her to safety. We have been informed that this is of the highest priority. My superior wants to send some agents in to find her.'

Valérie shook her head. 'How long will that take?' she asked abruptly. 'I've got documents that will get me there today. Your agents can try if I fail, but I'm going now and they'll never get there before me.'

'But Henry has gone down to Evian to get some identity documents for you. I'm expecting him back. Do you mean you have some already?'

Valérie nodded. 'I found identity documents that will get me in and out France and one that Hannelore can use. I came to tell you.'

'Very well. You try first, but my people will go in if you can't find her and get her out. This is vital for the war effort.'

'If I bring Hannelore here, will you get all three of them safely to England?' She looked out of the window at the leaden sky, impatient to leave but keen to see Clara once more.

'Yes, Henry will take them all to London. I promise.'

'Can I see Clara before I go, just for a moment or two?'

'Of course, I'll go and get her, and I'll bring you some tea to warm you up before you go out again.'

He left the room and Valérie picked up her coat and held it in front of the fire to try to warm it up. A few moments later, she heard the door open. Clara and Louis came in with a tray of tea. They looked much better than they had the last time she'd seen them, now dressed in normal clothes and looking calm and relaxed, unlike their earlier tense and jumpy behaviour. Clara smiled at her as she poured the tea and Louis pulled up a chair and sat down next to her. Out of his dirty old clothes, he looked like a normal teenage boy, wearing a thick jumper that was too large for him, but was clean. Valérie was sure that she'd seen Bill wearing the jumper before.

'I'm going to Paris now,' said Valérie. 'Is there anything else you can tell me that might help me to find Hannelore? We're just guessing that she's there and if I don't find her, Bill is going to send in some SOE agents.' Her memories of traitors and betrayals were rushing back. 'The more people who know, the more dangerous it becomes for Hannelore. If I can go in on my own and no one suspects me, then it's better than sending several people into the city because they might attract attention.'

Clara stared into the fire and then back at Valérie. 'I really don't have any more proof about where she could have gone, apart from the postcard you gave me where the hospital is marked. I've been trying to think about where she could stay and I remembered she did have a friend called Chantal where she might have gone. But I don't know her address. She was a nurse, but I don't think she was well herself so didn't work. I know her husband was worried that she would be taken to the camps.'

Valérie reached over and clasped Clara's hands. 'I'll do my best to find her and bring her back here. Bill has promised to get you all to England.'

Louis looked up at her, his face strained. 'Does that include me?' he asked. 'I don't have any secret documents and that's what they want. Are they going to leave me behind?'

The despairing look on his face filled Valérie with pity. 'Of course you're going too. Bill promised me that you will all go.'

'It's just that I don't have anybody else. The Nazis took away my parents and killed my brother when he tried to stop them. I can't go back there.'

Clara put her arm around his shoulders. 'I wouldn't leave you, Louis. If I'm going to England, you're coming too.'

He turned his face into Clara's shoulder and Valérie felt tears prick her eyes. They might be teenagers, but these young people had lost everything they'd known, home, family, friends. All they had left was one another. The urgency of what she had to do filled her with determination.

'I won't fail you, I promise,' said Valérie.

She shrugged on her coat and went out into the marble corridor, her low heels tapping on the floor. Immediately Bill was beside her.

'Henry will be sorry he missed you. I'll tell him what you're doing.'

'Thank you. I'll go back home to get my suitcase and then walk to the station.' She pointed back to the parlour. 'Did you give Louis your jumper?'

His plump face broke into a smile. 'Aye, I did that. Poor lad had nothing decent left to wear, so I gave him one of my climbing jumpers. If they kept me warm in a bothy in the middle of the Highlands of Scotland, they'll be fine for him here.'

She left him at the door, feeling more secure that Louis' future would be brighter than his last few years had been. She had to find Hannelore and the other half of the document and bring them to safety. The document could change everything by shortening the war and making sure other young people didn't lose their families. She glanced behind her and then pushed her bike through the gates, the guards nowhere in sight. There was so much sadness in that house, so much pain. She could improve their lives if she took a risk, her burning sense of purpose chasing away her fears. It wouldn't bring Philippe back but it might mean that others wouldn't suffer as they had.

THIRTY-TWO

VALÉRIE

Geneva

Valérie went home to collect her suitcase. Her father was in the kitchen having breakfast and she kissed him on the cheek before sitting down at the table and pulling a piece of stale bread towards her, spreading it with Agathe's plum jam to make it more edible. She was in a rush but knew she had to eat something first.

Under his watchful gaze, she smoothed down the skirt of the dark blue woollen suit she had decided to wear. With the white blouse, she felt she looked professional and business-like. The previous night she'd concluded that this was the best look for travelling in France. If she looked like someone respectable, with an important task to accomplish, it might give her more courage if she was interrogated about what she was doing and why she was there.

Her father glanced down at the suitcase and then back to her face. 'Do you really have to do this, Valérie?' But he knew the answer before she spoke.

'You know I do, Papa. So many families have been

destroyed by this war, their loved ones killed or taken away. I want to reunite someone Maman knew very well with what's left of her family.' *And I might just find out what really happened to Maman on the night she died*, she thought. She didn't want to upset her father but knew it wasn't enough any longer to have suggestions or suspicions, she needed facts about what had happened before she could get on with her life. She swallowed, unwilling to contemplate what kind of life she might have without Philippe. She just had to focus on the here and now and what she had to do; she would work out later which direction her life was going to take.

'You were always like that, even as a small child. If you wanted to know the answer to something you would keep pushing until you found it out. Please stay safe for me. With you, I have a family. Without you, I have no one.'

'I know, Papa.' She got up and kissed him. 'You don't need to come and see me out. I'll try not to be long, only a few days and then I'll be back. Say goodbye to Agathe for me.'

'Remember that the small hotel on the Rue Emile Gilbert, in the old streets across from the Place Louis-Armand, should be safe. It's only a short walk from the train station. The owner is Fabrice Vernier and his wife is Renée. They should remember me and make you welcome.'

Valérie nodded and turned to leave. She went down the hall and outside, stopping by the front door and glancing back at the window to the parlour, the room empty now but so familiar and dear. She'd never really appreciated the house where she lived, but she now looked at the tall frontage with affection. It was a place of protection and love.

She walked along towards the Cathédrale Saint-Pierre, before turning left down the hill past the Hôtel Les Armures.

'Valérie, wait for me!'

Henry ran down the cobbled street towards her, his coat flapping around his knees as he ran. 'I missed you, but Bill said you'd be around here.' He looked down at the suitcase. 'You're going already?'

'Yes, I'm going today. I couldn't wait any longer.'

'But how are you able to do this? I came to tell you that I couldn't get any documents from Robert.' His face darkened and the words came out slowly. 'I went to see him in Evian but he wasn't there. The restaurant has been closed down and no one would tell me where he was.'

She caught his arm. 'Is he all right? Do you think the Germans have got him?' She remembered Henry's friend, who ran the restaurant that served the best coq au vin south of Paris. A plump man who could steer his way delicately through his restaurant, a word for everybody and kind to all his friends.

He put his hand on hers and squeezed it. 'I was told he was safe but had decided to go into hiding. The Germans are getting too close and suspected some of his activities, so my source of fake identity documents has gone.'

Valérie took away her hand. 'As long as he's safe,' she said finally.

'So where did you get the identity papers?' he asked. 'You're too well known to use your own documents and get through the German border guards.'

She nodded. 'I hadn't realised that Jacob had given my mother some false identity papers. He wanted her to keep them until the end of the war, so I've just borrowed a couple of them to help me to get in and out of France and give Hannelore a new identity. I just have to find her, hope that she actually is where we think in Paris and will still be at the hospital Clara said she worked in before.'

His features hardened. 'It's too dangerous, there must be another way. I can't let you go into France on your own.'

Valérie shrugged off his hand. 'It's none of your business, Henry. This is my decision and you can't stop me.'

'But it isn't a game, Valérie. It's deadly serious and it's too dangerous for you.'

She turned and started to walk away from him but he blocked her path and she stopped in her tracks. 'Henry, leave me alone.' Her voice rose in anger. 'You have no right to tell me what to do, no right at all. I know the risks and accept them. I have nothing to lose.'

He ran his hand through his hair. 'I know I have no right but I care for you, Valérie. I don't want anything to happen to you.'

The tender expression in his dark eyes was unmistakeable.

'I know that this isn't a good time, with the loss of Philippe. It must have hit you so hard but there are other people who care for you.' He stepped closer to her. 'I've missed you so much, Valérie, I thought perhaps that...'

'No, Henry.' She cleared her throat, feeling she could hardly speak but knowing exactly what she had to say. 'I love Philippe. He might no longer be with me, might never be with me, but I'll never stop loving him and I'll never love anyone else. I'm sorry, but that's all I can say.'

He took a deep breath and looked at her, trying to see if he could persuade her to change her mind but she returned his expression with a fixed stare.

'Well, if you're determined on this, I can drive you to Bourg-en-Bresse. It will save you time. It will still take you hours to get to Paris. Goodness knows what delays you might face on the train, so the more time you have, the better.'

'Yes, please,' she answered, gratitude for his unexpected offer making her remember the times in the past when he had helped her. It seemed like another life led by a different person.

'My car is in the Place du Bourg-de-Four,' he said.

They walked back up past the cathedral. It was a cold December morning and she pulled her coat around her more tightly. They turned onto the square and she looked towards the Café de Paris. Its front door was closed with no sign of anyone outside. The car was parked down from the grocer's shop and Bernard came out in front of them, nodding a greeting. Before getting into Henry's car, Valérie watched Bernard pick up a box and walk briskly across the square and let himself into the café. She smiled as she thought about her two friends, who had finally made their peace with one another.

They got into the large car and Henry drove off down the square out of the old town. Valérie shivered at how close behind her she felt the German spies were, trying to discover what she was doing.

'I'm sorry, are you cold?' asked Henry, leaning across to the back seat to get a blanket. 'Put this over your knees.' All emotion was gone from his voice and he was back to the cool agent again.

'Thank you.' She looked at his profile as he concentrated on the road. 'So what have you been doing since you left Geneva?'

'I haven't just been working in Zurich. I've been to London a couple of times over the past few months and have met Jacob Steinberg.'

'What's he doing? Is it difficult for him being in England when he's German?'

Henry shook his head. 'Not at all, he's working for the British War Office. It's top-secret work, fluent German speakers are important for them. When they capture German officers and hold them in England, they have microphones placed in the buildings to record their conversations.'

'How is he? Did you talk about his time in Geneva at all?'

'No, he wouldn't talk about it. I think he found it very painful to remember that time. They were all so happy and it was all destroyed when the war broke out.'

'Even before the war.' said Valérie. 'I think it all went wrong even before my mother died.'

'I can't help you with that, Valérie. I wasn't here then.'

She stared at him, wondering if he was telling her the truth, the old mistrust about his motives flaring up again. She always suspected that he knew more than he was prepared to say, that all the SOE were hiding secrets, but at least she wasn't dependent on him to find out the truth.

'You know that's the other reason I have to go into France and find Hannelore,' she said. 'It isn't just the secret document. I must reunite her with Clara. And she's the only one who might have the key to the past and explain what really happened to my mother.'

He nodded but didn't reply. They sat in silence until they got to the border and Henry charmed the Swiss border guards, handing across their papers and taking them back after a cursory look by the guards. They drove slowly forward to the French side, which was much busier, the German guards looking grim and cold.

'I'll use my German papers again,' muttered Henry as he opened his window. He flashed his papers in front of the young guard, whose teeth were chattering with cold. The guard's reaction was instantaneous. Jumping back from the car, he thrust his arm out in the Nazi salute and barked out *Heil Hitler*. Henry spoke a few words of German and they were waved through.

Henry flashed her a calculating smile and she couldn't help but respond. 'Somebody's going to realise that you're not the person on these papers, someday,' she said finally, her words softened by a smile.

'I know, but I just like to see the reaction. Makes me feel important.'

His good humour faded as he drove up to the Bourg-en-Bresse railway station in the centre of the town. It was quiet, although a few Nazi soldiers were parading around the streets and swastika signs were hanging from the town hall and the other public buildings.

'You're going into the lion's den, Valérie. Keep your wits about you,' said Henry.

She stared at him, hearing the sincerity in his voice. 'I will,' she answered. 'Watching you this last year has given me some good lessons.' She kissed him on the cheek and got out of the car, her mind already turning towards what she had to do. She walked into the station building without looking back. She was telling the truth when she told him he'd given her lessons in espionage. One of these lessons was to keep cold and calm and not get involved with others. She wasn't sure she could do that, keep her emotions hidden, but at least she could try.

THIRTY-THREE

VALÉRIE

France

Valérie bought a ticket to Paris and saw there was a train waiting at the platform, two Germans guards checking papers at the barrier. She joined the queue of passengers and moved slowly forward. When she reached the front, one of the Germans held out his hand. 'Mademoiselle, your identity papers please.'

The guards were standing very close in front of her. Curbing the instinct to take a step back and ignoring their threatening stance, she handed over her identity papers confidently. She had to trust that Jacob's false papers were good enough to convince the guards.

He looked down at the photograph and back at her. 'And why are you travelling to Paris, mademoiselle?'

'I work for my father, he's a watchmaker and has sent me to meet one of his business contacts there.' She tapped her foot, as if impatient with the delay, and pretended to suppress a sigh. After what seemed like a long time, the guard handed her papers back abruptly and walked off without saying anything.

She breathed a real sigh of relief and climbed onto the train, hoping that she wouldn't have a long wait, although the line of people waiting to have their papers checked made that unlikely.

It was over an hour before she heard the guard's whistle and shouts for people to board the train. Despite her warm coat and gloves, she was frozen and wished that she'd taken Henry's blanket with her. As more people came into the compartment and it filled up, the door stayed closed and it became warmer. A final whistle blew and the train started to move off. All around her she saw local people, women with baskets, men going off to work and a group of young women laughing together in the corner of the carriage. Just before the train had left, four young German soldiers got onto the train and sat in the seats next to the young women, who watched them closely. One woman, more confident than the rest, leaned towards one of the soldiers. Her friend nudged her and whispered urgently into her ear. She was clearly warning her to be more careful, but her friend shook her head, ignoring the caution, and turned again to the young officer with a broad smile.

Valérie looked out of the window, not wanting to see what was going to happen, knowing that more people collaborated with the occupying force than helped the Resistance. French girls had German boyfriends while their parents worked with the French police to turn over to the Nazis the people they wanted to erase out of society. And the choice facing everyone was demonstrated by the young woman being pulled in different directions, between her cautious friend and the handsome German.

The train stopped and started many times as it wound its way north. The long journey began to feel endless and the warmth of the carriage escaped each time the door opened and a cold draught of air entered. Sometimes the train stopped at stations to pick up more passengers but other times it just stopped in the middle of the countryside for no reason. Once, she heard a shout and when she looked back, she saw a group of people being led off the train and towards a camp close to the railway line, the buildings covered with loops of barbed wire that stretched into the distance. It must be another internment camp, built to hold people before the Germans transported them to the concentration camps further east. She looked away when she saw a uniformed German push one woman to hurry her up through the cold. As she watched them, it started to rain outside and the pathetic group disappeared into the mist and falling rain, obscured by the weather and the raindrops rolling down the dirty glass of the compartment windows.

The conversation in the carriage had stopped as everyone watched the group of people stumbling along the side of the railway track towards the camp. As soon as the group were out of sight the conversation in the carriage started up again. Was that how it was in this country? Valérie wondered. They seemed to regard fear and bullying behaviour as normal, accepting that it would happen all around them and trying to get back to their own lives and concerns as quickly as they could.

By the time they arrived at Gare de Lyon station it was well into the evening. As the train pulled into the platform, Valérie got up from her seat and stretched her stiff muscles. Stepping down on the platform she gazed up at the stone arches of the station appearing through the steam from the locomotive. She heard the sound of laughter and saw the young woman who had been flirting with the German soldiers walk away with one of them, waving gaily at her friends who turned to go in the opposite direction.

Walking towards the concourse, she saw two German soldiers at the barrier leading to the next platform checking the papers of those making their way onto a train going south. Before she could move, a woman at the front of the queue waiting to board the train twisted round and ran away from the soldiers. With a shout of anger, they chased her across the large station concourse. While everyone was watching the terrified woman trying to escape, Valérie walked in the opposite direction across the concourse and out of the station.

In a moment, she was standing in front of the familiar tall clock tower at the Gare de Lyon looking across the Place Louis-Armand. Even this late at night the square was busy, travellers coming in and out of the city and café tables on the pavements full of German soldiers enjoying themselves. Although she had somewhere to go, Valérie felt very alone and turned determinedly towards Rue Emile Gilbert. She hadn't had anything to eat for hours so hoped she could get something at the hotel.

Valérie walked down the narrow Parisian street, its wrought iron balconies and ornate stonework stretching out in front of her. Halfway along, she saw the sign for the Hotel Ecureil above a finely carved stone entranceway. She went inside, past the tables of the restaurant at the side with people still lingering over a late supper, and towards a desk at the back of the hall. A man of about her father's age was standing behind the desk and he looked up at her suspiciously as she walked towards him.

'Mademoiselle, how can I help you?'

'Bonjour. Is it Monsieur Vernier? I'm looking for a room for a night or two. My father said I should come here. He's Albert Hallez from Geneva. He said he used to stay here when he came to Paris.'

The man's features lightened and he smiled broadly, coming round from behind the desk and shaking her hand energetically. 'So you are Albert's little girl? Not so little now, hein? Of course we have a room for you, I will get my wife to find the best room we have available tonight.'

He went behind the reception desk and shouted into the back room, 'Renée, I have someone here you must meet. You remember Albert, the watchmaker from Geneva that used to come here? His daughter is here now and we must find her a good room.'

As his wife came out and held out her hand she said in a quiet voice, 'I am Renée Vernier, you are very welcome, mademoiselle. We remember your father well. He was a good friend. How is he?'

Valérie smiled at the woman's warmth. 'He's very well, thank you.'

The front door opened behind Valérie and a group of German soldiers came inside and went through to the restaurant, sitting down at one of the empty tables. Immediately, Renée ushered Valérie into the back room and left her husband to take their order. When they were out of sight, she took a key from the board on the wall. 'Come on, my dear,' she said. 'Let me show you to your room.'

Valérie followed her upstairs, to a pretty room at the back of the hotel. Sinking gratefully down onto a wooden chair next to the window, she saw that it overlooked a lane behind the hotel that widened out into a small courtyard. 'Could I have something to eat, please?' she asked. 'The train from Bourg-en-Bresse took hours to get here and I haven't had anything since this morning.'

'I'll bring you something up here. It's late now and if you go downstairs on your own you might be bothered by those Germans so it would be better if you stayed here.' She shook her head. 'Travelling on your own like this, you need to be careful in the town. It isn't like Geneva, you know; there could be trouble at any time and you don't want to get caught up in it.'

Valérie pulled her coat tighter around shoulders and wondered if she would ever warm up. 'I know, madame, but I need to meet a friend here.'

'Where is your friend?' said Renée as she stood at the door, poised to leave.

'I think she's working in the Hôtel-Dieu hospital on the Île de la Cité. I'm not sure where she's living so I need to go and meet her when she's at work.' Valérie looked away from the woman's sharp gaze. 'We lost touch, with the war and everything,' she said weakly.

Renée stared at her. 'If you want to see her then you're better going out early in the morning, because she should be on her way into the hospital then. Is she a nurse there? Some of them stay in a hostel next to the hospital. The woman who runs it is a friend of mine.'

'I don't know what her job is,' answered Valérie finally, reluctant to divulge any details, 'but if I go and wait near the entrance to the hospital then I should be able to catch her.'

'I will get you some food and you can warm up. You look frozen, my dear. Once you've had something to eat you'll feel better.'

As she waited for her meal, Valérie looked out of the window at the building across the narrow lane running behind the hotel. She knew her story sounded unlikely and realised how she had jumped to take action when she wasn't even sure she would find Hannelore at the hospital. But what else could she do? She heard Renée walk back up the stairs and the faint sound of laughter from the restaurant below. She gave herself a shake. Her father had said she could trust these people, so she just had to believe that they hadn't changed their allegiance in the time since he'd been there.

By the time Renée opened the door to the bedroom, carrying a plate of steaming chicken stew and some fresh bread, Valérie had warmed up and taken her coat off. Renée put the plate of food on the small table in the corner of the room. The smell was impossible to resist and Valérie sat down to eat.

'This is lovely,' she said and Renée smiled.

'My son's wife comes from a farm north of Paris so we're lucky to have a regular supply of meat.'

When Valérie had cleaned her plate, Renée picked it up.

'I'll bring you some of the special apple tart I only keep for my best customers.' She hesitated and then carried on, 'There are more German soldiers around the station. People are saying that they're looking for a young woman. I know it can't be you, because they wouldn't be searching for a Swiss woman here, but if you find your friend, you should get out of the city as quickly as you can. You might not be the one they're looking for, but they'll stop anybody they suspect could tell them anything.' Her thin features sagged as she bent her head. 'We try to avoid any trouble but sometimes it seems like it's everywhere.'

'Thank you, madame. Even in Switzerland we have the same problems.' She thought about the German spies, how they were becoming bolder as they searched through her home city that was supposed to be in a neutral country. 'I'll be careful and when I find my friend, we'll go back to Geneva immediately.'

Renée pointed at the back window. 'If you need to come back to the hotel without anyone seeing you, there is an entrance to the lane on the next street, the Rue Michel Chasles. You can come at any time. If you knock on the back door of the hotel, either my husband or I will answer it.' The sound of laughter floated up again from the restaurant. 'You can avoid the people eating or drinking that way and can come upstairs without being seen.' She paused. 'If you need to leave suddenly, you can go out that way too. It doesn't look like it goes anywhere and is overlooked by all the buildings on the street, but you can get in and out that way without walking past the restaurant.'

As if she'd already said too much, Renée nodded to Valérie and left. More than ever, she realised that her father had been right to send her there. She was no longer doubtful that it was a safe place. She just had to make sure that it stayed safe and she didn't put her father's friends into too much danger. She got up to close the shutters more firmly, telling herself it was to keep the warmth in the room, but knowing it was to keep the dangers out.

THIRTY-FOUR

VALÉRIE

Paris

The next day, before it was light outside, Valérie crept down the stairs and into the room behind reception. There was no one else there and when she glanced into the restaurant, she could see that the front door was still locked. She heard a noise behind her and Renée came down the stairs and into the room.

'You must eat something before you go out, mademoiselle,' she said. She sounded so like Agathe that Valérie nodded obediently and sat down at the small table set against the wall. Renée handed Valérie some bread with jam and boiled up some milk for hot chocolate. After one mouthful, Valérie realised how hungry she was and finished the bread very quickly.

'Thank you, madame,' she said and got up, pulling her coat on. Renée opened the back door quietly and checked outside before she allowed Valérie to leave. 'Make sure you come back this way,' she said quietly. 'Turn left when you get onto the next street and left again, then follow the river to the Île de la Cité. You can't miss the hospital, it takes up a huge area in front of Notre-Dame.'

Valérie slipped outside and the coldness of the air caught her breath. Even in Paris, it felt like snow was coming and she wondered how much snow had fallen in the mountains above Saint-Maurice. The cold weather would be well established in the Valais mountains and in the Italian hills. She shivered when she thought about Philippe, and where his body might lie. What had happened to him? She couldn't bear the idea of him lying forgotten in the snow, but pushed away what else might have taken place. She thought about the lives of the other soldiers still protecting the Alps, before she realised with a heavy heart that she had less of a reason to be worried about the fort. Apart from Christophe, no one was there any longer that she cared about.

She looked along the street, trying to take her mind off her memories. It was getting a bit later now and more people were going to work. Some of the shops were opening their shutters and deliveries were being made. Walking up the elegant streets, she passed buildings that had been there for hundreds of years but were now draped with swastika signs. Several larger buildings looked heavily guarded. Head down, she walked briskly along the side of the Seine, feeling a prickling sensation down her back as she felt the stare of the German guards follow her. Every moment she expected them to shout after her as if they knew what she was there for, but she gave herself a shake to dispel her worries.

Reaching the hospital building, she recognised it from Clara's postcard. The hospital was much larger than she had imagined, and she walked around it, trying to decide which entrance would give her the best chance of seeing Hannelore arrive for work. In the end, she decided that Hannelore must be staying close to where her family had lived, so waited where the street led onto the bridge leading into the Marais district. She saw people making their way inside to work and looked for somewhere unobtrusive to wait, knowing that she could be there all day.

Across the ancient island in the middle of the Seine, the glorious frontage of Notre-Dame Cathedral rose majestically above the other buildings. Despite the huge uncertainty of what she was doing there, she couldn't help feeling a thrill of excitement at being in Paris. She spied a couple of benches next to the large entrance and walked to the nearest one. She sat in one corner, shielded by the branches of a tree, pulled her coat more tightly around her and settled down for a long wait.

For the next few hours, people came and went from the hospital, patients leaving to go home and worried visitors rushing into the entrance. As the hours passed and morning turned into afternoon, the skies clouded over and persistent rain started to fall. Valérie sat back on the bench, trying to get some shelter from the overhanging branches of the tree, but it gave her little protection. She would have to go inside soon if it didn't stop raining – but waiting inside the hospital would be too obvious so she would just have to come back the next day. Her heart sank. Maybe she was wrong; maybe Hannelore wasn't coming this way at all. Maybe she no longer even worked there. Valérie had been so sure that the hospital was the place to find her.

A group of doctors and nurses came outside and left the building, walking past her bench. Others came in to take their place and Valérie sat up in the seat, studying each face to see if Hannelore was among them. She was so busy looking through the group that she almost missed her. A small figure came out from the hospital, shoulders hunched in a blue coat, a matching hat clamped down over light brown hair. She walked quickly away from the building towards the bridge over the Seine, eyes fixed forward.

Valérie jumped to her feet as the woman came towards her and reached out her hand. 'Hannelore?' she asked quietly.

The woman stopped and looked up, her face blanching in fear and horror. Hannelore staggered backwards and put up her hands as if to ward away an evil spirit. 'Thérèse... but it can't be you. I saw you die that night,' she whispered.

'No, don't be afraid. It's me, Valérie. It isn't my mother, it's me.'

Hannelore looked into Valérie's face, her green eyes shining. 'You gave me such a fright, you look so like your mother. What are you doing here? How did you know where to find me?'

They walked across the bridge, Valérie checking they weren't being watched by anybody else, unable to stop the burst of excitement at finding Hannelore. 'It was Clara. She was sure you'd be here.'

'Clara? My niece, Clara? She's all right? I've been so worried about her, not knowing anything about where she was,' said Hannelore.

'Yes, she's in Geneva and safe for now, but we need to get you out of France to join her.'

Hannelore shook her head. 'I don't see how I'll be able to get across the border. The Germans have tried to stop me more than once in Paris and I've had to hide from them several times. I think they're getting close again. The minute I show somebody my papers it'll all be over. I've only been able to work here because the woman who runs the laundry desperately needs more people and she was prepared to turn a blind eye to who I am.'

'But it's fine,' said Valérie. 'I have identity papers for you with your picture and a different name, so we can go back into Geneva.'

'You mean I can get out of here?' Hannelore clutched her arm as if she could hardly believe what she was hearing. 'How did you manage that?' she asked breathlessly.

'I found them. Jacob left a set of them with my mother for

safekeeping until this war is over and two of them have our pictures on them – or rather, my mother's picture and yours.'

'Jacob,' she repeated as if she hadn't heard the name spoken for a long time.

Then suddenly they heard the noise of trucks coming up the road towards the bridge and Hannelore pulled Valérie into a side street, her voice insistent. 'We have to get out of here now. That's why I was leaving early today; I was told that the Germans were coming to the hospital to check who was working there. I think someone has given them information about me, so I can't stay any longer.'

They walked quickly away from the sound of the trucks, heads bowed against the rain, and Hannelore led her through the winding streets of the Marais district before they glimpsed two other lorries full of German soldiers on the road ahead of them. They ran away, the noises of the soldiers echoing through the city streets, over the sound of heavy rain. It was only mid-afternoon but the day light was already fading from the sky. This was a poorer district than the area around the hospital and Valérie looked at the rundown buildings for eyes watching them from inside the apartments. The streets were crumbling from lack of attention, the grey stone buildings unkempt and the wooden shutters worn and faded. There was none of the picturesque nature of the smarter buildings around the centre of the city.

'It's just here,' said Hannelore, stopping at a door halfway up the street and letting herself inside, panting slightly from running so fast. 'Come with me. I won't be long getting my bag. I'm always ready to leave here at a moment's notice. I've got used to that over the last few weeks.'

Valérie followed her inside, looking back to check that no one was watching them, but the street was empty and most of the shutters were closed, making the area feel cold and deserted.

Inside, water dripped through the ceiling in the entrance, an old bucket set out to catch the worst of the water. Valérie could hear dripping noises from other places in the building too. They ran upstairs to the first floor and Hannelore unlocked the door to the apartment on the left, walked through the hall and into the main room. Valérie looked around at the meagre accommodation – some worn chairs and a table the only furniture, apart from a sink and a small unlit stove in the corner. A woman, wearing layers of old clothes and a blanket over her shoulders, turned quickly to face them, her eyes wide with fear. She was thin, with straggly blonde hair pulled back from her face and looked desperately ill, her face sweating slightly despite the cold apartment.

'What's happened?' she said in a weak voice. 'Why are you back here in the afternoon? Who's this?'

Hannelore went towards her and held her hands. 'I need to go now, Chantal. I can't stay any longer. You'll be fine with Marc.'

At her words, a young man came into the room and turned to Hannelore. 'You're leaving now?' he said.

Hannelore nodded and gestured to Valérie. 'This is Valérie, the daughter of an old friend of mine. She's come to help me.'

As if she was too tired to take part in the conversation, Chantal sat down on the chair and leaned back, closing her eyes.

Valérie stepped forward and shook Marc's hand. 'Could I wait for Hannelore here?'

'Of course.' He waved his hand towards another chair and Valérie sat down, shivering in her damp coat. It felt colder inside the apartment than outside. When Hannelore went through to the bedroom at the back of the apartment, they sat in silence, Chantal's eyes closed. When Valérie's breathing returned to normal, she stood up to look out of the window at the street below. Suddenly she saw two men race down the street and then the sound of marching boots coming after them.

Chantal's eyes sprang open and she came to stand beside Valérie, holding onto the window sill. 'You have to leave. This happens when the Germans start searching around here.' She sighed. 'They've been back every few days, going into every house and arresting people. My husband and I will be leaving too.' She bent her head down and Valérie touched her shoulder.

'I'm so sorry you have to leave.'

Marc came up and put his arm round his wife's shoulders and she leaned into him. 'We're going today,' he said firmly.

Hannelore came running into the room, carrying a small suitcase. 'I have everything I need.'

'You'd better go out the back.' said Marc. 'You won't get out the front, they'll have blocked the ends of the street while they search.'

Hannelore embraced Chantal and Marc. 'Thank you for everything,' said Hannelore. 'I hope you get away safely.'

'It's me who should thank you. You stayed with me when I was all alone,' replied Chantal. 'Don't worry about us. Whatever happens will be God's will. Just take care of yourself.' She looked at Valérie. 'Both of you, be careful.'

Then they heard the noise of doors being rattled and loud knocking at the end of the street. Hannelore and Valérie ran downstairs to the hall and went out through the back door to the small lane running down behind the apartments and through the arch to the main street. They looked up and down the street but there were no soldiers in sight so they walked quickly, heading towards the hotel.

'Is Chantal ill?' asked Valérie as they tried to avoid the puddles on the street.

'She was ill when I got to know her in Paris. She has a disease that affects her breathing. When I was trying to leave Paris I saw her husband being arrested and had to come back to see she was all right. I had to stay until Marc came back but we'd already decided we had to leave. Her breathing is much worse now than it was before and the doctors are struggling to treat her. Marc thinks she'll be better in the countryside so they're going to the Loire Valley.'

Valérie just nodded. She hoped they would be all right but knew that nowhere in France was safe until the German occupation was over.

THIRTY-FIVE

VALÉRIE

France

They walked quickly through the back way to the hotel. At the first knock, Monsieur Vernier opened the door and ushered them inside. 'Go upstairs to your room,' he whispered. 'The German soldiers in the restaurant are looking for somebody.' He glanced at Hannelore. 'Go now and you won't be seen.'

They ran up the stairs quietly, stopping halfway when they heard a noise on the upstairs landing. They waited for a few moments to see if anybody came out of one of the rooms but there was no other sound and there seemed to be no one following them, so they carried on upstairs to Valérie's bedroom. Closing the door firmly behind them, they both sat down on the bed. Valérie waited for her breathing to get back to normal, her heart beating loudly in her chest. She didn't think anybody had seen them coming into the hotel, but they waited in silence for several minutes to check they were alone.

'How are we going to get to the station?' asked Hannelore, taking off her hat and tidying her hair with a shaking hand. 'If they're looking for me and have a description, we'll never manage to leave.'

'I'm sure we can think of something,' said Valérie. She knew it was dangerous, but she was still flushed with her success in finding Hannelore. Surely the most difficult part was over? Now they just had to plan how they were going to leave. She stood up and looked out of the window. 'There's only one train this afternoon going south that we can get. I don't want to go out but we'll have to if we're to get to Geneva tonight.'

Thinking about what Hannelore had said when she'd first seen her, Valérie turned away from the window. 'I'm sorry I gave you such a fright earlier. I forget how much like my mother I look. No wonder you thought it was her.'

Hannelore sighed. 'I'm all right now. It was just so sudden. I thought Thérèse was back with me again, even though I knew that was impossible.'

Valérie hesitated and then asked the question she had been holding inside for so long, desperate to find out the truth before anything else happened and the precious opportunity was lost forever. 'What happened to my mother? You said that you saw her die.'

Despite their situation, Hannelore heard the urgency in Valérie's voice.

'I was worried about her that night. She'd gone to collect some false identities from the man who prepared papers for Jacob. He already thought he was being followed but wasn't sure. I went to meet her so that she wouldn't be on her own coming back to meet your father. She'd told me where he would be meeting her. She was across the square in front of Cornavin station... I saw everything. She was walking across the snow when someone grabbed her arm as if to stop her from leaving. I went to try and help her but it was too far. Before I could get near, she'd pulled her arm away from him and started running across the square.' Hannelore's eyes filled with tears. 'Then she slipped on the snow and fell in front of a car driving up the Rue des Alpes onto the square. Other people came running to help, one of them was even a doctor. I remember him shouting for an ambulance, but nobody could do anything. When I looked back at the square, I saw the person who had grabbed her arm disappear into the darkness. No one apart from me saw him, but he caused her death.'

Valérie took a deep breath. Finally, she knew exactly what had happened to her mother. It had been an accident, just as she'd always been told. It had been an accident... but someone was to blame.

'Who was the man?' Valérie asked.

'When I described him – a thickset man in a black coat – Jacob said it sounded like one of the German spies who had been following him. He didn't think they were interested in anybody else so didn't warn your mother.'

She shook her head, remembering the painful scene. 'I lost my temper with Jacob, said some awful things, that it was his fault Thérèse was dead and that it was all over between us because he had failed to protect her.'

'You broke it off with him?' asked Valérie. 'Someone told me that he came looking for you.'

'He came back and tried to get me to change my mind, to come away with him to England because it was no longer safe in Geneva. My brother was already planning for us to leave Frankfurt to go to France. We thought it would be safer here than in Germany. But I couldn't forgive Jacob. He pushed David to smuggle more and more documents and secrets out of Germany through me, and his work, setting up bank accounts to stop people's money from being stolen by the Nazis, had become such an obsession that he didn't see that he was putting people in danger.'

'So, you came to France?'

'I stayed with my brother, his wife and Clara here in Paris

until it got too dangerous and the Germans started rounding up all the Jewish people in our neighbourhood. We knew we would be next. And we'd discussed what we'd do if we had to split up.' She glanced at her small suitcase. 'So, I have part of the top-secret document that has endangered all our lives,' she said bitterly. 'You must know about that, if you helped Clara.' Then she looked up at Valérie, hope lightening her voice. 'You said Clara was in Switzerland, but what about Ruth, my sister-in-law? She wanted to get Clara to safety but wasn't thinking about herself or her own safety.'

'I'm sorry. We don't know exactly what happened to Ruth but the Resistance believe she was taken away by the Germans.'

'So, Clara is all I have left,' Hannelore said quietly.

Before Valérie could answer, there was a knock at the door and Renée came inside, followed by two young men smartly dressed in suits and overcoats, carrying thin leather briefcases. Renée seemed younger and more alert, tension filling her body and making her voice quick and determined. 'They're saying that the Germans are looking everywhere for a young woman. You'll never get onto the train because there are so many of them at the station. They're asking everyone they meet for their papers, then they're taking away anyone they suspect.'

Valérie looked at her in horror.

Renée continued, 'Marcel and Jean-Claude are going to Dijon, so you can make the first part of the journey together. They aren't looking for two couples, so it might just get you through.'

Valérie shook her head. 'It's too dangerous,' she protested. But the taller of the two men stepped forward and spoke in a deep, confident voice. 'Don't worry about us, we go up and down this train line all the time. The guards are used to seeing us. They know that our business can benefit them too, so they are unlikely to stop us.'

Valérie looked from one to the other of them, still unhappy, uncertain of his assertion of being known to the German guards, but she realised that they had no choice. She glanced at Hannelore, who gave a slight nod.

'You need to go now if you're going to get the train. Good luck,' said Renée.

Valérie embraced her. 'Thank you for everything. I've left some money on the bedside table. I'll tell my father how you and your husband helped me.'

Renée gave a rueful smile. 'If we all survive this awful war, tell Albert to come back and see us. It's been too long.'

They all let themselves out of the room and went downstairs, meeting no one on the way. Valérie glanced at Hannelore, who looked for all the world like she was going to the gallows. Marcel paused as they stepped out of the back door and turned to her. 'Do you mind if I put my arm round you?' he asked hesitantly. 'No one will look twice at us if they think we're a couple out to get a train together.'

'Good idea.'

He put his arm round Valérie's shoulders as they walked along and she stiffened in the unfamiliar embrace, so unlike Philippe's, her nerves so tense that she felt rigid and awkward. A group of youths came towards them from the station and Marcel pulled her out of their path. She took a deep breath and tried to relax.

Valérie looked behind and saw Jean-Claude's arm casually thrown around Hannelore's shoulders. He said something to her and she laughed, showing no tension or fear, despite what she must have been feeling. Marcel squeezed Valérie's shoulder. 'It's just a bit of play acting,' he said smiling. 'You need to look like you're having a nice time with me.'

She returned his smile.

'That's better,' he said. 'Now, tell me all about watch-making in Geneva. That should take us until we get onto the train.'

They walked across the Place Louis-Armand, having silly conversations, occasionally breaking out into laughter.

'It's this way,' said Marcel, as they walked through the square towards the station. They passed a few shops and she gazed at the wrapping paper and Christmas gifts in the windows. It was the middle of December but she felt disconnected from the normal things in life, birthdays and Christmas. She glanced at Hannelore but the others weren't looking in the windows, just focusing straight ahead towards the station.

They walked into the station building, Marcel pointing towards the train. 'Come on,' he said in a loud voice. 'We'd better hurry or we're going to miss it!'

He steered his way past a large group of German soldiers on the left side of the station building and handed their identity papers to the two soldiers at the barrier to the platform. He whispered to Valérie as they waited for the papers to be checked and she giggled as if she didn't have a care in the world, although she could feel her heart thumping in her chest and her legs were shaking. The guard handed back their papers abruptly, as if he wanted to get rid of the young lovers, their light-hearted manner making him jealous and his job worse than usual.

Valérie took a deep breath as they got past the guard and turned back to watch Hannelore and Jean-Claude hand their papers over. This was the worst part. Valérie watched them, hardly able to breathe. The guards seemed to be looking at their papers for longer and one of them turned towards the group of soldiers as if he was going to call them over.

Before he could shout, Hannelore and Jean-Claude shared a deep kiss right in front of him. With a loud curse, he changed his mind and thrust their papers back towards them, virtually pulling them apart with his rough gesture. 'Get out of my sight,' he said harshly, 'I've had enough of you lot.' Hannelore and

Jean-Claude walked gaily towards the train and boarded it behind Valérie and Marcel.

Once inside the train, they moved up the carriages to put some distance between themselves and the soldiers and collapsed onto the seats. The disapproving glances from the other passengers as they passed gave rise to another fit of giggles from Valérie. Between her smiles she said quietly, 'This is exhausting. Can we stop laughing now?'

Marcel looked up the carriage and nodded. He turned to Jean-Claude and slapped him on the arm. 'That was close. He was about to get somebody else to look at your papers.'

'I could see that they were having an argument. One of the guards in the bigger group was ordering them to question every young woman getting onto the train while the other one was telling him only to question single women. He said not to bother us as we were two couples. So I decided to stop the argument by giving them a romantic scene. They were disgusted enough with both of you and I just made it worse.'

Hannelore smiled weakly at him, her good humour and laughter a distant memory. 'We couldn't have done it without you both. Thank you.'

By this time the train was almost full. The door closed and the train slowly left the Gare de Lyon station. As they pulled away, Valérie could see German soldiers marching six or seven single women out of the station. She shivered. 'What's going to happen to those poor girls? I hope they'll be all right.' The others didn't answer her and she continued to look out of the window as the outskirts of Paris were left behind.

When they reached Dijon, Valérie moved to let Marcel and Jean-Claude leave, but they shook their heads. 'Aren't you going now?' asked Valérie. 'I thought you said that you were on the train until here.'

'We're going to come with you to Bourg-en-Bresse,' replied Marcel. 'Just in case they're looking for young women on their own there too. We'll come out with you and stay until you get your connection.'

Valérie was about to argue and then thought better of it; the two men had saved them in Paris and could do so again in Bourg-en-Bresse. 'Thank you for everything,' she said finally.

'What's the plan?' he asked. 'Which way are you going across the border?'

'I want to go to one of the quieter border crossings north of Annemasse,' replied Valérie. 'I've been there before and the smaller crossings have very few guards. Once we get across, we can catch the tram from there into Geneva. I have to get Hannelore to the north bank of the lake but we can get most of the way by tram.'

After hours on the train, they finally reached Bourg-en-Bresse station and a German soldier came through the carriages telling everyone to get off. Valérie and Hannelore grabbed their small suitcases and followed Marcel and Jean-Claude off the train. Bourg-en-Bresse station was busy and Valérie was glad that Marcel and Jean-Claude could help them push their way through the crowds. When she was heading the other way, north to Paris, the station had been very quiet with very few soldiers around but now it was completely different. There was a tangible sense of tension in the station building, groups of German guards parading along the platforms and taking everyone off the trains to check their papers. The waiting room was full of people, old and young, groups of children and families whose journeys had been halted without warning.

At the exit from the platform, they showed their papers to the German soldiers, who hardly looked at them and waved them towards the waiting room with everyone else.

'This is where we leave you, we can get back another way,' said Marcel. 'It was good to meet you both.'

Valérie pulled Marcel into a hug and whispered into his ear, 'I can't thank you enough. You saved our lives.'

The two men disappeared into the darkness of the night. Valérie and Hannelore sat in the waiting room and Valérie studied everyone sitting around them, watching suspiciously and flinching at the slightest noise. Until Hannelore was out of France and safe with Clara inside the lake house in Geneva, guarded by the SOE, she wouldn't feel secure.

THIRTY-SIX

VALÉRIE

France

Valérie and Hannelore were squeezed in the corner of one of the benches in the waiting room and Valérie looked around to see whether anyone was looking at them. The departures board was completely empty and no trains seemed to be leaving the station.

On the bench next to her, a young woman was holding a boy aged about four or five years old. Valérie smiled at him and he returned her smile shyly, looking up at her from under his long lashes. His mother smoothed down his blond hair. Captured by his innocent charm, Valérie looked back up at his mother, her open smile and healthy complexion a marked difference to the thin waif-like figures sitting all around them.

'What's his name?' asked Valérie.

'Jean-Pierre, and my name is Rosalie.'

'I'm Thérèse and this is Véronique.' They'd been careful not to use their real names ever since they started using the false identity papers. They couldn't take any chances that they would be stopped because Hannelore and Valérie's names were known.

'You must be proud of him. He's a lovely little boy.'

Rosalie's friendly face fell in dismay. 'He's not going to be happy, though. I came here to get a local train to Annemasse but it looks like there's hardly anything going out there today. We heard that there have been explosions on the train lines between here and Switzerland, the Resistance are targeting trains transporting German troops.' They watched some German soldiers running into the station, guns at the ready and Valérie held her breath until they ran past. 'That's why there's such confusion here,' Rosalie continued. 'No one knows what's happening.'

Valérie sighed as she looked at the trains that were standing still, no drivers in sight.

Rosalie carried on. 'I was told that there was going to be a train to Annemasse this evening. My cousin works at the station and he said I should just come here and get on the first train that left.' She looked around at the crowds of people waiting in the station. 'But everybody else will try to take the first train; it's going to be so overcrowded I'm not sure we'll even get on it.'

Valérie turned to Hannelore and said in a low voice, 'If there is a train going that way, we need to get on it. We can't afford to sit here for hours, not with all these soldiers around. If they start to search everyone's bags, then we'll have a big problem.'

Suddenly, a guard shouted from the nearest platform. 'This train is leaving for Annemasse in five minutes. Anyone going to Annemasse or the stations on the way should get on now.'

In a wave of movement most of the people in the waiting room stood up and ran towards the barrier, leaving only a few people behind. Valérie saw that the Rosalie and her son were getting swept away by the crowd and she stuck out her elbows and grabbed the woman's arm. Hannelore took her other arm and together, they pushed towards the train. They helped the women and her son up the steps to the carriage and then they followed behind her, managing to get four seats together.

All the seats were quickly taken and the aisle of the carriage was full of people standing, with more on the platform trying to get on the train, when they heard the guard's whistle blow and the noise of the doors being slammed shut throughout the train. Valérie looked out of the window and saw German soldiers pulling a man and his family away from the carriage door. The man shouted angrily and lashed out at one of the soldiers who hit him with his rifle and knocked him to the ground. The rifle butt came away bloody from his wound and the people fell back from the train, afraid that the violence would spread. Rosalie was holding Jean-Pierre's head close to her so that he didn't see the man lying on the platform, his family crowded round him.

The train slowly pulled out of the station and everyone inside relaxed, either in their seats or sitting on the floor. The feeling of relief that they had managed to get on board united everyone in the carriage and Valérie saw them smiling to one another. They all looked like French country people, going home from visiting relatives or shopping. Rosalie swept back her dishevelled light brown hair that had fallen over her forehead. 'Thank you for helping us,' she said. 'We really had to get this train or it would be far too late for Jean-Pierre. We were visiting my mother today in Bourg-en-Bresse but we had to leave early to get home.' The train started to slow down, the carriages bumping together as it pulled into a small dark station where only a few people got off and no one got on. Valérie looked outside the window and could see nothing, not even the name of the station, and leaned back in her seat. This might not be a long journey in distance but the train was so slow it was going to take a long time. It was so dark outside that she frowned, hoping she could recognise where they were as they got closer to Annemasse and the border with Switzerland.

The carriage was quiet now and people were trying to sleep. Valérie still felt the tension of the station and she looked at Hannelore, who was fidgeting with one of the buttons on her coat, looking around nervously. Suddenly, she froze, her gaze fixed on the door at the end of the carriage. She clutched Valérie's arm in agitation. 'There are German soldiers coming down the train, checking everyone's luggage. They mustn't find the document in my bag.'

'It's not hidden?' asked Valérie.

Hannelore shook her head. 'Not really. It's in lining of my bag. If they search really carefully then they might find it.' Hannelore's eyes were darting around the carriage, looking for any way to escape through to the next car. Valérie watched the group of German soldiers led by a young officer dressed in a black coat and hat searching through passengers' belongings. She felt her heart beating fast and dread crept over her limbs. She looked at the carriage door, wondering if they could jump off but knew instantly that they would be seen and caught before they could get very far.

By this time, Hannelore was standing up and Rosalie was looking at her curiously. Watching the German soldiers working their way up the carriage, Hannelore pulled Valérie up too. 'We must go further down the train and hope we can get off at the next stop before they reach us.' As they bent down to pick up their bags, the train stopped suddenly in a screech of brakes and shouts of alarm from the passengers. Valérie caught the side of the seat as she was thrown violently to the side and held on tightly to stop herself from falling. She saw Hannelore thrown back on to the seat, her head hitting the wooden edging and bouncing back off the hard surface. She clutched the back of her head, her features screwed up in pain. As she pulled away her hand, the fingers were covered in blood.

Valérie looked further up the carriage and saw the German soldiers picking themselves up off the floor, the senior officer striding towards the door of the train throwing it open and shouting at his soldiers to follow him. Valérie knew she had to take advantage of the sudden change in their situation, her initial shock giving way to relief that the search of the German soldiers had been stopped. Ignoring the cries and moans of the passengers all around them, she pressed Hannelore's shoulder and handed her a handkerchief. 'Are you all right? Just wait here,' she hissed. 'I'm going to see what's happened.' Hannelore nodded and put the handkerchief on her wound.

Valérie went to the carriage door and jumped down onto the track, pushing past some other passengers standing there who were looking curiously towards the front of the train. Ahead, she saw a train coming from the opposite direction that had been blown off its line, the engine lying drunkenly on its side across their track. Lights from trucks and ambulances that had come to help the people on the derailed train lined the edge of the railway, and she could make out German soldiers sitting on the grass next to the track looking dazed, some of them in bandages. At the front of their own train, the driver was being dragged out of his cab by the German officer who had been searching the carriages. He'd done well to stop them from hitting the other train but it was going no further until they had removed the derailed train from the line. She also saw some passengers at the front of their train being helped out of the carriages and taken towards the ambulances.

Valérie looked at the scene for a few more seconds and then climbed back up into the carriage and crossed to the other side, opening the window and looking out. Unlike the activity and lights on the other side there was nothing but darkness, the trees swaying in the wind at the edge of the field next to the railway line. The sounds from the other side were muted here and Valérie went back inside the carriage to Hannelore. Rosalie was trying to comfort her son, who was frightened by the sudden movement of the train and the shouting and screams he could hear all around him. Valérie leaned down to whisper to Hannelore. 'We need to leave now. I can't see where we are exactly but we can't be far from Switzerland. There are too many German soldiers here and more are likely to come. We'll be stuck on this train for hours if we don't leave now. Can you come with me? You aren't badly hurt, are you?'

'No, I'm all right now,' she replied, her voice firm. 'It's nothing.'

Despite whispering, their words had reached Rosalie, who said instantly, 'If it helps, I know exactly where we are. We're near our farm; it's only a few kilometres from Annemasse. If you go out of the train and head through the trees, you'll get to the outskirts of the town, then you can decide how to get across to Switzerland. I'll wait here, my husband will come and get me. Everyone in the whole area will see what's happened.'

Valérie nodded. 'Thank you.'

Rosalie smiled. 'You've been very kind to us. Anything I can do to help.'

'Come on, we need to go.' Valérie picked up her suitcase and was about to follow Hannelore when she turned back to Rosalie. 'This will just weigh us down.' Before she handed it over, she took out the photographs of her family and put them into her pocket. 'You might be able to use some of the clothes, you look like you're about my size,' she said to Rosalie before they left the carriage.

On this side of the train she could just see the front of the derailed locomotive lying across the track, but as she had thought, all the vehicles were on the other side and it was dark here with none of the light from the vehicles reaching this far.

They ran across the field towards the trees before Valérie looked back at the trains and stopped suddenly. 'Keep going and hide in the trees over there. I've had an idea. I've got to get something and then I'll follow you.'

Ever since they'd got on the train she'd been trying to think about how they could get across the border. Only now did she realise what they could do. Bending low, she ran across the field up to the front of the trains, keeping out of sight and listening to the noises and groans from passengers being treated for their injuries. Just ahead of her, between the two trains, there was a pile of used bandages left behind by the emergency workers. Without hesitation, Valérie sprinted between the trains and grabbed a couple of the bandages then rushed back before anyone could see her. Behind the locomotive she breathed heavily as she listened for the sound of any shouts but no one came after her to see what she was doing. Her legs were shaking so much that she could hardly move for a few moments but then she pushed herself forward, away from the train, bending down and running across the field, keeping hold of the heavy bandages. Her hands were damp from the blood of the German soldiers who had been treated for their injuries. In the open field she was terrified that she would be seen by any of the German soldiers or emergency workers but could only trust she would be hidden by the darkness and they would be too distracted by the accident to notice her.

Once in the trees, she almost ran into Hannelore and grasped onto her arms in relief.

'What did you get?' hissed Hannelore. 'I can't see anything in the dark.'

'You'll see when we get into Annemasse,' replied Valérie. 'We're going to have to trick the German soldiers at the border if we're to have a chance of getting to Geneva.'

'Why did you give your bag away?' asked Hannelore as they walked briskly in the direction Rosalie had instructed.

'I didn't think we could get away with both of them,' replied Valérie. 'Mine just contained a change of clothes, yours contains something much more important.'

They walked doggedly on and soon came upon some buildings on the outskirts of the town. As they drew closer to the centre, Valérie made sure that they circled around the busiest streets and headed to the north of the town. As they passed an old, deserted warehouse, she stopped and went inside, indicating for Hannelore to follow.

She pulled a small torch from her pocket and shone it onto the bandages she had brought with her. 'They're disgusting,' said Hannelore. 'Whatever do you want these for?'

'Take off your coat and I'll tie one round your arm. You've been injured in the train crash. Your arm is broken and you're bleeding from other injuries. We're both Swiss, remember, so the first thing we'd do is try to get home. It's the best idea I can think of to distract the border guards and make them less suspicious of us. Hopefully, we'll have a better chance of getting across the border.' She hesitated and then carried on, 'If it gets difficult, you have to run and try and get across, leave me behind to deal with the guards. The most important thing is to get the document to the Allies, you need to remember that.'

She wrapped the bandage around Hannelore's arm, forming a crude sling, and put the second one, still damp with blood, round her waist. 'If someone tries to search you, scream in agony and squeeze the bandage. They should get a fright when they see the blood.' She draped Hannelore's coat over her shoulders and picked up her small suitcase. 'Hopefully they'll be so distracted by you and the state you're in that they won't even see the suitcase and try to search it.' Valérie looked at her handiwork and nodded in satisfaction, putting away her torch. 'The plan will only work if they've been distracted by news of the attack on the train. We'll go to one of the quieter crossings that leads straight onto a Geneva tram stop across the border. We just have to hope that all the German soldiers are trying to deal with the train crash rather than watch for people crossing the border.'

They left the warehouse and walked normally for the first few hundred metres and then stopped at the street round the corner from the border crossing. Valérie stretched her arm around Hannelore's shoulders, 'Lean on me and remember that you're in pain,' she instructed.

They hobbled towards the border crossing and Valérie saw that there were only two guards checking identity papers at the barrier, Swiss border guards lounging on the Swiss side a few metres away. She purposely went to the younger German guard and looked at him for any sign of sympathy but he just stared at her and stuck out his hand for their papers.

As Valérie handed across the false papers and took her hand away for a moment, Hannelore staggered and moaned. They saw a tram coming into the stop in Switzerland and Valérie plunged into their story. 'My sister was hurt in the train crash. You must have heard about it? It's been a huge disaster with a troop train and a passenger train caught up in it.'

The guard was looking at their papers and didn't reply. Valérie turned away from him to hide Hannelore's suitcase from his view. His colleague ambled towards him. 'What's going on here?' he asked.

'She says this woman was injured in the train crash, the one that we heard about.'

'Just check she's not hiding anything,' said the older guard, putting out his hand towards Hannelore's arm that was bundled in the bloody bandage. Valérie's desperation was overpowering. With a sinking heart, she watched the tram sitting at the stop, knowing they only had a few seconds to catch it. When the guard gripped Hannelore's arm and felt under her coat she screamed in pain. It was a real scream and echoed across the border crossing, making the Swiss guards look round. The German soldier pulled away his hand and saw that it was covered with blood. 'Mein Gott,' he cursed and jumped back, wiping his shaking hand on his uniform, his face a picture of disgust. Looking at Valérie, he said, 'Get her out of here before she collapses.' Turning to his colleague, he snapped, 'Open the barrier and let them through.'

Valérie propelled Hannelore through to the Swiss guards, flashed their identity documents again and almost ran to the tram, just managing to get on before the doors closed and it moved off. She breathed a sigh of relief as they left France behind. 'I didn't think that would work,' she said shakily. 'I can't believe I've got you into Switzerland.'

THIRTY-SEVEN

VALÉRIE

Geneva

They stayed on the tram to Cornavin station and then got off to change to the line leading up the Rue de Lausanne and the SOE manor house. They'd been very lucky to get the last tram from the French border to the station but the lights were now going off. There would be no more trams, and they would need to walk the last stage. As they crossed the road, Valérie looked at the people who'd got off the tram at the station stop, but no one took any notice of them, everyone hurrying home in different directions.

Hannelore was looking at her hopelessly. 'How long is the walk?' she asked forlornly.

'It isn't far, just up the Rue de Lausanne.' Valérie took Hannelore's arm and they started to walk together. It was a freezing night so Valérie knew they had to keep going, looking all around in case they were being followed. It was only a short walk out of the city, but she knew that too many people were trying to stop them. The streets were quiet, with hardly anyone out so late at night. When they reached the broad road at the edge of the trees that led down onto the lake, Valérie began to relax. No one had tried to stop them and she could see the light that had always shone from the manor house at night glinting through the trees. She knew that the light was against the blackout restrictions laid down by the Swiss authorities but Henry had told her once that they always left on a small light to guide people in need to the precise location of the house.

'Come on,' she said to Hannelore. 'We just follow the pavement next to the trees and the gate to the house is over there.' She linked their arms together. 'We're almost there, you'll be safe once we get to the house.'

A few steps along the pavement, she stopped suddenly when three men came out of the trees silently and blocked their way. Hannelore gasped and clutched Valérie's arm.

'I think I know him!' she said. 'I'm sure I've seen him before.'

Valérie's heart dropped as she saw Hans Meyer in the middle of the three, flanked by the younger German spy, Klaus, and Otto Hoffman, the consulate official who had been so helpful to her father. They all had pistols pointed towards them and she could hardly breathe.

She took a step towards Otto Hoffman and stared at his cold expression, trying to find some trace of humanity in his face.

'Are you a spy, like they are? I saw you following me but I thought you were different.'

When he didn't respond, she looked behind her to see if there was anyone who would help them but the pavements had emptied and there were no cars on the road this late at night. There was no one to hear her. She twisted forward again. If she screamed loudly enough for help, maybe Henry or someone else in the manor house would hear her.

'Get them away from the pavement and into the trees,' ordered Meyer, waving his pistol at them. She felt Hoffmann grasp her arm and pressure her to move off the pavement. She struggled against his strength, surprised that the small official had lost his habitual hesitancy, but she wasn't strong enough to pull free and he almost lifted her off her feet. Klaus pulled Hannelore after them. The two men stepped away from them once they were hidden in the trees but still kept their pistols raised, pointing at them.

Valérie rubbed her arms where Hoffman had gripped her, trying to force some feeling back into them, but, however hard she tried, she felt icily cold. What would they do next? She stepped closer to Hannelore who was staring fearfully at the pistols. When Valérie glanced over her shoulder, she saw that Hoffman had moved to stand behind them. There was no chance of escape.

She looked at Meyer, at his satisfied expression, and felt anger boil up within her, pushing away the fear. They were so close to safety that she couldn't fail now. They had to get away.

'What do you think you're doing?' she spat out. 'Let us go. You have no right to do this.'

'I have every right, mademoiselle, to do what I like with this woman,' he said in a quiet, cold voice. She shivered when she remembered the same implacable voice from outside the window of Monsieur Moulin's apartment. This man wasn't used to defeat, the assurance that he could conquer all before him chilled the blood in her veins.

'I know your friend here. She has something I want. And I would remind you that she is a German citizen, so I can send her back to a German-occupied country any time I like. The Swiss authorities will help me do it. They don't want to be overrun by Jews, just like everyone else.'

'You have no right to do this,' repeated Valérie. 'Let us go now.'

'And you, mademoiselle, you are an accessory to her crime. You will be arrested for breaking the rules of the Third Reich and imprisoned.' He smiled at her but the smile didn't reach his eyes. 'I have a car close by, so you have nowhere to go.' He waved his hand, as if he was now bored with the scene. 'Get the bag, Hoffman, we have no time for discussion. Klaus, go and get the car.'

Valérie saw Hannelore instinctively clutch her small suitcase closer to her. Before any of them could move, another voice cut into the still air.

'Drop your guns and move away from them, Meyer.'

Valérie stared into the trees where the voice had come from and saw a group of men walk towards them, Nicolas Cherix in front. She blinked a couple of times to try to identify the men behind him. Even though her eyes had got used to the darkness, she couldn't make out their features and realised some of them were wearing masks. She looked back at Meyer and Klaus and saw the pistols still trained on them. Hoffman was still behind them and she heard a click as he readied his pistol to fire. Time froze for a moment, and in the quietness, she heard the noise of a police siren in the distance, but it came no closer and was completely apart from the drama that was going on in the park. The Germans were caught but they weren't going to surrender without a fight and she and Hannelore might be the price of their capture.

'Drop your guns and we won't shoot,' ordered Nicolas again.

She saw a couple of other men behind Nicolas lift their pistols. One of them was tall and the way he held his gun looked very familiar. She narrowed her eyes to try to make him out more clearly, but her attention was caught when she felt a pistol being put into her hand. Hoffman had pulled her hands behind her back and was now giving her his gun. She didn't move and clasped the pistol tightly in her hand, suddenly wondering what was going on and trying not to let her sudden spark of hope show in her face.

Behind her, she felt Hoffmann raise his arms and she saw the two other Germans drop their guns and raise their hands.

'You're making a big mistake, Cherix,' said Meyer. 'You should not have interfered in something that does not concern you. We have reason to suspect this German citizen of betraying the Third Reich. We have every right to take her into custody and intend to do so.'

'Unfortunately for you, betraying the Third Reich is exactly what we want your citizens to do,' replied Nicolas coldly. He turned to his men. 'Take them away. I've heard enough of this filth. We need to get these hostages to safety.'

As the Swiss men moved closer, Meyer's face was twisted in fury and frustration. He was not used to being trapped and running out of options; the man usually in control was now like a wild animal and unpredictable. Valérie could hear his ragged breathing, his eyes searching for a way out. Before the men reached them, Valérie saw Meyer crouch down in a sudden movement and pick up the pistol that he'd dropped to the ground. He moved as quickly as a snake, raising his pistol towards Hannelore. He wasn't going to let her get away.

Before she could think, acting from pure instinct, Valérie drew the pistol from behind her back and pulled the trigger. The noise of the shot echoed around them, and a red stain spread across Meyer's chest. His face showed shock and disbelief before he collapsed onto the ground. Valérie dropped the gun, appalled by what she had done. She had killed someone. It was the first time that anyone had died at her hands and she felt sick as she looked down at the body lying in front of her.

A second shot rang out a few seconds later and the younger German fell down in front of them. Valérie snapped her head round, looking to see who had fired the second shot, but everyone was moving, and she couldn't identify the shooter.

In the calmness that followed, Nicolas walked towards them and, to Valérie's surprise, shook Hoffman's hand. 'Thank you for your help, Otto. We didn't know where they were going to set up the ambush, so your intelligence was vital.' Nicolas stretched out his other arm and held Valérie's shoulder. 'Are you all right?' he asked softly.

She nodded and watched Hoffman bend down to pick up his pistol.

'You helped me,' she gasped. 'You meant for me to shoot him.'

'There are many Germans who do not agree with this war,' replied Otto. 'The sooner it is over, the better it will be for everyone.'

Nicolas nodded. 'Otto has been working for Swiss Intelligence since he came to Geneva. We found out from him where Meyer planned to stop you from getting to safety.'

Otto smiled at Valérie. 'Your father told me that you were a good shot. Now I've seen it for myself. And don't feel sorry for him, many innocent people have died because of him. You did the right thing.'

'I do know him!' gasped Hannelore, who had come up to stand next to Valérie. 'He's the man who was following Thérèse the night she died. He's the one who caused her death. You and your father have got justice for her after all this time.'

Valérie looked on with loathing as Meyer's body was lifted onto a stretcher, and the strength of the feeling shocked her, tears pricking her eyes. She hadn't meant to kill him, it had been a completely instinctive reaction when she saw him pick up the gun and point it at Hannelore. But she couldn't be sorry, now that she knew what he had done. He had killed her mother, taken away years of joy and love that Valérie could never get back. And he hadn't even cared – individuals didn't matter to him.

'I need to go now, Nicolas,' said Otto. 'I can't be seen here. No one should know about my involvement in this.' He nodded to everybody and left.

Nicolas' men were starting to leave and Henry walked through them. 'Well done, Valérie. You've done it. We'll take over from here. Hannelore and Clara need to go to London to be with Jacob, and we'll take the document there too. I'll make sure they get out of Geneva safely.'

Valérie embraced Hannelore, who hugged her tightly. 'You'll be safe with Henry and you need to go and get Clara, find your family again. Just do me one favour.'

'Anything,' said Hannelore. 'I owe you so much. Not just for saving my life but for rescuing my precious Clara and bringing us together again. I am forever in your debt. What can I do?'

'Forgive Jacob. Don't punish him any longer for what happened to my mother. It wasn't his fault, so don't blame him for that night. Will you promise me?'

'Yes. I promise. I can't afford to lose anyone else I love.' She pointed over at the place where Meyer was shot. 'You've saved me in a lot of ways, Valérie. When this war is over, I promise I'll come back to Geneva with Jacob and we'll find you.'

Henry led Hannelore towards the manor house without looking back.

Only Nicolas remained with her and she started to move towards him. Then, over his right shoulder, a tall figure walked through the trees towards them. The flash of memory she'd felt when she saw him standing with the gun flooded back. Not believing what she was seeing, she took a step forward as the man emerged from the darkness in front of her, smiling as he always had.

'Philippe!' she cried and ran into his arms. 'They all said you were dead, but you're here, you're alive!' She clutched his arms, and looked into his face, unable to believe it was him, and then, with a sob, she threw her arms around his neck. He kissed her deeply, like a man who had been lost forever but had now come home.

As she felt his arms around her, all the hopelessness of the last few weeks lifted and she could see her future clearly again; it was a future that included him, her love.

Desperate to find out how he'd come back to her, she moved back in his arms and asked, 'What happened to you? They told me you had died in an explosion.' Her voice cracked and she couldn't carry on. He pulled her close again before he answered.

'We were hit, but not too badly. It looked much worse than it was. Some locals heard the noise of the explosions. They found us and took us away before the Germans came to investigate what had happened. I was unconscious for several days and it was only when I came to that I realised where I was and could get word to Stefano that I was alive. He and our guide Alessandro came to get us.'

'And Yves is all right?' asked Valérie, holding her breath for his answer.

'He's safe at home. He took the brunt of the explosion but he'll recover. We were lucky that we didn't lose anybody.' He took a deep breath before continuing. 'The Germans rounded up the local people and shot them in revenge for our escape and for their dead comrades. Many of the local people had fled the area because they knew there would be reprisals but some of the old folk wouldn't leave their homes.'

Not wanting to dwell on the cruelty of the Germans' actions, he pointed to the road and the car that had just drawn to a halt. 'My father said he'd send a car for us. Come on, let's get out of here.'

They ran out of the trees towards the car waiting to pick them up. Valérie glanced back again to where the bodies of the German spies had fallen. 'I need to go and tell my father what really happened to my mother.'

'Yes, and I need to talk to him about how quickly we can get married. I'm not going away again without you being my wife.'

Despite the darkness in the car, she could hear the smile in his voice.

They reached Valérie's townhouse and jumped out of the car to go inside. Before they reached the door, Albert came running out, seeing Valérie first. He clutched her close and then looked over her shoulder and saw Philippe. He blinked a few times, as if he couldn't believe what he was seeing, then pulled him close with his other arm. 'You're alive, my boy,' he cried. 'You've come back to us.' He turned back to Valérie. 'I was so worried about you. Come inside and tell me everything.'

They sat in the parlour in front of the embers still glowing in the fireplace and Valérie drank in the familiar room, the photographs on the mantelpiece and the much-loved old furniture, suddenly aware of all she could have lost. She recounted the events of the past few days to her father, feeling lost in a warm haze of relief and happiness. It was as if she'd been given a second chance at life. The document was safe, all of it, and it might just be the key to ending this brutal war. And the man she loved was here, right here with her, not cold and still on a mountaintop in Italy. He was home.

Then Valérie remembered the other truth she had heard that night. She looked at her father, full of happiness and gazing at them both with pleasure, but she knew that she had to tell him what had really happened to her mother. He saw her face grow more serious. 'What else did you find out, mignonne?'

'It's about Maman.' She stretched out and grasped his hand, rubbing his fingers as she thought about the words she should use. 'I found out what happened to her on the night she died.'

'Tell me,' he said.

'It was an accident; that much is true. She did fall in front of the car on the icy station square, but someone else was there and she was running away from him.'

'Who told you about this?'

'Hannelore. She was there too and had gone to meet

Maman because she was worried about her. You're right that she was collecting something for Jacob, but he didn't know that she would be followed that night.'

'Who caused the accident? Did Hannelore see the man?'

Valérie's gaze didn't waver. She didn't want to bring all his pain back but he needed to know, just like her. 'Yes, she did see him and it was a German spy.' She suddenly realised that she was clutching his fingers painfully when he breathed in sharply and she released them. 'But he's dead now,' she continued. 'He can't hurt us anymore, Papa.'

Her father opened his mouth to ask more but then changed his mind. As long as the man was dead and wouldn't threaten his family any longer, that was all he wanted to know. He bent his head and wiped his eyes and the embers in the fire falling down in the hearth was the only sound that filled the room.

Valérie turned to look at Philippe and tried to think of a way to bring her father back to the present. 'When did you get home?' she asked him, thinking of his grandfather and his certainty that Philippe would come back. 'They must have been overwhelmed.'

He smiled, picking up on her need to change the subject. 'I walked in on them last night. My father and mother were overjoyed but also astounded when I told them what had happened.' He shook his head, remembering the scene. 'But my grandfather surprised us all, he was pleased to see me and all he would say was it was about time I came home, as if he knew I wasn't dead.'

'He never believed you had died,' said Valérie. 'It was almost as if he could sense you were still alive.'

Philippe spoke directly to Albert. 'I'm sorry I didn't come and see you yesterday, sir, but my father insisted I hide my presence until tonight. He and his men had been waiting for Valérie and Hannelore every night for the last few days in case they came back. The SOE knew that the German spies were watching for them and were determined to protect them when they did come back.'

'And then I realised that one of the men with the Swiss Secret Service was Philippe.' She stretched out to hold his hand tightly.

'And as ever,' he joked, trying to lighten the atmosphere, 'your aim was quicker than mine.' Suddenly, he yawned.

'You must be exhausted,' said Albert. He looked at them both and stood up. 'You must stay here, Philippe. You can sleep on the sofa tonight and we can sort everything out tomorrow. I'll go and get some blankets.' He left the room and they heard his footsteps on the stairs.

Valérie leaned her head on Philippe's shoulder. 'At least I'll have you for a few days before you have to go away again.' She felt him kiss her hair.

'The major said I could stay for a bit longer before I had to go back.'

She lifted her head sharply.

'You were at the fort?' asked Valérie.

'It was on my way home. After we got back to Locarno, Stefano and I went there. He wouldn't let me go myself, he had been so relieved to see me, so sure that I had died and he had survived that awful day.' Philippe smiled. 'He said he wasn't going near Italy again for a long time. And he's going to get married to Francesca, the woman he went to try to find in the first place and the one who helped save him. So, we'll have two weddings after Christmas.'

'Two weddings?' echoed Valérie.

He nodded. 'I went to get the marriage licence today. And there's something else I need to tell you. I have somewhere for us to live.'

'Philippe, how can you have done that so quickly?'

'My father told me that he and my mother have decided to move out to the farmhouse in Vessy to live with my grandfather.

He really can't be alone anymore, and my mother has decided she's had enough of living in town. We can have their flat in the old town. We'll want our own place in time, but it seemed a good idea to use it for now. You'll be close to your father and his workshop.'

'So, it's all sorted?'

'Yes.' He gathered her into his arms. 'I'm going to marry you before anything else comes between us.' He kissed her hair and she snuggled down into his arms, feeling in that moment that whatever challenges and risks they had to face in future, at least they would be together.

EPILOGUE

HANNELORE

South of England

Hannelore sat in the living room warming her hands next to the blazing fire, the heat in stark contrast to the cold grey January day outside. Showers of sleet and rain were sweeping the English countryside north of London. She looked up at the sound of laughter coming from the kitchen, where Clara and Louis were with the housekeeper. It sounded like they were trying out their English on the kind matronly woman who'd been introduced to them by Henry. They were in one of the houses run by the SOE near London, Henry had explained. It was near where Jacob was working for the British government, and he had arranged for them to meet. She looked up nervously when she heard the front door open. Valérie's pleas were still ringing in her ears but she didn't know if it was too late for her and Jacob, whether too much time had passed for them to cross the chasm she'd created between them.

When she looked up again, the door to the living room was open and Jacob was standing staring at her, not moving into the room. He was clean-shaven and looked younger and thinner than the man she'd left so long ago, as handsome as ever and wearing a well-cut suit and tie.

She knew that it was up to her now to break the silence, but she was scared that she might have lost him forever. She stood up awkwardly, her legs shaking so much that they were hardly able to carry her weight, and she tried to move towards him, but stopped, not knowing if she would reach him. Almost instinctively, he strode towards her, held out his arms and closed them around her to hold her steady. She could smell the familiar cologne he always wore and closed her eyes, safe in his arms.

'I've missed you so much,' she whispered. 'It's been so long.'

He guided her back to the sofa and they sat down together. He didn't look up at her but down at their clasped hands. 'It's been a long time and you've gone through so much. At least now you're safe in England.'

'Have you any information about what happened to David and Ruth?' she asked. 'David was captured by the Nazis and taken away. I don't know about Ruth, after I left her I heard nothing.'

'I'm afraid I have no news, Hannelore. They were probably sent to one of the concentration camps. Until this war is over, we'll never know where they went or what happened to them.' He squeezed her hands and she looked into his dear face.

'I'm sorry Jacob, sorry for what I said about Thérèse. I was wrong to blame you for her death.' She shook her head, trying to think back to the night when she'd seen her friend die. 'I know now it wasn't your fault; you couldn't have known that the German spy was going to approach her that night. I was upset and had to blame someone.' She held his face in her hands, trying to make him understand. 'I was wrong and I'm sorry.'

He inched a bit closer, lifted his hand and touched her hair tenderly. 'I thought then that it was all over between us, but you're here now and have come back to me. What does it mean for us? What are you saying?'

She stared at his top button, her shyness stopping the words that she'd waited so long to say. He looked at her with longing in his eyes but he hadn't said he loved her.

'I'm saying that I was wrong not to come with you when you asked me. The last few years have taught me not to throw away people you love; too many of them could be taken away not to keep hold of the ones who are still there.' She smiled at him through her tears. 'Do you know who told me that? It was Thérèse's daughter Valérie. She said that I had to tell you I was wrong to blame you for what happened to her mother.'

'Valérie?' asked Jacob.

'She's a very brave woman now, working for the Resistance to get French refugees into Switzerland. She came into France to find me and took me back to Geneva. I'd never be here if it wasn't for her.' She squeezed his hand tightly. 'And we both got out of France thanks to you. Valérie found the false identity papers you'd hidden in her mother's books and used them to get past the German border guards.' She smiled ruefully. 'You saved my life just as much as Valérie did.'

He wiped away her tears gently. 'But I'm too old for you. You can't want me.'

'I don't want anybody else. It's always been you and always will be.'

She knew that her words had got through to him this time and he crushed her against his chest, kissing her deeply.

As the evening went on, they sat together before the fire, sharing their stories.

What seemed like a long time later, Henry came back into the living room, followed by Clara and Louis.

'I'll leave you now,' said Henry. 'You can stay in the house until you find somewhere of your own.'

'I've found a place already,' said Jacob. 'It was too big for one person but for us all' – he waved his hand to include Clara and Louis – 'it would be perfect.'

Clara came towards Hannelore and Jacob. 'Do you want us to stay with you? I thought that maybe now you have Jacob, you might want to be alone with him. You might not want us.'

Hannelore reached out her hand to her niece. 'You're all my family. I'm not letting any of you go now.' She looked up as Henry turned to leave. 'Thank you for getting us safely here.'

'I did the easy bit. It was Valérie who reunited you,' he replied.

Turning, he left the room, a solitary figure walking down the hall and out of the front door.

A LETTER FROM DIANNE

Thank you so much for reading *A Light to Guide Us Home*.

If you enjoyed it and want to keep up-to-date with all my latest releases, just sign up at the following link. Your email address will never be shared and you can unsubscribe at any time.

www.bookouture.com/dianne-haley

This is my third story about brave Swiss citizens helping Jewish refugees escape from occupied France, despite the opposition of the Swiss authorities and often at great risk to themselves. It also shows the perilous conditions in north Italy late in 1943 after Mussolini was deposed and the Italians switched sides to support the Allies. Even though it was a neutral country throughout WW2, Switzerland could not avoid witnessing the agonies of its neighbours.

If you enjoyed the story, I would be very grateful if you could leave a short review. I appreciate all feedback from readers. It makes such a difference helping new readers to discover one of my books for the first time.

You can also get in touch on my Facebook page, through Twitter, Goodreads or my website.

Thanks,

Dianne

KEEP IN TOUCH WITH DIANNE

diannehaley.com

 twitter.com/dhaley30

Printed in Great Britain
by Amazon